PRAISE FOR MARK LAWRENCE

'I enjoyed the hell out of *One Word Kill*. Mark is an excellent writer.'
—George R. R. Martin

'*One Word Kill* is the kind of story that will stay with you for a lifetime.'
—Robin Hobb, *New York Times* bestselling author

'A completely absorbing tale that perfectly captures the fear, awkwardness, cynicism and optimism of adolescence.'
—Anthony Ryan, *New York Times* bestselling author of *The Legion of Flame*

'*One Word Kill* grabs hold of you and won't let you go until you've finished the last page. It's everything that I look for in a book, and like the best of reads, one that stays with you long after you've finished reading it.'
—John Gwynne, author of The Faithful and the Fallen series

'Mark Lawrence balances big ideas with small, personal stakes very skillfully.'
—*SFX*

DISPEL ILLUSION

MARK
LAWRENCE

47N⬛RTH

Published by 47North, Seattle

www.apub.com

Amazon, the Amazon logo, and 47North are trademarks of Amazon.com,
Inc., or its affiliates.

ISBN-13: 9781542016322 (hardcover)
ISBN-10: 1542016320 (hardcover)
ISBN-13: 9781542094016 (paperback)
ISBN-10: 1542094011 (paperback)

Cover design by Tom Sanderson

Printed in the United States of America

DISPEL ILLUSION

THE STORY SO FAR

Here I present a catch-up of the previous books to refresh your memory and avoid having characters undergo 'as you know' conversations. This is in no way a substitute for reading *One Word Kill* and *Limited Wish*. It is meant to help those who have already read books one and two.

Nick is a mathematical genius who lives in Cambridge and has turned twenty-two between books two and three. The year is 1992.

Nick's D&D group consists of his two schoolmates, John (handsome, rich, somewhat shallow) and Simon (antisocial, obsessive, has a brilliant memory), plus his girlfriend Mia (witty, imaginative, streetwise). Their former dungeon master, Elton Arnot, has withdrawn from the group because the death of his father, a security guard, made him unwilling to risk the rest of his family through continued association with Nick.

Demus is Nick aged forty. In book one he comes back from the year 2011 in order to convince Nick and Mia to record her memories so that they can be reinstated after she suffers a terrible accident in the future.

In book one Demus steers Nick and his friends into stealing an advanced microchip needed to complete the memory storage device. During this robbery Demus and Elton's father are killed by school psycho-turned-would-be-drug lord Ian Rust. Rust also dies.

Six months later, in book two, Demus is involved with Nick and his friends when they discover and undo a potentially world-ending paradox. The paradox involves two timelines that fail to separate properly after a decision Nick makes.

In book two we meet the older Rust brother, Charles. He is employed by Miles Guilder, a rich and unscrupulous businessman who funds Nick's research and is very keen to drive it forward with reckless speed. Also heading the experimental side of the time-travel project are Professor Halligan and experimentalist Dr Ian Creed. Success so far has been very limited.

You can enjoy the book without thinking too hard about the mechanics of time travel, but for the curious, here is an optional reminder of the technical side of things:

Every action splits the timeline into many new timelines, one for each possible outcome. When someone travels to the past, their arrival should immediately start a new timeline so that paradox is impossible. They can kill their father long before they were born because the father they are killing is the version on this new timeline, not the father who created them. That father exists in their past and you cannot change your past.

We learn in book one that Nick Hayes lives in a very special, possibly unique, timeline where going back into the past does *not* split the traveller off on to a new timeline. Nick knows this because he remembers himself at forty coming back to 1986 and interacting with himself at fifteen.

However, the past still cannot be changed. If the time traveller does anything that is incompatible with their own past – killing their own father before he meets their mother, for example, or simply not doing something that they remember seeing their older selves do – then at that point they create a new timeline and split off on to it.

Demus (Nick at forty from 2011) can come back and remain on the timeline he remembers, but his actions are constrained by the need for unfolding events to match his memories of the time (when he was Nick). If what happens does not match his memories, then the world has branched on to a new timeline and his actions cannot help the Mia he knows in the future. Similarly, he can't do anything that is incompatible with the world he knows in 2011. For example, he can't kill someone he knows is alive then, or save someone he knows is dead then. If he did, he would split on to a new timeline.

At the end of book one Nick uses the memory storage device to erase his memories of the events during the robbery at the microchip laboratory and of a number of days before that. This is in order to match the gap in Demus's memory and to spare him the detailed knowledge of exactly how he dies.

In order to make sure that Nick's timeline and Demus's timeline continue to be the same, Nick will have to become Demus as he grows older. This means he will have to invent time travel. Nick doesn't want to go back and die saving Mia, but he does want to save Mia, and if he doesn't go back as Demus and do what he remembers happening then that would create an incompatibility – a paradox – which would resolve itself either by destroying the timeline, or by it turning out that Demus's memories are delusions, which would mean Mia could not be saved after her accident.

CHAPTER 1

1992

The two saving graces of explosions are that from the outside they're pretty and from the inside they're quick. The one I was in was taking forever, though, and had none of the fiery goodness of the typical Hollywood offering. When time explodes it tends not to create exciting fireballs, and most of the shrapnel inside the Winston Laboratory was crawling through the air at a pace that would make snails look zippy.

I was closer to the detonation than any of the others, since I'd been running towards the array of electromagnets with the intention of turning them off. Dr Ian Creed and a lab technician named Dave were another ten yards further back, and a scattering of researchers stood among the workbenches another ten yards beyond that.

The huge magnets had been reduced to jagged iron shards and were being flung out on trajectories made hard to predict owing to the powerful magnetic fields still trying to haul them back together.

My brain had skipped a beat between running towards the assembly and being hurled back by the leading edge of the shockwave, and my next coherent view of proceedings had been as I hung in the air, apparently frozen in place, facing a similarly stationary array of sharp metal brought to a halt some small fraction of a second before, which thankfully avoided them punching a variety of fatal holes in me.

It took, or seemed to take, an age before my body-time caught up with my brain-time. The fracturing of the time led to all the various components of the explosion following their own internal clocks, and while the distribution appeared random, it was clear that the living pieces in the mix were operating on the fastest clocks. My father once told me that the equations that govern the universe don't care about 'now'. The mathematics of time don't care about 'now', they just ask what value you want to set 't' to. There's a special connection between consciousness and time. Einstein said, 'Time is an illusion', and the great Douglas Adams had even greater doubts about lunchtime. The more I dug into the mathematics of time, the more I found I was digging into the connections between the universe of atoms and fields and the universe of wet squishy consciousnesses. Life in general, and human intelligence in particular, had once seemed an inconsequential complication in the world of physics; but the more we learned, the more intelligence had revealed itself to be a fundamental mystery at the heart of everything, deeper than the dances of stars and galaxies.

As mentioned, I had a lot of time on my hands while waiting for my body clock and brain clock to synchronise. When at last the former caught up with the latter, I struggled to get my feet on the floor and began to run.

The thing about being incredibly fast compared to your surroundings is that it doesn't really work like it does in the comic books. The air doesn't want to get out of your way. It's still on slow time, and running at 300 miles an hour is just as hard as standing still in a super-tornado with 300- mile-an-hour winds trying to knock you down. Plus, the floor can't give you the friction you need to accelerate. It turns into an ice rink while the soles of your shoes melt.

Dr Creed and Dave weren't moving as fast as I was, but they were moving a hell of a lot faster than everything else in the room. I saw them try to shout questions, but of course by the time any sound they made reached my ears we would all be mincemeat. Further back, the rest of the staff were still as statues. The fact of the explosion hadn't even registered on their faces yet.

I ran, but my progress seemed painfully slow. It was exhausting, too. By the time I reached the first bench, panting and gasping, I was thirsty and bored. The fear and adrenaline had been run right out of me. I reached for a plastic cup of coffee that hung frozen in the moment on its way to the floor. Dry-mouthed, I tried to take a swig, but the plastic fractured beneath my fingers, unable to drag the weight of coffee through the air towards me at the speed I wanted it. Even if the cup had been made of iron, the liquid would have refused to pour at any rate that wouldn't make a glacier look swift.

As I wrestled with the cup a jagged shard of iron passed sedately beneath my arm.

'Shit!'

Turning my head I saw the shrapnel cloud had stolen into motion. Not all at the same rate. Some pieces tumbled through the air as if they were sinking through mud; others crept forward only slightly faster than the minute hand on a clock. The rest hung there silently, biding their time. A small piece swept by my ear at the speed a bowling ball approaches the pins.

Unable to find the traction to outpace the oncoming storm I started to turn, contorting my body to allow the fragments past me rather than through me as they caught up. I danced my curious jig as if weightless. When I took both feet from the floor, gravity reeled me in so slowly it might as well have been turned off.

A piece of metal almost too small to see cut a line across the side of my hand. It really hurt and drew my attention to the bright motes streaking towards me. They could be just as fatal as a book-sized chunk if they tore through my head or heart, and no part of me wanted to find out if I could survive a dozen needle-size holes punched entirely through the slightly less vital parts of my body.

The sound of the explosion reached me, impossibly deep, shaking my chest. I was slowing down and still the metal storm continued its slow-motion tumble around me. Gravity's grip on me strengthened and I let it start to take me down as I passed the workbench.

Pieces of shattered magnet began to zip by with high-pitched whines, too fast to avoid. Fortunately, they were fragments that I had already spotted before their sudden acceleration and had contrived not to be in the path of.

As I hit the floor I began to hear the screams and shouts of my co-workers, my own clock having slowed enough to allow soundwaves time to do their job. I lay there while things hissed past. The workbench exploded into splinters as a chunk of metal tore through all the wooden and plastic shelving beneath, shredding equipment. I found my arm peppered with secondary shrapnel.

And suddenly it seemed to be over. The echoes of devastating impacts died away, leaving a deafening silence.

I edged my head above the benchtop and blinked to see a cloud of glittering pieces still hanging there at the centre of the explosion. Without warning, one hissed by overhead to punch a hole in the warehouse roof fifty yards behind me. I glanced back at Dr Creed. All of us seemed to be in synch now, moving in regular everyday time as far as I could tell.

He met my eyes above the bench he had been hiding behind, then yelled, 'Run!'

We both followed his advice, heading for the closest exit while behind us the cloud of frozen pieces sporadically popped back into regular time, like kernels of corn popping in a saucepan, and zipped out to destroy something.

It wasn't until I reached the door and glanced back that I saw that Dave was lying close to where I last laid eyes on him, his white lab coat all red now.

◆ ◆ ◆

'So what happened then?' John asked, his hand still in a pack of Quavers that he had forgotten all about.

'The cover-up began, of course.' I leaned back in my chair. This must be what it was like to be the dungeon master, all eyes on me. Simon and Mia watched me across the gaming table: a much bigger affair than the one in Simon's bedroom. John had secured his job at the merchant bank immediately on leaving uni but he'd only been at it a month and, however huge his starting salary, there was no way his dad hadn't paid for his ridiculously expensive Putney flat overlooking the Thames. 'I have to believe that there will be an inquest into Dave Weston's death, but Guilder has the funds to grease an awful lot of palms and the lack of morals to have those he can't buy intimidated. With monsters like Charles Rust on his payroll he just has to say what he wants and how many legs he's prepared to have broken to make it happen.'

'I still don't understand why he's so set on pushing the experimental side of things before you've nailed the theory down.' Simon turned his gaze back to the dice. It took a lot to distract him from a game of D&D, especially now that his vast acreage of spare time would drastically shrink when he took up his accountancy job at the end of the summer. I'd done well to sidetrack him this long, but now that the exploding part was over he wanted to get back to the game.

'And I don't understand why you would do an idiot thing like run directly at equipment you thought was about to blow up!' Mia said, rather more heatedly than Simon.

'I didn't think it was going to explode right there and then! Well . . . I did a bit, but I thought I could pull the wires before they set it off. And to answer your question, Si, I don't understand it either. I used to think it was just greed. I thought he just wanted to stay ahead of any competition and nail down all the financial rights. But now it seems like an obsession.'

John shrugged and returned to his Quavers. 'People get obsessed with money, even when they already have more than they know what to do with.' He looked pointedly over at Simon's character sheet, where Fineous the thief had gold coins listed by the thousand along with a profusion of gems and jewellery.

'Someone needs to look after it all,' Simon replied with unfeigned innocence. 'And who is least likely to have the treasure stolen off them?'

I snorted. 'That sounds reasonable until you realise what he's saying is that if you or I were carrying it, he would just steal it off us.'

We settled to the game, the same campaign that Mia had been running for six years now. Somehow we'd managed to maintain it through sixth form and university, and now into the start of various careers. My own life during that period had been rather more static than the others', since I'd gone to Cambridge at sixteen and was still there at twenty-two, still bashing my brain against the same problem. The newspapers, and occasionally my colleagues, liked to claim I was making breakthroughs every month, pushing back mathematical frontiers and casting light into dark corners of our understanding. To me it felt more as if I were chipping tiny pieces off some vast marble block, hoping that something beautiful lay deep inside and that, at the end of my efforts, I would stand back to behold a magnificent statue rather than just a big heap of marble fragments.

Mia set the scene for us. Her biggest strength as a dungeon master had always been her ability to create the atmosphere and play the parts of everyone we met. It was a talent that, honed by years at a theatre school, had recently secured her a job as the understudy's understudy in *The Mousetrap*, Agatha Christie's murder mystery, which was in its fortieth continuous year in the West End. It was only a temporary arrangement since the understudy had broken her ankle, and really Mia was too young for the role; but even so, it was a prestigious thing to have on an actor's CV, and if the planets aligned to give her a shot on the big stage I knew she would do well.

Ever since we had lost Mia's old character, Sharia, during our escape from The University years ago, my mage, Nicodemus, had been obsessed with undoing her death. We had seen her lose her grip on the serpent that carried us up one of the alchemist's towering chimneys and fall hundreds of feet to her death in the great hearth. Death, however, isn't always the final word in a game of Dungeons & Dragons. High-level clerics can call on their gods to raise the recently dead, and still more powerful clerics can even resurrect someone from a single dry bone. We, however, didn't have so much as a hair from Sharia's head and, even if The University had kept hold of her corpse, it would be suicide for us to go back there having seriously pissed off two of the handful of guilds that controlled the place.

In any event, my mage would much sooner fix the problem himself with magic based on human ingenuity, cleverness and the occasional eye of newt than go crawling to the gods and their overly smug representatives. Unfortunately, 'fixing the problem' had taken the best part of six years so far.

'I still say,' said John, leaning back in his gaming chair, 'that getting Sharia back by using time travel seems like a really unimaginative solution given, y'know, your day job.'

'And I still say that hitting every enemy repeatedly with your sword until they die is a pretty unimaginative solution to every combat you've ever entered.' I picked up the lead figure representing John's warrior, Sir Hacknslay, and tested its sword for sharpness against my fingertip.

'Touché.' John grinned.

'And before *you* start complaining, Fineous . . .' I forestalled Simon with a raised hand. '. . . we are definitely *stealing* this time crystal. It's going to take a master thief, so it's going to be all about you.'

Simon pursed his lips and nodded. 'Good.'

'So all we need is to break into the Tower of Illusion, steal the time crystal from the great Hoodeeny, go back in time, save Sharia and we're done.' John rubbed his hands together. 'Easy.'

CHAPTER 2

1992

Mia rented a room in a rather grotty house-share in Wandsworth. The back garden surged against the kitchen windows in a green sea of bramble and saplings that made it next to impossible to open the door. Rumour had it that there was a decaying Ford Fiesta out there, but even in winter the vegetation hadn't died back enough for me to have ever verified the fact.

'Tea?' She rooted around in the fridge, hunting for her own milk among the sour-smelling bottles labelled for various of her housemates. Three of the four of them were actors, the other two 'resting', while Mia with her understudy-understudy gig and the occasional call to be a background figure in an advert for peanuts or some new line of clothes came the closest to actual employment.

'Coffee, please.' I sniffed and wrinkled my nose. 'Black.'

We retired to her bedroom with our drinks. It was a lot cleaner than the kitchen, which seemed to be a place where they only acted at housekeeping. 'Nice posters!'

'Max let me have them. He's the floor manager.'

Mia had put up three large posters advertising stage plays from last year's season. I wouldn't have wanted them in my room, but then again, the walls in my Cambridge flat weren't peeling and mouldy. I sipped my coffee and said no more. Mia had strong views about making her own way and past attempts to help her financially had ended poorly.

Mia turned the TV on and joined me on the mountain of cushions heaped upon her bed. The news burbled at us from her black and white while we reclined, shoulder to shoulder, in a comfortable silence. John had sent us all packing at eight when his latest girlfriend, Carly, had arrived. Carly was a model, apparently, but I think by that she meant she had paid to have a photographer make her a portfolio rather than that she walked the catwalk with Naomi Campbell. Mia was prettier, though admittedly not nearly as tall.

I'd been happy to call it a day for the same kinds of reasons as John, I suspected. I was eager for my night with Mia to begin. Simon sulked, of course. He missed the days when it was the dawn chorus breaking in through the curtains that let us know our D&D session might have gone on a little too long.

'You did a good job today,' I said, and laid my hand on her leg.

'It was fun.' Mia nodded and sipped her tea.

'No, I mean you did a great job. Not just acting out the city folk and whatnot, but you told a great story. You made it all hang together.'

Mia smiled, glanced my way, then returned her attention to the weatherman.

'I mean you should think about writing plays, not just acting in them. You have a real talent for both.' I kissed her hair. 'Turn it off. I want you under the covers where the weather doesn't matter.'

Mia turned to meet my lips with hers. 'We can leave it on. In case I get bored.' She pulled away with a grin before I could grab her.

Out in the hall, the phone began its annoying electronic chirping. Fortunately, in a house where would-be actors are always waiting to hear from their agents, no phone is left to ring for long. Someone thundered down the stairs, clattered against the phone table and snatched up the receiver. A moment later they banged on Mia's door and a rather sullen voice announced, 'It's for Nick.'

'Crap. It's probably Simon wanting to discuss D&D strategy.' Mia had finished the game with all our characters trapped in an underground cave. I rolled off the bed. 'Hold that thought. I'll get rid of him.'

'What thought?' Mia called after me. 'I was thinking about the chance of rain in the southern counties . . .'

I reached the phone in time to see Mia's housemate Melany retreating up the stairs in her threadbare nightie and enormous fluffy slippers. 'Hello?'

'Nick! You have to get here! Now!'

'Ian?' It sounded like Ian Creed from the laboratory. 'How did you get this—'

'Just get in a car and get here!'

'I don't have a car. Has something happened? I told Guilder if he pushed things after Dave died I was going to—'

'We've had a breakthrough! Nobody is hurt. Just get yourself down here. You'll want to see it.'

'You could just tell me . . .'

'Has to be seen!' And, annoyingly, he hung up on me.

It takes a lot to distract a twenty-two-year-old from sex with his girlfriend, but I couldn't leave it hanging. Ian had sounded excited and he wasn't a man given to excitement. The word at the lab was that when his wife of nearly twenty years told him she was having an affair, he said it was a 'poor show' and went back to reading his newspaper. Someone probably made that one up, but the fact that it was so widely believed gives you a measure of the man.

'So, I have to go . . .' I told Mia, finishing off my remaining coffee in two gulps.

'Sure.' She surrendered with so little fight that I felt slightly insulted. 'I'm coming too.'

'You are?' I blinked.

'You're working on time travel, Nick. If Dr Roboto is losing his shit then it must be something awesome. I want to see!'

'I guess. Sure.' I warmed to the idea. 'Do you think we can get a train this late?'

'John will drive us.'

'John? But Cindy—'

'Call him. They're probably on to the cuddling by now and he'll be glad of an excuse to leave. Tell him it's a historic moment. Also . . . isn't she called Carly?'

'Hmmm.' I still remembered Dr Creed and Professor Halligan freaking out because they'd managed to create a discrepancy of seven nanoseconds between two clocks. That was six years ago, though, and things had moved on since then. 'I'll try him, but I don't think he'll go for it.'

It turned out that Mia knew John better than I did. Within thirty minutes we were in his brand-new Mondeo heading north towards Cambridge considerably in excess of the speed limit.

'Take it easy, Boy Racer.' I braced myself to keep from sliding around on the back seat, Mia having called shotgun. 'It's not like rushing a pregnant woman to the delivery suite. The police won't let you off when you explain that the emergency is a scientific breakthrough.'

'I'm going to try it anyway!' John accelerated. 'Aren't you excited? You've been at this forever. It's about time you got something properly science-fiction out of it all.'

'You mean better than my forty-year-old self popping up out of nowhere?'

'Well, we didn't actually get to see him do the popping – he just rang the doorbell. And he just looked like . . . some guy. You've no idea how boring merchant banking is. I want to see something cool like that explosion you were telling us about.'

'You really don't.'

'Well, OK, not that. But something space age!'

Cambridge was mostly asleep when we arrived; the pubs had turned out, the drunks had ambled off into the night. We pulled into the brightly lit visitor parking bay outside the Winston Laboratory just before midnight and presented ourselves at the security gate.

'You know I can't let those two in, Dr Hayes.' The security guard wasn't one of the ones whose names I'd memorised. I didn't know the night staff. Most of my work was done at home with pencil and paper, or sometimes in the university computer lab running simulations on a Sun Workstation. I very rarely came to see the mechanical side of things. We theoreticians don't like to get our hands dirty.

I frowned at the guard. 'You know I can go back in time and beat you up when you were a kid, right?'

The man gave me a blank stare. He had a bland, humourless face and a look that said the world had yet to impress him.

I sighed. 'Tell Dr Creed I'm at the gate and that I'm not coming in without John and Mia.'

I went back to join the others while the guard telephoned the lab. Overhead, a handful of stars were outshining the urban glow in a clear sky and the day's heat had retreated, leaving a cool edge to the breeze. It took a couple of minutes, but soon enough Dr Creed came bustling out across the tarmac to join us.

'Nick! Glad you could make it!'

'Ian.' I shook his hand. The years had put a touch of grey in his thick black hair, but he was still the same serious, barrel-chested little man who I'd met when I first came to the lab at sixteen. The broad grin trying to escape his beard was most unlike him. 'You know Mia? And this is John: the only reason we could get here so fast. I promised them they could both come in.'

'Guilder won't like it . . .' Creed frowned. Then he grinned again. 'But who cares!' He waved us through. Again, most unlike him. I'd been gearing myself up for a fight. As the 'talent', I got to act like a prima donna quite often, though if it got in the way of the experimental progress that Miles Guilder was so set on, he would have Charles Rust pay me a social call. The last visit had been two years ago and I'd been careful since then not to push things far enough to get another one. There wasn't much that made it worth having that grinning one-eyed psychopath turning up on my doorstep.

We followed Dr Creed into the lab, finding the large warehouse space fully lit, though there appeared to be nobody at work on any of the equipment. Glancing at the ceiling, I could see the patches over the holes where shrapnel from the last explosion had punched through.

The place had its own unique scent: a mix of stale coffee, burned plastic, solder and more astringent components, most likely toxic. It felt to me like a laboratory should feel – large but crowded with dangerous-looking equipment. The whole place was a hulking behemoth, pregnant with experiments, now dedicated to trying to squeeze out a single invention.

'Come on! Come on!' Creed waved us along. Normally his short legs had him trailing me, but tonight he was practically running.

The original bank of computers had been upgraded several times, and the capacitors whose current they controlled now occupied a third of the lab's acreage. They looked like great white oil drums on metal legs, a forest of them gently humming. Get within ten feet of one and the hair on your arms would begin to stand on end. Each one cost as much as a three-bedroom house.

'Through here!' Creed led us through the chain-link fence enclosing the inner 'secret laboratory' and into the area cordoned from view with office partitions.

'There!' he announced with pride. He gestured at the equipment looming before him, then put on his glasses and bent to examine the readout on some dials.

In front of us were six huge electromagnets arranged in the same pattern as the ones that had exploded four days ago, killing Dave Weston. Each of the magnets weighed well over three tons, and the forest of cables around them made it hard to see into the space they enclosed. The cables allowed for precise control of the magnetic field at the centre of the array. The various solutions to my equations yielded ever more efficient ways to pulse current through the set-up, thereby building the necessary resonances that allowed us to dump enough energy into the target area to vibrate space-time. And, if everything went right, that pulsation of the space-time membrane would grow so large as to break off a self-contained bubble, thus making our own time machine from the very stuff of the universe.

'There's someone in there!' Mia said.

Through the tangles of cables, some thicker than both my thumbs together, I could see she was correct. The back of someone's head could just be made out. It looked as if they were sitting on a chair. Dr Creed beckoned us round to a place where the cables had been tied back to allow a clearer view.

'Professor Halligan?' Mia seemed unsure. It was definitely him, though. His face was peculiarly immobile and twisted into a disturbing grimace.

'Professor?' I pushed in alongside Mia and called again, but Halligan didn't so much as blink.

'He's time travelling!' Dr Creed declared triumphantly. 'Travelling through time!'

'Shouldn't he just vanish, then, and appear in the future?' John asked.

Dr Creed peered up at John over the top of his glasses. 'Why on earth would he vanish?'

'Well . . . I . . .' John fished for an answer better than *because he had seen it like that in a film once.*

'He's moving forward in time,' Mia said, rather more thoughtfully, 'but so are all the rest of us. So's the chair he's sitting on. If he's going into the future faster than we are, then . . .'

Dr Creed came to watch the professor with us. 'He's going forward twelve hours. So he should be back with us at eight o'clock tomorrow morning. Until then, no time will have passed for him. To the professor it will be exactly as if he has just 'popped' forward half a day. But of course, his body still exists in the meantime. And there it is. After all, forward time travel is just an advanced form of waiting.'

'I'm surprised he isn't naked,' I said. The others gave slightly repulsed looks. 'Well, Demus said . . .' I trailed off, remembering that Dr Creed had no idea who Demus was and should certainly not be told that I had already come back from the future to visit myself. But Demus hadn't brought back the technology he needed with him, which implied that he couldn't bring anything but himself. And although I had wiped most of his visit from my memory, Simon, who forgot nothing ever, had since repeated back to me some of what I'd told him about what Demus had said. Simon reported that Demus said he had returned buck-naked, Terminator-style, in front of a police station on Watkins Street at three in the morning of 1 January 1986. So, while I was grateful to find Professor Halligan fully clothed, I was also surprised to see it. Maybe non-living things were easier to bring forward in time than backward.

'Can we touch him?' Mia asked.

'You can try.' Dr Creed seemed to be enjoying himself. He hauled back on one of the bands that held the cables apart, widening the gap enough for us to slip through one by one.

Halligan looked so unnatural that I didn't really want to touch him. Part of me wondered if he'd been replaced with some kind of wax replica. Close up, the light seemed to do weird things where it reflected off his skin, a bizarre kind of shimmer as if he wasn't quite there. The others sensed it too, and hesitated.

'Is he safe?' asked Mia.

'He is.' Creed nodded. 'Check his watch, too.'

Halligan had both his hands raised as if in horror, or possibly to signal that he had changed his mind. On his right wrist three watches were visible above the cuff of his jacket, one digital and two clockwork. All three showed two minutes past eight. I reached out to touch his left hand. The air seemed to thicken around my fingers until at some fraction of an inch from his skin my fingertips met a smooth barrier they couldn't push past. Oddly, I could touch the watches and even move them slightly.

'Ha!' Creed barked. 'See? The time differential won't allow matter to reach him. Or light. What you're seeing are reflections from the surface created around him. That's why he looks a bit . . . shiny. The watches aren't frozen in time; the magnetic flux just broke them when I threw the switch. His clothes aren't travelling with him, either – they're just hanging on him. You could set fire to them and they'd burn away but it wouldn't hurt Halligan! You could hit him with a hammer, shoot an artillery shell at him. Wouldn't do a thing. I tried with a diamond drill just—'

'You shouldn't be able to do this,' I said. 'Not with just the power you have here.'

'I know!' Creed beamed. 'The experimentalist proves his worth! I mean, we knew that it would take less power to send someone forward than backward, and we knew that shorter trips would be easier again, but even so it's a huge breakthrough!'

I blinked and backed out through the gap, leaving Mia and John to poke the professor. 'Why on earth did Halligan let you do this to him?

You're lucky the whole lot didn't blow again! And you know it wasn't the explosion I was really worried about.' My main concern had been that an imbalanced attempt could cause a lasting discontinuity in space-time. A crack. And if that happened, I hadn't the mathematics to predict what might leak through. 'It was a crazy risk. And who knows how he's going to be tomorrow morning, assuming he comes out of it at all?'

'Guilder.' Creed said the man's name as though it explained everything.

'He's an old man in a wheelchair.' Actually, he wasn't much older than Creed, but I wasn't feeling particularly diplomatic. 'I know he's good at making threats, but he's hardly going to have you killed, and *this*, this right here, very well might.' I waved my hand back at the looming magnets.

Creed looked guilty. 'He's using the carrot *and* the stick now. You know he's dying. I think he just wants to see the project realised before he goes. He offered us both a quarter of a million pounds to make this work. We knew we were close. I didn't expect to be this close, though!'

'Well, congratulations.' I said it through gritted teeth. I'll admit some part of me was wondering where my quarter of a million pounds was. 'Let's hope Halligan comes through unscathed. At least he volunteered to test it himself.'

'Well, there were a few guinea pigs first.' Creed looked guilty again.

'What! You're telling me that—'

'Actual guinea pigs! Not undergraduates.'

'Ah . . .'

'Guinea pigs? Where?' Mia emerged, followed by John, having grown bored of the frozen professor.

'They, uh, scampered off.' Creed glanced out the way we'd come in.

'So, it's done then?' John asked. 'We can all zip off to the future and claim our jet cars?'

Creed shrugged and began to lead us out towards the main lab. 'It needs scaling up and testing. We need to be very sure that the subject stays locked to the planetary spatial trajectory.'

'The what now?' John asked.

'He means that if we just sent someone a day into the future, then when they resumed experiencing normal time they would find themselves floating in the vacuum of space,' I said. 'The Earth would have moved on, following its orbit around the sun. Clearly Halligan is moving with the rotation of the Earth about its axis, the sun and the galactic core, but if there are even tiny discrepancies they could accumulate to a significant error over the course of years or centuries.'

'Oh,' said John. He glanced back at Halligan. 'You know, I wasn't very impressed to start with, but I have to admit it was pretty cool when we took the chair away.'

'You did what?' I looked back in. They'd pulled the chair out from under Halligan and left him sitting on nothing. 'Oh, come on! This is like the moon landing. You can't have him fall on his arse when he arrives.' I had to force a smile from my lips, though. Halligan did look pretty funny.

Creed just shook his head. 'I'll take care of it. And you, Nick, should get on with working out how we did this. I can show you the adjustments I made, but you're right, according to the current theory our power supply shouldn't be able to advance him more than a second at most.'

I agreed to get on the case as soon as I'd had some sleep. I hardly needed encouragement. It was the biggest advance we'd had in years.

I emerged from the wall of partitions, leading John and Mia, and approached the gate in the chain-link enclosure with Creed escorting us.

'You're right about the reappearing in space bit,' John agreed as we headed for the exit. 'That sounds bad. Sign me up for the spatial coordinates thingy when I go to collect my robot slaves.'

I grinned. 'The future folk might give you a hot cybernetic girlfriend . . . or they might cook you on their post-apocalyptic barbeque, but either way you won't be coming back with your bounty. The coming back problem is rather more difficult and requires a lot more power!'

'I thought you said that the universe doesn't care about now,' Mia said. 'Time is just a number in the equations.'

I nodded. 'I did say that.' John may have scraped into Oxford and Mia might have gone to a performing arts college, but there really was no mistaking who was the clever one. 'But sadly there's something called entropy and if you try to run time backward then entropy *really* doesn't like that.' I paused at the exit and looked around at the empty workbenches. 'We should go get some sleep if we want to be back here for eight. You can resume your affair with my couch, John.'

'Halligan really needs to be watched,' Creed said. 'I was hoping . . .'

'Nothing doing, my good doctor,' I said. 'You're getting paid two hundred and fifty thousand quid for this. The least you can do to earn it is stay up and keep an eye on Professor H.'

CHAPTER 3

1992

John woke us the next morning, banging on the bedroom door. 'Wakey, wakey! We've got important science to go and see!'

'Uh?' Mia groaned and rolled over next to me.

I sat up, yawning. John had never been so keen on science up till now, but I guess since we had torn him from the lovely Carly the night before he was making sure Mia and I didn't get to roll around in my bed while he languished on the sofa.

'Wakey, wakey!'

'OK! OK!' I yawned again and stretched, looking down at Mia and wondering whether I really did want to go and see an old professor unfreeze. Mia looked very tempting with one slim arm reaching out across my pillow. The black shock of her hair seemed to beg my fingers to run through it, and traces of yesterday's make-up had given her panda eyes. 'Time to get up.'

Mia was a deep sleeper. Removing the duvet was the first stage in waking her off-schedule. If you didn't take it beyond arms' reach she would assure you she was awake and in the process of getting up, then drag it back and fall asleep again in the space of five seconds while your back was turned.

I bundled the duvet into the chair and stood to see the view. 'The things I do for science.'

Mia patted ineffectually around the bed for the duvet, then cracked open one grumpy eye.

'Up and at them!' I said.

'I can see you're already *up*.' She spoiled a seductive smile by yawning hugely halfway through it. 'Come back to bed and cuddle me.'

I almost did, but John banged the door again. 'Breakfast's on fire. Little help?'

We arrived at the laboratory full of tea and burnt toast and with five minutes to spare. John had been very proud of his breakfast efforts. There had also been something that was allegedly scrambled egg but seemed to be made of rubber and eggshell. We'd choked down some of the least inedible parts to spare his feelings. I patted my trousers for my pass and found a triangle of the least carbonised toast instead. I'd been throwing it in the bin when John came back from the loo and I'd slipped it into my pocket to hide the fact. The daytime security guard knew me well enough, but still wouldn't let me in without a pass. He said that John or Mia wouldn't get in even if I'd had my ID. I made a fuss until he called through for confirmation. With the deadline for unfreezing fast approaching, the small shouty voice on the other end directed him to 'Open the damn gate.' I hurried through apologetically with the others on my heels.

'Whoa, nice Roller!' John whistled at a gleaming Rolls Royce in the car park – not the typical commuter choice for graduate students and researchers. The chauffeur stared at us over gloved hands, gripping the wheel as if daring us to smudge the wax job.

'It means Guilder's here,' I said.

Sure enough, we found Guilder waiting with Dr Creed in the inner laboratory where Professor Halligan was still motionless, though his chair was back underneath him now.

When I first met him, Guilder had been a big man with an intimidating physicality to him. He'd had that kind of restless energy that makes you think someone is never far from violence. But over the last few years he'd been brought low by some unspecified neurological condition that had gradually robbed him of his strength, wasted the flesh from his bones and sat him slack-jawed in a wheelchair. You only had to look at those stony grey eyes, though, to be reminded that Miles Guilder was still a man to be feared. The fact that Charles Rust stood behind him in a tailored suit, his thin hands on the handles of the chair, only served to underscore the threat that always accompanied the man, even when alone and chair-bound.

'Late to the show,' Guilder greeted me, his voice weak and breathy where once it had boomed.

'Slightly early by my watch.' I moved to get a view of the space between the towering magnets. 'Are we expecting any flashover, Dr Creed?'

Guilder narrowed his eyes. 'Flashover?'

Creed waved the idea away, glancing at his watch. 'Spare energies released when the subject returns to our timeline. They should be minimal, though this is the longest journey we've made so far.'

'And the first human one.' I was going to elaborate, but Creed looked at his watch again and shushed me.

'We're expecting him back in twenty seconds.'

We all looked at Halligan, frozen in his slightly comical horror.

'T-minus five, four, three, two, one!'

We all looked that bit harder.

'See, now *that's* what being late looks like,' I said. Despite the joke, I was worried. In real life, when you miss a target you tend to be able to assume that you will at least get somewhere near what you were aiming

26

at. If I aim at the bullseye I may miss, but I can be fairly sure my dart will hit somewhere on the board, and even if I'm having a particularly off day I can still pretty much guarantee that it will at least hit something in the pub. When mathematics goes wrong the consequences can be more severe, rather like the dart missing the bullseye, the board and the pub, and hitting a three-toed sloth instead, somewhere in the Bolivian jungle. Or perhaps drifting away through interstellar space off the shoulder of Orion. I had to hope that the error here lay with the experimental side: a calibration a percentage point out, the power surge a touch too high, that sort of thing.

We watched in silence for what felt like a long time. John wandered off and started poking at abandoned equipment. He picked up some kind of helmet.

'Well?' Guilder demanded.

'I . . . uh . . . well.' Creed flipped through his lab book as if a good answer might appear before him.

'What's the longest this might take?' Rust asked me. Apparently he had been authorised to ask obvious questions on his employer's behalf.

'Well, on the assumption that protons decay, we can expect the heat death of the universe to occur in around . . . well, it's a one followed by about a hundred zeros years. And after that the concept of time becomes somewhat problematic. So before then.'

With effort, Guilder turned his head. 'Dr Creed?'

Creed had retreated behind his workstation monitor. He glanced across at John. 'Put that *down*!'

John, now wearing the helmet he'd picked up, looked rather sheepish. 'Sorry . . .'

But Creed was already tapping his keyboard energetically, looking for an answer for Guilder. 'I—'

A flash of bluish light, a shockwave and a scream interrupted him.

Turning, we found ourselves being stared at by a very surprised-looking Professor Halligan, the surprised look enhanced by his hair standing up as if full of static. He looked dishevelled and somewhat disoriented, like a man who's been through a full cycle in a tumble drier.

'Did . . . did it work?' he asked.

'It did!' Dr Creed pushed through us to reach the professor. 'We did it, Bob! We made history!' He took hold of the professor's hand, ostensibly to shake it, but perhaps also to convince himself it was touchable once more. 'You were one minute and eleven seconds later than expected, though.'

'Hmmm. Have to work on that.' Halligan got to his feet. 'Nick! Good to see you. And . . .' He blinked. 'You've brought friends.'

John guiltily put the helmet back on the table.

Creed and I helped Halligan out from the cradling grip of the magnets. We ducked beneath and stepped above the mass of cables to where Guilder waited in his wheelchair, watching with a strange kind of hunger in his eyes.

We retired to one of the workbenches and a graduate student brought coffees. Guilder whispered something to Rust, who elaborated for our benefit.

'Mr Featherstonhaugh and Miss Jones here will have to sign non-disclosure agreements and then they will have to leave.' His singular snake-like eye slithered across John, then Mia. The use of their surnames was to leave us in no doubt that he knew who they were and where to find them. He drew out the first multi-page document and offered a pen to John, indicating where to make his mark. 'Sign here.'

'And don't come back,' Guilder gasped. Despite his frailty he still managed to give me a hard stare.

John and Mia knew better than to argue. They signed their names on the dotted line while the rest of us looked on in stony silence. Well, my bit of it wasn't stony, but it was silent.

'I'll be out of here in ten minutes,' I said when the paperwork was being folded into the inner pocket of Rust's jacket. 'I'll catch you guys at the flat, yeah?'

Mia gave my hand a squeeze and went on tiptoes to peck a kiss on my cheek. 'Don't be long!'

And off they went.

◆ ◆ ◆

A flash of bluish light, a shockwave and a scream.

Turning, we found ourselves being stared at by a very surprised-looking Professor Halligan, the surprised look enhanced by his hair standing up as if full of static. He looked dishevelled and somewhat disoriented, like a man who's been through a full cycle in a tumble drier.

'Did . . . did it work?' he asked.

Dr Creed pushed forward. 'It d—'

'Never mind about any of that!' John, still wearing that stupid helmet, grabbed my shoulder and dragged me around to face him. 'We've been through this at least *seventeen* times already.'

'Ha! Ha!' I spoke an unconvincing laugh, annoyed that John couldn't see how big a deal this was.

He sighed. 'You have a piece of toast in your left pocket. Dr Creed was about to say, "Bob, we made history!" And Guilder out there has instructed his pet killer to get Mia and me to sign non-disclosure forms that I guess he must always carry around in his inside jacket pocket. He offers us the use of his pen – it's blue with gold bands.'

'I . . .' I blinked. 'You saw me trying to hide that toast.'

'I didn't. But I couldn't know about the other stuff, could I?'

'You could guess them . . . if they're even correct. You—'

'We go through this *every* time,' John said desperately. 'We have five and a half minutes until it repeats. I'm the only one who remembers anything. We don't know why. This, maybe.' He rapped his knuckles on the helmet. 'It's got . . .' He glanced at Creed, '. . . field dampeners in it?' A shrug. 'Anyway. You've been working on a solution using another set of pulses through the magnets.' John swivelled towards Professor Halligan, who had staggered out to join us. 'You always ask, "Was it the flashover?" at this point. The answer is "Yes" and Nick gets more done if you don't make any more interruptions.' Turning back to me, John continued. 'You asked me to memorise a set of equations and numbers to get you up to speed with your thoughts so far. Not sure I've got them all straight, but here goes.' He took a deep breath and began to recite.

It seemed that John had made some errors in his recital, but it wasn't gibberish and I made sense of it. With practised efficiency he furnished me with paper, pens, a calculator and a workstation, which he unlocked using Dr Creed's password. I didn't have time to write any code but the machine linked into the World Wide Web and the Lynx browser enabled me to navigate through literally hundreds of pages of information held on computers all across the planet. Well, mainly in America. Most of the pages were either academic or pornographic. If you had the time to wait, then all manner of naked women would appear line by line on your screen as if a blind were slowly being lifted.

'Nick! We're on a clock here!' John clicked his fingers between me and the computer screen.

I set to work, knowing that if I didn't also find time to impress any progress on to John's mind in an easily conveyed manner, I would have utterly wasted my efforts. I raised my head from the equations John had dictated and gazed across at Mia and the others, who stood in hot debate back by the magnet array.

'About now,' said John, still at my shoulder, 'you're thinking that if this is just going to repeat over and over you could take some time out and experiment. You're thinking that this is consequence-free play time.' He tapped the page before me. 'While that's true, you told me to tell you that without this reminder you would "take the time to play" on every cycle and never find a solution.'

I sighed and returned to the sums. Quite what the others did with their five minutes I'm not sure. I was wholly focused on the problem.

'A minute to go,' John said.

'That was never four minutes!' I looked up from my page of squiggles.

'You always say that. Now hit me with what I have to remember for next time.'

'OK. Listen carefully.' And, forcing myself to go slowly, I began to tell him.

◆ ◆ ◆

A flash of bluish light, a shockwave and a scream.

Turning, we found ourselves being stared at by a very surprised-looking Professor Halligan, the surprised look enhanced by his hair standing up as if full of static. He looked dishevelled and somewhat disoriented.

Halligan opened his mouth. 'D—'

'Don't care.' A wild-eyed John, still wearing that stupid helmet, grabbed my shoulder and dragged me around to face him. 'We're in a fucking loop and this is like the hundredth cycle. Shut up and listen.'

He began to spout out high-speed mathematics, stuff he couldn't possibly have understood. I was amazed he could have even memorised it. It seemed to be connected to a temporal overspill. The others stood, bewildered, as John led me away to a workbench, still reciting facts at ninety miles a minute.

'You said you would need to send another pulse through to break the cycle and you narrowed the parameters down to . . .' He began to scribble down figures.

'But what—'

'Ssshhhh!' He slammed a hand to the desk. 'I got a decimal point wrong on the last cycle and Mia and Halligan were killed in the explosion.'

I shut up. Rust wheeled Guilder over to watch us, the others following. Somehow John's uncharacteristic intensity silenced all of them.

I focused on the paper before me, figures and equations swimming, sweat trickling from beneath my arms and down across my ribs as I strained to make sense of what looked like hours or even days of work.

'One minute left. You have to tell me what new stuff to tell you next cycle.'

'Already? You're fucking kidding me?'

'Fifty-five seconds.'

'I think this should work. Let's give it a try.'

'You said that last time. Fifty seconds.'

'No, I'm sure of it. This will work.'

'You said that too. Forty-five seconds.'

'Lemon, kumquat, banana! Did I say that last time?'

'Actually, it was "Lemon, lemon, banana." Forty seconds.'

'Get away from the magnets!' I shouted. 'Get behind something!'

I gave them fifteen seconds then hit the 'run' on the current sequence I'd coded into the workstation. Behind me the great banks of capacitors, all sizzling with stored current, dumped their load of electrons into the thick copper cables linking them to the electromagnets. A whine built rapidly, the huge chunks of iron creaked in their housings bolted deep into the concrete floor . . . and . . . nothing happened.

'Shit . . .' I picked up my notes and squinted at the last equation I'd written. 'I think—'

'Five seconds.'

'Two.'

'One.'

'Oh, dear God! Thank Christ for that.' John collapsed dramatically to the floor, letting the helmet roll away. As I helped him back to his feet, he pulled me in close and hissed, 'Rust has a gun. He's a head-case. Don't let him—'

'A gun?' I hissed back. 'How do you know?'

'He fucking shot me! Twice!'

'Christ! Why?' I pulled away, but not too far – he still looked unsteady.

'It bloody hurt, too! In case you were wondering . . .'

'*Why* did he do it?'

'I made the mistake of pointing out that there were no conse-quences in a loop. I only made that mistake once!'

The others had gathered at a lab bench where some cold coffees still stood. Halligan raised a quizzical eyebrow and beckoned us over.

'C'mon.' I went to join them, John following, making sure he had me between him and Rust at all times.

Guilder had John and Mia sign non-disclosure documents and sent them packing. John practically dragged Mia out with him. She looked apologetically over her shoulder. 'See you at the flat. Don't be long!'

We watched them go. It was a shock to see that it was dark outside. Like when you come out of a cinema and the world has changed while the film held you timeless. I don't think Dr Creed or any of the others noticed.

'Non-disclosures? This is huge!' Professor Halligan declared as soon as the distant main doors began to close on Mia and John. 'We can't keep a thing like this quiet! The government will—'

'We can and will,' said Rust, gesturing toward Guilder to indicate that he was speaking on the man's behalf.

'This is dangerous is what it is!' I raised my voice to get the floor. 'I can't believe it's my job to be the grown-up here. We were all caught in a loop there, in case you didn't notice. And if it hadn't been for John messing about we would have kept on failing to get out of it in our allotted five minutes. Christ knows how long we've been stuck in there.

And what if it had been a five-second loop? We've no idea how long these things take to unwind – if they unwind at all, that is.'

I looked at Guilder for some kind of response, but he just shook his head and waved Rust on.

Rust continued as if I hadn't spoken. 'You've been well paid to ensure your discretion and those monies would need to be returned, along with additional severe financial penalties, if you were to break our agreement. In addition, there would be other severe penalties which I myself would be delegated to hand out. Trust me, gentlemen, you do not want to go there.' Rust raised a hand against any protest. 'These experiments have been well documented and filmed. Your place in the history books and your undoubtedly deserved share of a Nobel Prize are assured . . . but must be delayed a while yet.'

Halligan blustered. 'But why? And how long do you think those kids who just walked out of here will hold their tongues? And Nick here, he didn't sell his soul to you.'

Rust shrugged. 'I trust them.'

This sounded wholly unlike Rust, who I doubted had ever trusted another human soul in his life, but it also sounded unlike Guilder, who sat there studying me. They were right to trust me, of course. I had no interest in making my work public. Publicity meant government interest, and that meant regulations, it meant losing ownership of the work, it meant being watched and controlled more thoroughly than Guilder could ever achieve.

It worried me, though. My memories of the whole paradox incident that came to a head just after I arrived in Cambridge were hazy in the extreme, and fleeting. When we solved the problem it had technically stopped having ever existed, but however well we had managed to stitch reality back together, a few stray recollections seemed to have found their way through the gaps. Had the same thing happened to Rust or Guilder or somebody else involved in the whole strange business? Did they know I came back to 1986 from 2011? Or did they have other trump cards in their hands?

'Look, I've got to go.' I wanted to see if they would let me.

Rust's eye flickered towards Guilder. 'Sure, Nick, you run along.'

I made for the door, keeping a brisk stride and calling back. 'And for God's sake don't throw the switch on any more tests before I figure out what went wrong with that one!'

'Sure thing, Nick,' Rust called after me. 'We'll be around to pick you up at 9 a.m. sharp.'

I turned at the door, halfway through, and shouted back, 'Pick me up?'

'Nine sharp! Mr Guilder has something to show you. Bring your girlfriend if you like.'

With that I pulled the door shut behind me and ran for the main gate. I knew the sort of things Rust liked to surprise people with, and if Guilder thought he could show me a pile of money big enough to get me on board the crazy train, he had another think coming.

CHAPTER 4

1992

According to my watch, reset against the laboratory clock, it was just after 11 p.m. by the time I got back to the flat. John was already bedding down on the sofa, pleading exhaustion. I felt as if I'd only just choked down the breakfast he'd incinerated for us. Mia was as wide awake as me.

'Well, if you'd had to suffer through those same five minutes a million damn times you'd be exhausted, too.' John yawned mightily and set his head on the pillow. 'That was some weird shit. Someone should make a film like that. Only not just five minutes. Draw it out so there's time to do something. A whole day on repeat.' He yawned, mumbled something else, then closed his eyes.

I retreated to the bedroom with Mia, closing the door as quietly as I could.

Mia sat on the bed and patted for me to join her. 'So not sleepy.'

I took her up on her invitation. 'Good.'

◆ ◆ ◆

When the bell rang, Mia and I were ready to go. We hadn't done much sleeping. Even when we tried, we just couldn't. It was like how John described jetlag, something neither Mia nor I had had the chance to experience. Either way, by 6 a.m. we were physically exhausted and mentally buzzing. By nine we were practically waiting at the door, ready to see whatever it was Guilder wanted to show us. Mia reckoned it might be a sports car or an actual bucket full of cash. Some kind of bribe, anyway.

For his part, John slept like he was in one of those stasis pods in *Aliens*. I hated him in the way that only someone who can't sleep hates someone who won't wake up can. He hadn't been invited on Guilder's little trip, so after shaking him, taking his blankets and doing my best impression of a very annoying alarm clock, I left him to it. He grunted some sleepy dismissal at us as we left.

The man at the door was the chauffeur we'd seen the previous night, a small fellow with curly grey hair and pale eyes, younger than his looks might first imply. He looked at us not with the disdain that a rich man's servant reserves for social inferiors, but with the mild disgust that is usually kept for dog mess in the street.

Guilder's black Rolls Royce looked wholly out of place parked in the slightly rundown residential street where I rented a flat on the second floor of a terraced townhouse. The chauffeur opened the car door and Mia and I bundled in, finding ourselves opposite Guilder in his wheelchair and Rust beside him. The interior had been adapted to allow the chair to be wheeled in and secured.

'Good morning.' Guilder wheezed the words out with effort. 'Trouble sleeping?'

I narrowed my eyes in reply. Being sick didn't change the fact that Guilder was a bastard. It just made him a sick bastard. He employed psychopaths and used them to terrorise people to do what he wanted them to. I wasn't exactly a stranger to illness myself. I'd never felt it gave me a licence to treat the rest of humanity like dirt.

'We have a long drive,' Rust said. 'Should be there by lunchtime.'

'You could just tell us where we're going and what we're going to see,' I said.

'Allow. A dying man. A little drama.' Guilder leaned back and closed his eyes.

I found myself yawning, tired at long last. I put my arm around Mia and looked out to watch the world go by.

◆ ◆ ◆

'Getting close.' Something prodded my leg.

I cracked an eye open and yawned again. '. . . must have dozed off . . .' Guilder had used his cane to poke me. I turned my head and found Mia was resting hers on my shoulder, so fast asleep that she'd actually dribbled a bit on my T-shirt. 'What did you say?'

'Almost there,' Guilder repeated.

Mia lifted her head, blinking. I guess we both must have fallen asleep, though I never would have thought that possible with a creature like Rust staring at us. I imagined that if he ever slept it would be like a snake, motionless and with his eye open.

We were somewhere rural. Fields, hedges, cows, brilliant yellow rapeseed. The car made a sharp turn and we were no longer on a met-alled road. The suspension absorbed most of the lumps and bumps but I could hear stones pinging up from the tyres to hit the undercarriage, and the hedges on both sides reached out to scratch at the paintwork with twiggy fingers.

'Where are we?' Mia asked.

'Not far south of Bristol,' Rust said. 'Mr Guilder owns fifteen square miles out here. We're on his land now.'

We rumbled on for a while, making several turns. At two points Rust had to squeeze out to open and close gates. That lazy weakness that often visits on waking after a daytime sleep had me in its grip and I was prepared to sit and yawn and lean against Mia, who seemed content to do the same to me.

At last we stopped in a small clearing in front of a patch of woodland. It seemed out of place among the intense agriculture of the area. The outer trees seemed young, mostly saplings. Perhaps Guilder had forbidden his tenant farmers from clearing them . . .

'The last bit's on foot.' Rust slid across the seat and opened the door.

Mia and I got out the other side while Rust positioned a ramp and wheeled Guilder from the car. It would have been a nice day for a walk. Lazy summer heat, a light breeze, crops, the warm slow press of green things rising from soil. I'd been too long poring over papers; it was good to be out among the bees and birdsong, good to fix my eyes on distant things.

A concrete pathway, painted in camouflage green and brown, led from close to the car and allowed Guilder's chair to be wheeled in among the trees. Mia and I followed on for fifty yards or so, in among thicker, older trees, until the path ended abruptly on a brown metal plate the same width as the path and about six feet long. Rust wheeled Guilder on to the plate and put the chair's brakes on.

'One at a time here,' Guilder said. 'Try . . . not to fall . . . off.'

He took out a device that looked like the garage door remote controls you see in American films. When he pressed the button the metal plate beneath him began to descend, thankfully with none of the shuddering that garage doors usually display. Guilder disappeared smoothly from sight down a rectangular concrete shaft just a hair's breadth wider than the plate.

We moved in close and watched him go down. A dank smell rose from the hole, and water stains fringed the walls where rain had trickled through the gap between the platform and its housing.

'Is this his James Bond supervillain hideout?' I whispered to Mia.

She sniggered. 'He just needs a fluffy white cat in his lap!'

As Guilder went deeper the shadows swallowed him and a sense of unease rose through me, extinguishing my good humour. I took a step away from the edge, worried for a moment that Rust might just set his hand to the small of my back and pitch me in.

A minute later the empty platform rattled back into view.

'You next, Nick.' Rust gestured for me to take my place.

I hesitated, meeting Mia's eyes.

Rust snorted, reading my mind. 'This isn't the fox-chicken-corn puzzle. You either have to leave Mia alone with me at the top or alone with me and Mr Guilder at the bottom. If I wanted some of Miss Jones I would have taken it a long time ago.' He nodded again to the platform. 'Get on.' The amused malice in his eyes reminded me of his brother, who certainly had had designs on Mia.

'Go on,' Mia said. 'I'll be fine.'

With a sigh I took my place and almost immediately the iron plate began descending again. I watched the world reduce to a shrinking rectangle of daylight. For a while I had nothing to study but the walls. The water stains followed me for a surprising distance and after that it was just featureless concrete and the two notched steel tracks that some toothed wheels beneath my feet must be engaging with in order to raise and lower the platform.

Finally the shaft opened up into a dimly lit natural cave where Guilder sat waiting. He sent the platform on its way back up as soon as I stepped off it. I watched it go until it vanished into the ceiling, making the cavern even dimmer.

'I knew I . . . was dying . . . seven years ago.' Guilder looked up at me. In the half-light his wasted face took on a ghoulish aspect. 'I started financing . . . Halligan at about the same . . . time that a brilliant fifteen-year-old was told . . . he had cancer.'

'That doesn't make us friends,' I said.

'It creates . . . a shared understanding . . . of the value of time,' he wheezed back.

I couldn't deny that. Demus and his revelations had been a lifeline to me just as the world had become a very dark place. If I had had nothing to do but contemplate my fate, I couldn't imagine how I would have kept from falling apart. The fact that Demus existed had saved my body from self-destruction, but it was the *idea* that he existed that had saved my sanity.

We watched in silence as Mia descended into view. When she stepped off the platform Guilder made no move to send it back up.

'Not bringing your pet snake down?' Mia asked.

'I employ Charles . . . to keep me safe,' Guilder said. 'Here, I feel safer . . . knowing he is . . . up there.' He raised a shaky hand, indicating a concrete walkway. 'Push me.'

Evidently wheeling himself off the platform had been his limit, so I did the honours. I had to be careful not to steer him off the edge on to the natural rock, where the ground was too uneven for the wheels. Mia followed close behind, one hand on my upper arm. The sporadic lightbulbs just gave a sense of emptiness, their illumination failing to reach the opposite wall.

As we followed the path it got darker and darker until I could barely see the concrete ahead of us. The only sound was Guilder's breathless voice, pausing every few words as he gasped for more air.

'It took me a long time to find this place. It's a previously unknown cave system. Caves are not uncommon in this region. It's the limestone. I had extensive surveys carried out on the land I owned. Purchased more land. Commissioned more surveys. And here we are. My secret cave.'

'Like Batman!' Mia observed.

Guilder ignored her. 'I started looking as soon as Robert explained that those travelling forward in time would not vanish from our world but would merely pass through it in a greatly accelerated manner. It occurred to me then that a man wishing to leap forward a significant number of years would require a safe and secret place in which to do it. Imagine if I were to simply begin the journey in one of my houses. Who is to say that my enemies might not take possession of me and entomb me in a wall? Who is to guarantee that the time to which I travelled would be one in which I would be welcomed? Better to be in control of when and if I chose to make myself known.'

'You?' asked Mia from the darkness behind us. 'Why would you—'

'He's dying. He wants to travel to some time when they can cure him.' I wondered how I hadn't figured that one out ages ago. I guess I had been so fixed on the idea that Guilder's unseemly haste had been driven by a greed for more money that I hadn't really thought about other motives. Besides, for the first few years he had always seemed to be in rude health and yet obsessed with forcing the rate of our experiments beyond all reasonable caution.

'Correct.' Guilder's wheels bumped against a low barrier. We had come to the end of the path. A single low-wattage bulb managed to create a small island of light for us, showing nothing but a few yards of smooth stone floor strewn with stones dumped by whatever river had carved the place way back when.

'You're not worried that the elevator will break or run out of juice while you're down here for decades?' I asked.

'There are several of them, all very well concealed, and powered by generators with ample fuel,' Guilder told us. 'And the way we came in would be buried after I began my journey.'

'Entombed like an ancient pharaoh,' Mia said. 'With all you need for the afterlife.'

'Precisely,' Guilder said. 'Getting out is not the problem.' He pushed a smaller button on his control. 'This is.'

Floodlights burst into life on all sides. I covered my eyes, letting go of the wheelchair and cursing. For a few moments all I could do was press my knuckles to my eyes; then, hearing Mia's exclamation, I started trying to peek between my fingers. It seemed as though we weren't alone. I could make out figures ahead of us. Lots of them.

'What the . . .' With a tear running down my cheek and blinking away more, I lowered my hands.

'Why are they naked?' Mia asked.

It wasn't the first question I would have asked, but it was on my list. Scores of naked people stood in front of us in an ordered queue like they were lining up for check-in at the airport. And they weren't the nice kind of naked you can see in top-shelf magazines. This was real people naked, young and old, fat and skinny, droopy and pert.

'What on earth have you been doing?' I asked.

'Me?' Guilder managed a hollow laugh. 'Nothing. They were here when we breached the chamber. All one hundred and seven of them. Like a fucking terracotta army.'

CHAPTER 5

NINETEEN YEARS LATER

2011

I always held out hope that we had jumped the tracks somehow, that somewhere along the line our lives had diverged from the script witnessed by Demus. Nobody likes to believe that everything they ever think or do, no matter how spontaneous it seems, has already happened and was bound to follow its path. Twenty-five years had given me plenty of surprises, plenty of times to stare into the mirror, even as Demus had slowly written himself into my reflection, and to say to him that surely I was the first and only one to have experienced the moment that had just passed. Could the man who came back to visit me when I was just a child, sick and terrified of dying, could he have already lived every second of my life? Had he already made love to Mia, cried with her when she miscarried their child, accepted the Fields Medal for mathematics, sailed the South China Sea, stared in wonder at dawn breaking over the shoulder of Kilimanjaro? Was it true that everywhere I went, he had been there first?

I hoped that we were free of Demus and his lies, that we could live our own lives and make our own destinies. But until we were done with the year 2011 we would never be sure. This was the year Demus said he had come back from; this was the year his Mia was supposed to have her accident. If we passed through it safely, we would know that we had escaped him. We would know that somewhere in the intervening quarter of a century of free choices and random events, our paths had strayed and our lives had become our own rather than something held in trust, a torch to be passed over when we had run our leg of our own particular human race.

I'd grown to hate Demus with a passion. He could have saved Mia both from the accident itself and from the lifetime spent knowing that it was headed her way. He could have done it with a few words. He just had to tell me to do something that he hadn't done. Anything. If I knew he had never sung in public I would have done so, thereby ensuring that I wasn't him, and that my Mia wasn't his Mia. Instead he chose not to. He chose to sit back and let it all happen, and for that I couldn't forgive him. What made his Mia more valuable than mine? What made his love for her deeper than mine? Because whatever he might think on that score, he was wrong. Mia and I may have left the melodramatic rapture of teenage love behind us, but what remained had wrapped itself around our bones. We had something deep and rarely spoken, the shared scars of early trauma, the ache of children that never came, an enduring delight in each other's company. And, of course, I still wanted to take her to bed whenever the opportunity arose.

'Nick?' A hand shook me. 'Nick! Did you hear anything I said?'

I looked up. Neil Watkins, assistant director at the National Institute for Temporal Studies, had hold of my shoulder. 'They've been trying to reach you. Mia's been in an accident. You need to get to the hospital.'

CHAPTER 6

1992

'How could they just be here already?' I blinked and tried to keep my eyes from returning to the naked people. The line of mainly pale flesh exerted a strange pull, like a road accident. 'Halligan and Creed only did their experiment yesterday!'

'They were all here when the chamber was first entered last November,' Guilder said.

'And you're sure there's no other way in?' Mia asked.

'We've found another way since. There are extensive tunnels. One leads to a well-hidden crack in a small cliff face in some old-growth woodland a quarter-mile west of here. It's just about large enough for a man to squeeze through, but the moss all around showed no signs of disturbance.'

My gaze had returned to the figures while we waited through Guilder's laboured explanation. Mia had actually gone up to the first of them, a middle-aged man, and was feeling his arm. 'He feels like Professor Halligan did. But how far in the future are they trying to go, and why here? How did they even get the equipment in?'

'And who did it?' I asked. 'Have they been spying on our work?'

I went to join Mia. The cave wasn't as silent as I had first thought. From further back came the slow dripping of water. It was cold after the sunshine above and goose bumps had risen across my bare arms. An icy drop of water hit the back of my T-shirt and suddenly I had great sympathy for the naked crowd before me, standing here in the dark year after year, come what may.

'I've had the faces of these people photographed and circulated discreetly in the hope of finding their identities,' Guilder said.

'And?' I asked.

'If you and Miss Jones would go and study the two figures at the far end of the line, you should be able to tell why it has proved so difficult to discover who these people are . . .' Guilder said. 'I would come with you, but my wheels weren't made for such explorations.'

'You could just tell us,' Mia said.

'Humour me?' Guilder managed a smile. 'Would any of this have been as much fun had I just told you about it in Cambridge?'

I had to admit it was an impressive and fascinating thing. I was glad I'd come.

I tilted my head at Mia. 'Coming?'

And we set off around the edge of the cavern.

None of them were children, and most were older rather than young, though none were really elderly. Two of the women were young and gorgeous. The whole thing made very little sense to me. The queue led back towards the far end of the chamber, beyond the area illuminated by the floodlights. The end of the line stood in shadows. We closed in on the last pair, numbers 106 and 107. A man and a woman, neither of them young nor old.

'Fuck me!' I stopped in my tracks.

'What?' Mia nearly walked into me.

Words escaped me.

'Bloody hell!' Mia pulled up short beside me. 'Is that . . . ?'

'It's Demus, yes.' I hadn't seen him in six years, but now he stood before me, with a full head of hair and all his worldly goods on show, there was no mistaking him.

47

'So who's behind him?' She leaned to look past, eyes widening.

'Wow.' I stepped forward and stared, wishing the light was better.

'At least I kept my figure,' Mia said.

'Yes, you did!'

◆ ◆ ◆

Guilder waited patiently for us to return. We came back with furrowed brows, lost in thought. Mia had questions, of course, and so did I, but I cautioned her to wait. Guilder probably had the place bugged and I didn't want to give the man any more cards than he already held.

'So, you see,' he said. 'They're not going into the future. They're *from* the future and they're heading into the past.'

'Well, technically they could also be from the future and be heading back into it after a visit to some earlier year,' I said.

Guilder shook his head. 'You go back, you start a new timeline; they wouldn't still be in our timeline for the return journey. I shouldn't have to remind you of your own discoveries, Dr Hayes.'

I said nothing. Guilder didn't have to know about the peculiar arrangement of our own timeline, which allowed me, and seemingly anyone else who tried, to come back to it and not start a new timeline as long as they didn't do anything to contradict what had happened in their past.

'The real question is, why are Miss Jones and yourself the last two travellers?'

'Well,' I said. 'If you wait long enough, you'll find out.' I regretted the words as soon as they were out of my mouth.

Guilder didn't seem to take offence, though. He twisted his mouth in a rare smile. 'I don't think I have that option. My doctors have given me a few months. Six, at most.'

'That begs a different question then. Why did you wait until now to show me this? Has Professor Halligan seen it, or Dr Creed?'

48

Guilder watched me for a moment with those stony eyes of his. 'Knowledge is power, and I like power. Unfortunately, in this particular game almost all the knowledge is locked up in that extraordinary brain of yours. So, forgive me if I hang on to my secrets a little long. But I doubt the reality of this cave has any bearing on your mathematics. I brought you here to remind you that there is an end product and to prove to you that you achieve it. This seems to be a fact that is now set in stone, or at least in a stone cave.' He managed a dry chuckle. 'So my push for results clearly gets us somewhere.' He took a moment to recover his breath before trying to turn his chair. 'Take me back to the lift, if you would.'

As I pushed him back along the path, he explained the reason for the visit. 'I'm going to bring Halligan and Creed here, of course, but you're going to have to be the one to arm them with the techniques they need to understand what's going on here. Knowing when these people have come from and where they are going might be the beginning of giving us a why. I've identified at least twelve of them. All extremely wealthy individuals. At best estimate they are all around twenty years older in the cave than they are now.'

Guilder allowed us to go up first. By the time he rattled back into view the sun had almost managed to erase the subterranean chill from my bones, and Mia had realised that two old men she knew were going to be seeing her naked on a regular basis.

We ate in the beer garden of a roadside pub not far from the caves. Possibly we were still on land Guilder owned. It felt odd to sit there with a half of lager and a ploughman's lunch across the table from Rust and Guilder. I imagined them as the snake and the spider: Rust driven by a cold hunger, remorseless and ready to strike at any moment; Guilder more inscrutable, his motivations hidden, possibly alien. Like a spider, he would sit still when you watched him, making no move but full of a menace that was hard to explain. But that wasn't the real threat. The true fear was what would happen if you looked away. The sudden scurry. And when you looked back, he would be somewhere new, the distance between you devoured. Perhaps even on you. Metaphorically speaking, of course.

Neither Guilder nor Rust made any conversation. When healthy, Guilder had been full of the energetic can-do charm that businessmen exude, but with him the steel was always there under the velvet, and the face he showed to the world was not his own. For Rust, words were just another weapon, to be brought out when required but serving no other purpose. He had saved me once, after my might-have-been daughter manipulated his past, putting him in my debt according to his own bizarre life rules. But that debt had been paid, and we were never anything even distantly approximating friends.

'What if the press get hold of it?' Mia was saying as we got back into the car. 'We'll both be nude on the *Nine O'Clock News*. They'll do tours round the cave for sightseers. We'll be like the waxworks at Madam Tussauds.'

None of that really concerned me, though. All the long drive back to Cambridge I sat deep in my thoughts, mumbling the barest of responses to the occasional half-heard comment from Mia. Demus has said that he arrived in January 1986 in the small hours of the morning, naked and just outside the Watkins Road police station. Had he been lying? Why would he? Was this a second trip? But he wouldn't have made any other trips ever again after that visit. He died. So was this a visit to the past made before he came to see us? And again, why?

How could he just have appeared at the police station if the solution to time travel that he invented was the one we saw in the cave? It would mean that from the moment he appeared outside the police station until the moment in the future that he left from, there would be a naked Demus standing in the street. And if that were the case I think I might have heard about it by now . . .

So . . . what the hell was going on?

We got back to Cambridge by late afternoon and Guilder's chauffeur dropped us in the street where he had picked us up that morning.

'You've been very quiet,' Mia said, climbing up the steps behind me.

'There's a lot to think about.' I watched the Rolls Royce pull away.

Mia opened the main door and led the way upstairs. 'What does it mean? What we saw in the cave? We're there, Nick. I come back with Demus? That means it works, right? The whole thing about storing my memories. I get better after the accident.'

'I don't know.' I really didn't. 'Just because they're in a line doesn't prove that's the order they left in. And we don't know when the Demus we saw there actually left the future. And even if the me and you we saw there really did leave after the accident . . . well, just being able to stand up doesn't prove your mind is restored.'

Mia reached my floor and turned, rolling her eyes. 'How about a little optimism?'

'The optimist sets themself up for disappointment. I'm just aiming for a little realism. We have a hundred and seven naked people travelling backward through time in a cave, and two of them are us. That's about all we know for sure.' I moved past her, wanting a cup of tea and a comfy chair before continuing the conversation.

'Well, I—' The door to the flat stood ajar and, seeing it, Mia fell silent.

We went inside to find everything on the floor. Papers, books, clothes, the contents of cupboards, the furniture turned over with its linings slit, the carpets rolled back, floorboards lifted.

'John?' Mia called, but it wasn't the kind of flat you could get lost in. 'John!'

'They've taken him,' I said, anger rising.

'Who?'

'Guilder's people, of course.'

'Guilder did this? Why? What's he done with John?'

I nodded. 'He's always kept a close eye on my work. You know he has me followed. He's in my computers, too. His hackers are quite clever, but I have them boxed out of areas they don't even know exist—'

'John!' Mia shouted. 'What about John?'

I frowned. 'This is obviously a message. He has my flat broken into quite often. Usually it's hard to even notice they were here. This is about ownership. Like a dog pissing on a tree. Maybe John will . . .' I heard footsteps on the stairs.

'Jesus! What happened?' John stood at the still-open door looking astonished.

'John!' Mia rushed over to hug him. He looked even more surprised, but didn't object. 'Hey! Hey! Everyone's OK, aren't they?'

'Where were you?' Mia asked.

'Well . . .' John coloured. 'There was a girl from downstairs who wanted to borrow some sugar. And . . . well, we got talking and she took me out for a coffee, then we went to see *Batman Returns*. I just said goodbye to her at her door. Jenny. You must have seen her, Nick. Hot blonde! She lives just below you.'

'A forty-year-old accountant named Kevin lives in the flat below mine,' I said. 'I think he's gay.'

'But. She said . . .' John looked around at the chaos. 'Oh . . .'

We all set to tidying, trying to get things back in order. At least they hadn't broken anything, but even so it made me angry. Angry that after all these years I still hadn't found a way out from under Guilder's boot. This whole journey of mine had been punctuated by people who thought they could impose their will on me, from Michael Devis and his schoolyard bully mentality, through first one Rust brother then the other, to Guilder who, despite never lifting a finger against me, was the biggest bully of them all.

'You and Mia naked in a cave?' John stopped midway through restocking my kitchen cupboards with the assorted tins that had been pulled from them. Mainly mushroom soup, with a few tins of baked beans for visitors. Nothing but haute cuisine chez Hayes. 'Seriously?'

'Seriously.' I was stuffing reams of old bills and bank statements back into the right drawers.

'How does that even work?' John asked.

'I don't know.' I'd been thinking the very same thing myself. I'd spent forever wrestling with the mathematics of the thing without ever giving serious thought to what it would look like. I thought I knew. I thought Demus had told me about his solution. And then there had been my almost-daughter Eva's more sophisticated form of time travel. I guess I had invented the bicycle and she had invented the biplane.

'But . . . if you can see people travelling back in time . . . I mean, how does that work?'

'You understand that asking the same question twice doesn't mean I will change my mind about not knowing the answer?' I forced the over-stuffed drawer shut, making a mental promise to have a cleanout. One day.

'But . . .' said John, who was seriously beginning to test my patience. 'If you came back from a hundred years in the future that would mean that there would be a "you" standing there in that one spot for a hundred years—'

'Stark naked!' interrupted Mia, who seemed to be taking the naked part rather personally.

'Naked,' agreed John. 'But when you get to the time you're aiming at . . . you would have to leave behind this image of you standing there, because it's going to be there for a hundred years.'

'It's worse than that,' said Mia. 'Imagine there is one of these . . . what? Time trails? Of you. And you know about it. Then what happens if you decide, "No, I can see that I am supposed to go back in time in this spot, but I don't want to." What happens then?'

53

'Or,' I said, 'if you do decide to go back but from some different place. What if you step into the time machine in London, somewhere where there has never been a sign of one of these time trails? I like that, by the way – I'm calling them time trails from now on. It's official.'

'Cool.' Mia grinned. 'It's like I just named black holes.'

'If black holes made zero sense at all,' John added.

'They kinda don't,' said Mia.

'Anyway.' I straightened up with a double armful of bedding. 'None of it makes much sense, but what it's hard to argue with is that there are a hundred and seven nudists heading back through time in a cave under a field not far outside Bristol, and I'm one of them.'

CHAPTER 7

2011

'Mia Hayes – she was brought into A&E not long ago. Where have they taken her?' I leaned over the reception desk at Addenbrookes Hospital, trying and failing to force myself to calmness.

'Let me check for you, sir.' The woman at the desk wore the neutral expression of someone whose job sets them face to face with a dozen desperate people every day, each of them sure that their matter of life and death is somehow more vital, more urgent, than those of the others all around them whose lives must be just as important to them and have been just as broken. 'There's no record of her being assigned to a ward. She must still be waiting in A&E.'

'Still? But she was—' I bit back the words. I didn't know what the situation was. I had just assumed. I'd been waiting so long for 'the accident'. And here we were in 2011, a quarter-century after Demus had told us it was going to happen. Only a few months remaining on the clock.

'It's through there, sir. Just follow the signs to Accident and Emergency.' The receptionist pointed with her pen and gazed past me to the next in line.

I followed the signs, doing that almost-walk where all that holds us back from a flat sprint is the misplaced sense of embarrassment that so often keeps people in check. It's as though somehow we think that if we throw decorum to the wind and run, the universe might disapprove and raise the stakes still further, greeting us with a greater disaster than we might find if we just walk there like civilised human beings.

I wound a long path past endless doors with cryptic names above them, coming at last to the A&E reception. I saw Mia immediately, sitting on a crowded row of fixed seating amid daytime drunks, young mothers with croupy babies and old folk nursing unspecified injuries or sucking on oxygen as if it were all that sustained them.

'Mia!' I rushed over, emotion suddenly catching up with me in the home straight. If I lost her, I didn't know what I would do. Some vital part of me would shatter. Not enough to kill me, perhaps, but enough to leave me broken. Waiting for my days to run out.

'Hey! I'm alright. I would have called you, but I broke my phone. And maybe this . . .' She tried to raise her right arm, which I belatedly noticed was in a sling.

'What happened?'

She looked confused. 'It's a bit of a blur. I got hit by a car.'

'Christ!' A cold sick feeling took hold of my stomach. 'Did they catch the fucker?'

'Well, it wasn't her fault. The driver, I mean. I ran out into the road without looking.'

'Why?'

Mia's confusion became something closer to worry. 'Someone tried to grab me on that little road behind the supermarket on the high street.'

'What kind of someone?'

'A young man . . .' She frowned as if trying to remember. 'It's lucky I took all those Krav Maga classes. I don't think he was expecting a fight . . . But he was so fast! I—'

'What did he look like?'

'He came at me from behind. I never would have got away, but two men came out of the warehouse door at the back of Tesco and they must have seen him just about to grab me. One of them shouted a warning. And after I'd elbowed the bastard in the face and twisted away, the other two rushed him.' She shook her head as if trying to rattle more of the memory loose. 'I should have stayed and helped, I know, but in the moment all I could think of was to run. Then when I reached the high street and looked back, I saw him coming down the alley after me, head down, limping but fast, no sign of the two warehouse men. I think they must have hurt his leg, though. So anyway, I kept on running. And a car hit me. Stupid, I know.'

I asked the only question that mattered. 'Was it him?'

'It's been a long time. And I didn't see his face.' Mia shuddered. She stared at nothing as if trying to summon back that last image, her glimpse of the man chasing her. She spoke slowly, weighing her words. 'I think it might have been.'

'Shit.' I looked around the A&E waiting room with fresh eyes, trying to identify anyone who might be more than they seemed. I'd worked hard to make sure that when they finally arrived, there wouldn't be any help waiting for them; but these were resourceful men, and desperation is a powerful motivator. 'He'll have followed the ambulance to the hospital. We need to get out of here without being seen. And quickly. How's your arm?'

'The triage nurse said it wasn't obviously broken, but I haven't seen a doctor yet . . . I'm sorry, am I boring you?' Mia punched my shoulder with her good arm.

'Sorry.' I looked up from my iPhone. 'I'm on Google Earth, looking at the layout of the hospital. I'm going to call the lads in on this, and all the hired help.'

'We might be overreacting?' Mia frowned. 'I mean, it was just a glimpse. Dark hair, slim, young.'

'Maybe.' I frowned, too. The police artist's impression would fit about five million British men.

'He was probably just after my handbag.'

'I had two men following you, Mia.'

'I told you not to do that!' She punched me in the same spot, but harder.

'Well, I did. I worry, and we only have a few months before we're clear of this. Anyway, the point is, where were they?'

'What are you saying?'

'I'm saying that I think he took them out first. They were professionals. Hard men. Perhaps he got hurt. Perhaps that was why he was limping, and perhaps that's why you managed to get away in the first place.'

'Oh.' Mia looked properly scared for the first time.

'And if any of that's true, we're going to need everybody and everything if we're to stand a chance of stopping him.'

CHAPTER 8

1992

For a week after confronting myself in Guilder's secret cave, I ignored my usual work concerning how to crack the intractable problems of time travel to the past, a much trickier beast than simply accelerating travel into the future. Instead I devoted myself to figuring out the mechanics of the process, given the assumption that the difficult part of actually making it happen had been solved. Being presented with irrefutable evidence of a thing you're trying to make happen having definitely happened always concentrates the mind wonderfully.

By the time Friday came around and I boarded the train to London, I had broken the back of the problem. I stayed with Mother that night and spent the evening dotting mathematical i's and crossing mathematical t's. By the time Saturday came around, I was ready to explain it to someone.

'Hey, Simon.' Simon always opened John's door on D&D days. You could be forgiven for thinking that he lived there. Apparently, John disabled his doorbell every Friday night and around nine the next morning he would plug it back in, whereupon it would immediately ring and he would go to the door to find Simon waiting there for the D&D session starting at ten. Mia and I never asked quite how early Simon actually arrived, but the fact that John was organised enough to disable his bell suggested that the answer was 'very'. It was just good fortune that Simon always put his faith in technology and never thought to knock.

'I'm excited to hear about this cave,' Simon said.

'All will be revealed in a minute.' I ushered him back into the hallway.

'Good.' Simon gave me an odd look, then smiled at Mia, before finally turning and leading the way into the luxury of John's apartment.

John was waiting at his posh oak gaming table with bowls of snacks laid on and Coke cans at the ready.

'The cave!' said Simon, even before I'd properly settled into my chair.

'Well, I guess John told you about it,' I said. 'I've got some proofs sketched out now, so I think I understand the mechanics of it all.'

Simon frowned. 'What are you talking about?'

'The secret cave with all the naked people in it . . .' I frowned back. 'What are you talking about?'

'The cave all our characters were left trapped in at the end of last week's session, of course.' Simon blinked in surprise.

'So you're not interested in my—'

'Fineous is trapped,' Simon explained, speaking slowly as if I might not be able to follow, 'in a cave. Mia said the air could run out at any time.'

'I said it would last at least a week.' Mia shook her head, smiling.

'A week ago!'

'I want to hear your proofs, Nick.' John pulled the tab from a Coke and leaned back in his chair to slurp it. 'Not the boring stuff, though. Just the edited highlights.'

'Right, then.' I gave Simon a look, daring him to object. 'It's a bit crazy, but that's what happens when you mess with time.'

'I noticed.' John took another slurp.

'Well, normally, if you go back in time you vanish and nobody – past, present or future – ever sees you in your timeline again. That's because the act of you arriving back in the past splits off a new timeline.

So you can murder your father before you were born, should you be moved to do so, and there's no paradox because you arrived from a different timeline where he remained unmurdered.'

'Is unmurdered a word?' Mia asked.

'Big picture. Keep your eyes on the prize.' I tapped the table. 'So, this stuff in the cave is because our timeline isn't normal. It's . . . knotted. Something very weird happened to it, which is why Demus was able to go back to 1986, talk to himself, i.e., me, and remember doing so. As long as he did nothing to contradict what he knew had already happened he stayed on the same timeline he left.

'Now, people who go back in time and do so in the way that Demus did are the ones who then leave a trail through all the time they travel through. And that trail is the solid image of them, like the ones Mia and I saw in Guilder's cave.

'If you want to go back to your own timeline you have to go to the far end of a trail that you have already left through the years, a trail that has been waiting for you. And then it all works. So one day, it seems, Mia and I will go back to that cave, step into our timelines and travel back.'

John burped loudly. 'Same question I had in Cambridge: what if there's a trail with your name on and you refuse to use it?'

'Good question. The answer is that it vanishes. But it does create a persistent low-level paradox field, and too many of those can be fatal, so it's best avoided.'

'How many of these persistent low—'

'PLLP fields.'

'How many of those things would it take to kill someone?' John asked.

'Oh, I mean fatal as in "to life in general", not a particular someone. If they go critical, they would unzip all matter in a volume expanding at the speed of light.'

'Right . . . how many?'

'Don't know. Paradox mathematics is too difficult for me. We'd have to ask the daughter I might have had. Eva did seem to have a real talent for it.'

'Sounds a little dangerous,' Mia said. 'How are you going to fix it?'

Simon interrupted me. 'I have an idea.'

'Yes?' I hoped it was better than the ones I'd come up with so far.

'Fineous searches the walls of the cave for secret doors.' Simon reached for his small mound of six-sided dice.

And just like that, he sidetracked us all into having fun.

Simon's idea wasn't actually that bad. Nobody had helpfully built a secret door to the outside world in the cavern we'd been trapped in by a cave-in, but there was a very hard-to-spot crack behind a small waterfall at the far end. By dint of a lot of squeezing and pushing, and later the judicious use of a shrink potion not unlike the one in *Alice in Wonderland*, we managed to emerge into the dungeons beneath the Tower of Illusion, just as we'd been planning all along.

My mage came through last. 'You squeeze really hard,' Mia said, rolling some dice behind her screen. 'You're certain for a moment that you're going to be wedged in the crack forever. Things start going weird and blurry. And then, with a sudden pop, you're through and clear with just grazed ears to show for it.'

'That was the last of the shrink potion,' I told the others.

'What have we got left?' John asked.

I looked down the long list of bottles we'd taken from the workshop of an alchemist who had tried to have us killed. Almost all were erased now. 'A potion of fire resistance and . . . a potion of truth.'

'That's it?'

'That's it.'

At first the Grand Illusionist's dungeon appeared to be an actual dungeon for prisoners. It was all cells, their heavy doors lining the sides of dark and stinking corridors. We peered through the small barred windows into quite a few, but most were empty. Several contained the mouldering bones of previous occupants or, worse, their ghosts: translucent white memories of their misery, haunting the same place that they had haunted in the flesh during the last months or years of their lives.

'A cheery place,' John said. 'Sir Hacknslay takes the lead with Boris.' He pushed the small figure of painted lead that represented his warrior to the front of our group, and set beside it an axe-wielding barbarian in a bearskin cloak.

'Fineous lurks at the back, behind Nicodemus,' Simon said.

'Boris?' I asked.

'He's at the front with me.' John tapped the figure.

'Who the *fuck* is Boris?'

John and Simon both looked up from their study of the map.

'What do you mean, "Who the fuck is Boris?"?' John set his finger to the figure.

'I mean, who the fuck is he? We've never met a Boris. I've never seen that figure before.'

Simon frowned. 'Maybe he's been ensorcelled.'

'Boris has?' I asked.

'No, you. You, Nicodemus.' He picked up a character sheet I'd not noticed before. 'We've had Boris since just after the Tower of Tricks. He saved us all when the pirates had everyone captive. Boris! Mad axeman. Scared of rabbits.'

'Oh, right. *Scared of rabbits.*'

Simon let out a breath. 'Good, you remember.'

'Bollocks I do. Mia set you two up to this.' I glanced at her bemused smile. 'Boris is some kind of illusion we picked up back in the cave.'

'Or,' said John, 'Mia set you up to this. Told you to pretend that you didn't remember Boris because something got to Nicodemus back in the cave.'

I snorted. 'Nicodemus has the highest intelligence in the party and he's a magic-user. He's the one least likely to fail a saving throw against this sort of thing.'

'Actually, it's very slightly less likely that both of us failed together than you did on your own,' said Simon, doing his human calculator thing. 'Basically, it's fifty-fifty.'

'Yeah, but I *know* I'm not acting. I know Mia didn't put me up to this.'

'I also know I'm not acting,' John said, staring at me. 'Boris is my favourite member of the party. A real man's man.' He blinked suddenly as if remembering something and turned to Simon. 'Maybe Nicodemus has forgotten drinking that potion of forgetfulness.'

Simon shrugged. 'Makes sense.'

I laughed. 'Nice one.'

'So you don't remember?' John leaned over and tapped the potions section on my character sheet.

I looked. 'There's just two potions and neither of them are forget—'

John tapped harder. 'That just means you didn't forget to rub it out.'

There, where his finger had been, were the rubbed-out traces of another potion. I could make out the 'f' at the start and one . . . maybe two 's's at the end. 'I admire your efforts,' I said, shaking my head.

'So, are we going to get on with this or not?' Simon asked, leading from the back again.

'I'm not going anywhere with this fake.' I moved Nicodemus further from the barbarian. One swing of his axe could leave the party with two halves of a magic-user, and Nicodemus was definitely more effective whole than as the sum of his parts.

'So use one of those scrolls of "dispel illusion" you bought,' Simon said.

'Hmmm.' The two scrolls had cost an arm and a leg. That axeman still had me thinking about body parts. It had proved ridiculously hard to get hold of the 'dispel illusion' spell anywhere near the tower, and even more strangely impossible to get the less powerful 'detect illusion'. There had been additional strife as the only thing that allowed Nicodemus to use illusionist spells from scrolls was a headband that Fineous had lost two fingers stealing and that sported an enormous diamond at its centre. Fineous had wanted to sell the thing and put the proceeds towards finding a cleric who could restore his missing digits. But, no, I needed it so that we stood a chance on this mission to the Tower of Illusion to restore Mia's character to life.

'Cast "dispel illusion" if you're so sure,' repeated Simon.

'I think not. We don't have enough to waste, and we're going to need them later. Plus, "Boris" isn't doing any harm just yet. Who knows, he could prove useful. Might kill some illusionary monster for us with his illusion of an axe.'

'Well played, sir!' John said. 'Neatly got yourself out of having to prove yourself wrong.'

We pushed on through the dungeons, taking any stairs that presented themselves so long as they led up. I gave Boris ten gold pieces by way of apology for doubting that he was real, but mainly to check if he was solid. Solid illusions are much harder to cast and maintain than ones of the more ghostlike variety. Adding sounds and smells comes somewhere between those two levels of difficulty. I guess that technically, when an illusion shares all the aspects expected of something real then it is hard to say that it's not in fact real, even if you are the one who magicked it into being. The only difference between an illusionist's very best work and reality is that the illusion can be undone with the right spells – or rather that there are more spells that will undo it, as a fireball will burn up both sorts of real.

Before long we came to an enormous chamber sporting no fewer than eight spiral staircases going up. We crossed the chamber to inspect the only other exit, a long tunnel leading off on a gentle upslope to what looked suspiciously like a distant circle of daylight.

Although we wanted to come up into the tower, we all agreed that going outside to covertly establish its location relative to us would help us choose which staircase to take.

I say we *all* agreed because everyone but Boris did, and Boris wasn't real. In fact, I had been in two minds about going until he said it wasn't safe to go outside.

'Yeah, not taking advice from a figment of someone else's imagination,' I said, and started heading straight towards the distant daylight.

'Have you considered,' Simon said, 'that one of your time experiments may have bumped you on to a different timeline in which Boris has been a part of our D&D game for years? I only ask because it's an interesting alternative, not because I don't think Mia is sneaky enough to have cooked this up with you.' He shot her a narrow look.

If it had been John who said it, I would have brushed it off immediately, but Simon was terrible at acting and this seemed quite polished. 'I'll give the matter due consideration.' I moved my mage Nicodemus toward the tunnel Mia had added to the map for us.

'The whole length of the tunnel fills with flames. They shoot from the walls, ceiling and floor.' Mia indicated the region affected. It started just a yard in front of Nicodemus.

'Can I feel the heat?' I asked.

'You can. You can also hear the roar of the flames and smell a charred odour on the air.'

'I disbelieve it,' I said. 'I'll have a go at disbelieving Boris, too, while I'm at it.' Illusions can be disbelieved. You can get a saving throw on a D20, and having high intelligence gives you a better chance at making the object of your disbelief vanish, but the more powerful the illusion the less chance you have.

Mia rolled some dice behind her screen. Even if neither Boris nor the flames were illusions, she would roll just to stop us deducing the truth. 'Nothing changes.'

'Damn.' John moved Sir Hacknslay to join Nicodemus before the flames. 'I'll try, too.'

More rolling. 'Nothing changes.'

Sometimes you have to up the ante. You can get additional chances to break an illusion using just your mind, but you have to risk something more each time. 'Nicodemus closes his eyes and walks forward slowly, telling himself that the flames aren't real.'

Mia rolled again. 'He gets very hot. The skin on his face feels as if it is starting to blister.'

'The flames aren't real. The flames aren't real.' I advanced the figure.

Mia rolled again. 'He's in real pain now. Take a point of damage. The others can see that his hair is crinkling up and smoke is rising in wisps from his clothing. He's very close to the fire now.'

'Drink your fire resistance potion!' Simon said.

'That would just be giving in to the illusion.' I reached forward to advance Nicodemus. 'It would raise my saving throw and waste a potion to boot!'

'Use one of the scrolls!' John urged. 'I mean, step back first, or it'll spontaneously combust.'

'I've only got two "dispel illusion" scrolls!' I said.

'So cast one!' Simon shouted, no doubt worried that some of the few party valuables he wasn't yet carrying might burn. 'You'll still have one left and you'll know, one way or the other.'

Sometimes you need to believe what your senses are telling you. Sometimes you need to go with your gut.

'What you gonna do, Nick?' Mia asked.

'Nicodemus runs forward.' I pushed the figure into the flames.

CHAPTER 9

1992

The next time I visited Guilder's cave I made the journey alone. I hadn't learned to drive – you hardly need to in London or Cambridge – so I took the train to Bristol and got Dr Creed to pick me up. He and Professor Halligan had moved shop to our evil villain's subterranean lair in the hope of making measurements that might allow them to reverse-engineer some of the physics. They could, of course, have easily outnumbered the naked time travellers with world-class scientists eager to help, but Guilder insisted on secrecy and paid well to keep it.

Even so, understanding scientists as I did, I knew that no amount of money would keep either man quiet about their own successes for much longer. You don't enter a career in research science for the money. If that's what interests you, then banking is the way to go. More than Guilder's millions, both Creed and Halligan wanted the acknowledgement and admiration of their peers. Both were terrified that somehow, even though there was no sign of it in the literature, some other group would scoop them and claim the discoveries for themselves. Someone else's name would be carried into the future, forever attached to the work.

'So . . . what have you found?' I knew they had discovered something. Creed was bubbling with it, though keeping his lips firmly pressed together.

'You let Guilder drive you for hours without making him spoil his big reveal. You can wait another forty minutes for our bit of theatre.'

I sighed. '*Show, don't tell* is advice for writers, not scientists.' Even so, I didn't argue. I liked to reveal my own discoveries with a touch of drama, after all.

After twenty minutes I started turning round in my seat. The same black car had been on our tail for several miles of winding country lanes and multiple turnings – one of those new four-wheel drive things everyone had started calling SUVs. 'I think we're being followed.'

'We are,' Creed agreed, unconcerned. 'Guilder's men follow us to make sure we're not followed. That man has dangerous levels of paranoia!'

Dangerous was the word.

We parked close to the small wood, waiting by our car as a black Land Rover with tinted windows passed slowly by: maybe the same car that had followed us, maybe another of Guilder's patrols. When it had vanished around a corner, we slipped unobserved into the trees. The wood seemed quiet today; no birds, no bees, just branch and bush seething all around us in the grip of a cool northerly wind. Creed had his own controller for the elevator and went down first. I joined him in the darkness below shortly after, finding the silence and stillness eerie after the animation of the wood above us.

'I don't like this place.' Creed seemed glad to have my company again. 'Never been good with underground places, and those travellers, well, they unnerve me. No logic to it, but that's how it is.' He hugged himself and led off along the concrete path.

We joined Halligan in the well-lit 'statues' cavern.

'Ah, young Nick!' Halligan straightened from his work at a folding table where he had been inspecting one of Creed's constructions. A forest of cables snaked underneath it and out across the damp floor. 'Good of you to join us. Though, of course, you've been here the whole time, too. Along with Miss Jones.' He waved an arm towards the silent onlookers.

He and Creed had been calling Mia 'Miss Jones' a lot lately, even though they both knew her and called her Mia to her face. I suspected it was a professional distancing of themselves, given that they had spent several days in a cave with an older version of her standing nude before them. I wondered if they would start to call me 'Dr Hayes' next.

'So.' I hugged myself, wishing I had remembered to bring a coat. 'What've you found?'

Creed stepped up with some lumpy white object in his hand and a sheaf of glossy photographs. 'Would you be so kind as to remove your left shoe and sock?'

I frowned, then with a shrug set to unlacing the shoe in question. 'Is this some kind of weird initiation ceremony for a new underground cult?'

They both ignored me. Creed motioned for me to sit in one of the camp chairs by the table. 'Guilder expected me to come down here with a lorryload of electronics. He probably wants me to get out my sonic screwdriver and reverse the polarity of the neutron flow . . . But experimental science starts with the basics. Simple observation. I've been having a very close look at this place and the surrounding tunnels. More specifically . . . the mud.'

'The mud?' I had to admit that this was also more basic than I had expected. I sat in the chair as directed, sock and shoe in hand. Creed crouched before me, took my ankle and lifted my bare foot to rest alongside the white object he had in hand, which I could now see was some kind of plaster cast.

'It looks like a good match to me!' Creed announced. 'Have to take some measurements for the record.'

'That's a footprint,' I guessed.

'Indeed. But if this is yours … haven't you seen what it means?'

'That these time travellers are not immediately starting new time-lines!' I tried to sound surprised.

'Yes! It goes against all our theories!' Halligan interjected. 'These people. This older you . . . they could be here in this timeline right now. You could have been in the woods just now, spying on yourself. It's incredible!'

'Wow!' I strained my acting muscle still further. 'Incredible.'

Halligan nodded enthusiastically. 'Realistically, though, I doubt many of them do much more than say hello to someone before they break continuity and start a new timeline. The longer they stay on our timeline the more chance there is of them causing a split.'

I gave a wise nod. 'It would be very difficult to hang around for long.'

'We found the footprint here.' Creed pulled out what looked to be a map of the cave system and pointed to a number of X's in one of the tunnels leading from our chamber. He put the paper on the table, then busied himself with his tape measure and callipers. I tried not to squirm, but my feet have always been ticklish. 'I've found quite a few footprints, but this was the clearest. It's in a depression in a passage about a hundred and fifty metres from the rear of the cavern. It's yours, and what set me looking for it were the faint impressions leading away from you and Miss Jones, or at least from your time trails, as I believe we're now calling them.'

'Right!' I got it. 'These people are all headed for the past, so they will already have walked out of here. I'm surprised you found any of my footprints among the crowd.'

'Well, maybe we just got lucky. Or . . . maybe you made an effort to leave an impression . . .'

'Because you've told me about it now,' I said. 'And in the future I will remember it, and when I go back to however many years ago I'm heading, I could have left this footprint,' I tapped the plaster cast, 'just for you to find.'

Creed frowned, puzzling through the logic. 'But . . .'

'Hurts your head, doesn't it?' I grinned. 'So, you've established that the travellers do in fact leave at some point in the past.'

'More than that. We can see that there are holes in the queue, implying that some of the travellers weren't coming this far back. Six gaps, in fact – we assume left by travellers who will arrive at their destination time in some year we've yet to reach, and so their time trails don't reach this far back. We did wonder if they might have been physically removed in some manner, but time trails seem impervious to force.'

'They're rooted in the Earth's gravity well, so, yeah, without removing most of England along with them, they aren't going to shift.' I looked at the row of faces before me while putting my shoe back on, and wondered how far back the most adventurous of them had aimed. History always felt like a dangerous place to me, and emerging naked from an underground tunnel in the 1700s or any date before that seemed rather suicidal. Getting burnt as a witch might be a distinct possibility. Most of them were probably headed back to try something again, or to change something, perhaps just to tell someone once more that they loved them, or just to take a missed opportunity and tell that someone for the first time. Maybe some planned to return to a lost child. Or spend time with an underappreciated parent, or save someone close from a mistake. Most of them would alter the past in a way that created a whole new timeline and set them off towards a new, changed future. But some, like Demus, would try to be part of what had already happened, and thereby retain the possibility of changing the future they'd abandoned. 'So hit me with the *but wait, there's more* section of this presentation.'

Creed and Halligan exchanged a glance. The professor nodded, then grinned as if he were a schoolboy rather than a world-famous mathematician. 'There *is* more!' He took the photos from Creed's hands. 'We've been able to do some dating and we found that at least one of the travellers left their spot within the last few months! We had an actual time-traveller in our "now"! And it's possible that they've done nothing to break continuity, in which case they could still be in our timeline. Theoretically we could find them and speak to them!'

'That would be something.' I tried hard not to sound blasé about it. It would only be my third encounter with a time traveller but given that the first two were me and my own paradoxical daughter, and that I'd spent a long time with both, it really wasn't that exciting a prospect. 'And what do you mean by "dating"?' I asked. 'You guys have become expert trackers in less than a week? You have a machine that tells you how old footprints are?'

Halligan tapped the topmost photo.

'What am I looking at?' But then I saw it: the track of Guilder's wheelchair intersecting the faint impression of a bare foot. The kicker, though, was that if you looked closely enough you could tell that the footprint lay on top of the tyre mark. 'Do you think Guilder knows?'

'If he doesn't, he will soon.' Halligan pointed to one of the video cameras bracketed high on the cave wall. 'The real question is, does he have that person, or persons? Did his men catch them before they could leave? And that really depends on how quickly after the discovery of the cave our traveller arrived at their destination time and tried to leave.'

I nodded. If Guilder had hold of a traveller, he could learn all manner of things about whatever operation my future self was running. He would know more about it than I did. And that could only be bad.

The distant rattle of the rising elevator plate interrupted any further thoughts I might have had on the matter.

'That's not right.' Creed immediately started back towards the entrance, a definite urgency to his stride.

73

I followed closely enough to see Creed break into a run as he spotted the elevator platform being swallowed by the shaft and rising out of view. Creed gave a despairing shout and raced to the controls.

'I expect someone's just summoned it.' I didn't think there was a real prospect of being trapped in the caves, but Creed's fear was beginning to infect me.

We listened to the silence after the plate drew level with the ground fifty yards above us and stopped.

Halligan joined us with a puzzled expression. 'What's up?'

'Not us,' Creed muttered.

More silence, staring up at the shaft while Creed pushed uselessly at the buttons on the control panel.

I flinched at the clanking sound of the plate descending again. Creed managed a strangled laugh of relief. And all three of us waited to see who our guest was.

The sight of Charles Rust's sharp face and malicious smile, while perhaps more welcome than the elevator never coming down again, was certainly not what I had been hoping for. He wore his customary dark tailored suit and black eyepatch. That single snake eye of his found me immediately, despite the swift transition from daylight to gloom.

He stepped off lightly as the plate descended its last foot. 'Nicholas, just the man I wanted to see.' Glancing towards Halligan he added, 'If we could have the room.'

The fact that both Halligan and Creed crowded on to the elevator plate in defiance of its stated weight limit and safety instructions left me in no doubt that Rust had given them his intimidation speech at some point in the past. However Creed felt about caves, it was clear that he was more keen to get away from Rust than from any sense of claustrophobia.

Rust let them rattle their way up into the cavern's ceiling, content to watch me, unspeaking but smiling that little smile of his that probably meant he was thinking of ways to hurt me.

'This couldn't have waited?' I asked.

'My employer is running out of time,' Rust said. 'Which is why he spends so much money researching it.' He set off along the path to the statue cave. 'Walk with me.'

He halted at the front rank of travellers, which I was grateful for. I didn't want his cold gaze slithering over Mia and me at the back.

'Mr Guilder is worried,' Rust said.

I didn't answer. A man in his position had a lot to be worried about.

'A clever young man like yourself will have figured out Mr Guilder's plan for self-preservation by now.' Rust fixed me with his singular stare. He often referred to my age as if we were a generation apart, though in truth he was only seven years older.

'He told it to me himself. He wants to jump forward to a time when doctors are able to cure him.' Rich people had been trying to beat the clock for ages. In California there were freezers full of the heads and bodies of those hoping to be defrosted in an age where they could be resurrected. I guess the ancient Egyptians had been trying much the same thing with their mummification and bottled vital organs. Freezing heads wasn't much of a step up from removing the brain through the nose with a sharp hook and sticking your kidneys in an earthenware jar. I didn't ask why Guilder was worried. What disturbed me was that he might have figured out why he should worry.

'Mr Guilder has noted that you and the lovely Mia are the last in this queue,' Rust said.

'How observant of him.'

'And that nowhere else on the planet or in our history has any other discovery similar to the one in this cave been made.'

I tried to hide my nervousness in a shrug. 'There's a kind of self-regulating loop at work. If there were historical records from the sixteenth century of a "witches'" cave full of time-trails, then nobody in the future would choose that cave to head back to the past in. They wouldn't want the sort of reception they might get. So almost by definition, the places travellers use will be ones that stand the test of time.'

Rust eyed me in that predatory way of his that always made my throat constrict and my words dry up. I knew him to be capable of all the horrors I could imagine and quite a few more besides.

'You're lying.'

'I'm not.' I was, though, and the denial I managed to squeak out was not convincing. The truth was just what Demus had told me on our very first meeting. And I believed it not because I trusted him, but because I'd worked out the mathematics for myself. It is a lot easier to prevent time travel than to achieve it. The mathematics are simpler to work out. The idea is simpler to implement, requiring less advanced technology, and the energy requirement is much smaller. It just so happened that I was so far ahead of the competition, partly because of the head start that Demus had given me, that, based on the evidence before us in the cave, I was going to be able to invent and implement backward time travel before anyone else discovered the means to stop it. I, of course, knew how to stop all time travel right now. It just required a network of fairly simple temporal disruptors, each of which required an engine not much bigger than that of passenger train and would, for several thousand square miles around them, increase the energy requirement for time travel from the already 'extreme' to 'unfeasible'. In short, it is a lot easier to close the door to time travel than to open it, and soon after Demus departed 2011 that door must have closed for good.

'You know how I know you're lying?' Rust asked.

'I'm not lying.'

Rust shrugged. 'It's good that you don't know, or it would be harder for me to keep on spotting it.' He stepped closer. Uncomfortably close. 'You have a tell. Like a bad poker player. I know when you're bluffing, Nick.'

'I'm really—'

'Mr Guilder is planning to take his trip into the future very soon. He's tasked me with ensuring that the journey goes smoothly and as far into the next century as planned. Some of his other researchers have suggested the possibility that some kind of barrier could be erected, preventing travel in either direction.'

'Other researchers?' The idea that Guilder might have other academics studying the same thing should have occurred to me already, but somehow it hadn't. The sin of pride, I suppose. But nothing in the open literature indicated anyone was considering a barrier, let alone close to discovering the theory behind it. 'What others?'

'Several prominent mathematicians and physicists in America. Others in Switzerland, France and Poland.' Rust ran his strangely grey tongue over narrow yellow teeth, keeping his gaze on me. 'The thing is, it seems strange to Mr Guilder that more than one of these very clever scientists has, on the basis of the early work of yours released to them in strict confidence, independently suggested that some kind of barrier could be constructed. Whereas not one of them has come anywhere near to a solid solution to travelling forward in time any faster than you and I are doing right now . . . And while you've already solved that problem, you've said yourself that going in the opposite direction is much more difficult.'

'It is.' Going forward in time presents no paradox issues. It's the equivalent of having a long sleep. Einstein showed it was possible before the First World War. When you wake up in the distant future you're a curio, an anachronism. Everyone else knows things you want to know. Going back, on the other hand, makes you a rock star. Suddenly you know things nobody else knows. You have all the secrets. You're unique and powerful. If Demus hadn't been constrained by his desire to save his Mia he could have used what he knew to become the richest, most famous, most influential person on the planet. 'Much more difficult.'

'And over there . . .' Rust pointed to the top of Demus's head, visible at the back of the ranks. '. . . is proof that you achieved your goal. You're heading back somewhere . . . back past 1992, at least. Where do you think you might be heading, Nick?'

'I don't know. I guess I still have twenty years or so to make up my mind on that.'

'But the real point here' – he jabbed my chest with a sharp finger – 'is that you made it. Your future self left next millennium and came back to this one, and after that the door seems to have closed. And that worries Mr Guilder. What if the door is closed both ways? What if medical science twenty years from now still can't cure him? You see my problem here, Nick?'

A sudden terror gripped me. 'He sent you here to kill me?' Guilder didn't really need me any more. For him, backward travel was an optional extra rather than the goal. I backed away towards the table covered with Creed's gadgets. I didn't want to die in this cave. I didn't want to die anywhere, but somehow the idea of dying in the chilly depths of the earth, and having Rust be the one to do it, made it worse. 'You can't! It doesn't happen like that!'

Rust took something from his pocket and calmly unfolded it. A knife, gleaming in the floodlights: a small, wickedly sharp blade, not the sort that offered a quick exit. 'We carve our own future, don't we, Nick? Isn't that what you say? Every choice splits the world?' He waved an arm at the naked travellers. 'When I split you open, another me will decide to let you go, and all this will belong to that Nick instead. Isn't that how it works?'

The back of my legs bumped against the table where Creed had been working and something delicate fell to the floor with an expensive crunch. Against all sense, instinct had me turning to save it. Despite already being too late and the move presenting my back to a psychopath with a knife, I was on my knees among the power lines reaching for the device before I knew what I was doing. A second later I saw my chance. I took a handful of cables, gave a sharp yank, and in an instant all the lights died.

Rust rushed forward with a shout of annoyance, but I was already rolling away, toppling the table in the process. I heard him trip over it with an oath.

'This is stupid.' Rust clattered about, presumably tangled in the table and powerlines. 'Where are you going to run to?'

I wasn't running anywhere. That would make noise that he might follow. I was crawling determinedly in a direction I hoped would take me to the far end of the cave. My main fear was that Rust would reconnect the lights and find me still crawling across the mud floor before I reached the tunnels.

'You'll get lost and die in these tunnels if you run off!' Rust shouted.

I kept crawling. I'd decided I would rather starve in the dark than give Rust the satisfaction of slicing me up. I discovered the rear wall by banging my head against it. I managed not to cry out in pain, but just barely. Feeling my way along the rock, I soon located what I hoped was the tunnel I was looking for. I got to my feet and began to hurry as fast as I dared, arms raised defensively before me.

'Guilder didn't send me to kill you, you idiot!' Rust's shouts faded in the distance. 'He needs you—' Another turn of the passage swallowed his voice.

It's a scary thing being alone in the dark: cold, wet and lost. But it's a very different kind of fear to the one you experience when seeing a steel blade in the hands of a man who wants to cut you open with it. Yes, I had seen myself in the cave coming back through time, but that wasn't a guarantee of survival; just an encouragement. I wasn't indestructible. If I jumped off a building, I would die. It would mean that I had somehow split the timeline without Demus to help me and that the man in the cave wasn't truly me. I couldn't run blindfold into traffic. And I couldn't let Rust stick me with that blade.

I moved on slowly now, feeling both walls of the tunnel for any side passages. All my senses strained to extract something of use from the blind dark. I'd run without a plan, driven by terror, but I wasn't without hope. The map Creed had pulled out to show me where they had found Demus's footprint had shown me rather more than that. It had shown me the way he went in order to get out at a time before Guilder installed his handy elevator. I'd only had a brief glance, but I have a good memory and now I was squeezing it hard to extract every twist and turn of the tunnel that I hoped I was in, and that would eventually emerge in a nearby forest.

I banged my head on the rock again, three times, and stubbed my toe, which hurt even more. Speed was important. Speed could get me killed, too; more likely by getting me lost than by braining me on a low ceiling, though both were possibilities. But speed could also save me. If I was too slow, I'd find Rust or one of his associates already waiting for me at the exit.

The thing about maps is that what looks like three inches on the page might be three hundred yards or three miles on the ground, or in this case underneath it. And when you can't see where you're going, three miles can seem like thirty. I pressed on with blind faith. After all, a timeline with my name on it was waiting back in the cave, and I was determined to be the Nick Hayes who set it off in 2011 and rode it back to 1986.

As hard as I tried to keep my mind on the business of not leaving the main tunnel and not dashing my brains out on rocks above, my thoughts still wandered. I needed a plan. If I ever reached the surface again, that would only be the start of my troubles.

I figured that, for once, time was on my side. Guilder was clearly running out of it and planning to make his move. If I just stayed unavailable for long enough – a few weeks, perhaps – then everything should sort itself out. Guilder would either shuffle off his mortal coil in the present, or sling himself into the distant future. And if he hit a barrier not long after my departure in 2011, well, he would just have to hope they had the cure for whatever ailed him by then. If I set the police on Rust for good measure, that should keep the man busy, and also dissuade him from killing me since he would be top of the suspect list. Rust was a curious creature: a bastard, yes, but one who lived by his own set of rules based on debt and obligation. It seemed likely that once Guilder was gone, Rust would have no reason to pursue me. I hoped so, anyway.

After several lifetimes spent stumbling through pitch-black tunnels, or perhaps half an hour, I found the way growing narrower, the floor underfoot more muddy. Soon I was splashing through icy ankle-deep water while the rocks grazed my elbows on both sides. The narrowing continued inexorably.

'Shit. Shit. Shit.'

The water had reached mid-thigh and was heading towards the zone where men are wont to gasp and to start walking on tiptoes. Worse still, I had had to turn sideways to fit along the passage. One ear slid over wet stone while the rock on the other side was so close I could barely get my hand between it and the other ear.

There are various processes in life where you're carried on past the point of no return despite yourself, and you find that the only option is to plunge on. An argument developing into a fistfight gathers its own momentum; ill-advised sex, too: with both of them you reach a point where pulling out ceases to be an option. The tunnel was threatening to become my third example. Could I back out now, wet and shivering, and try to find an alternative route, blindly feeling my way and having lost all faith in my flash reading of the map? Or did circumstance compel me to push on, even as the rocks threatened to trap me in a grip that would no longer allow any retreat? Would I wedge myself into some dark crack and leave a skeleton to moulder away as the centuries ticked by?

The tunnel was slightly wider lower down, so I started to crawl, my mouth just above the water, head scraping the rock above. The crack began to tighten even at this level, and it occurred to me that soon the mechanics of crawling through tight spaces would only allow me to inch forward, with reverse gear ceasing to be an option.

I'll admit to panic, to tears, and even to appeals to any god who might be listening. But in the end, it was the memory of Rust's knife and his evident pleasure at the thought of using it that drove me forward. That, and the faintest hint of motion in the air. I crawled and wriggled and splashed and during a shivering pause for breath I hoped that none of the travellers had been fat, because if they had it would have required a long diet before they escaped this way.

Reason suggested that the travellers would have practised this exit, and that it would be a bastard to get through; otherwise, the cave they travelled in would have been discovered in antiquity. So I squirmed and cursed and scraped myself across cold damp rock and wept, and finally left the icy water behind as I struggled into a wider space.

Something else was different here, but it took me an age to figure it out. The difference was that I could see! Kinda. I could see the faintest of shapes. Light – well, a handful of photons at least – was leaking in from somewhere. I advanced faster than was sensible and came to a sudden, painful halt against a sturdy metal grid.

'Bastard thing!' I backed off, rubbing my arms and forehead, before returning to inspect it: a rectangular grid of bars, each about half as thick as my little finger, the gaps between them large enough for four fingers to pass through, but not a hand.

'Crap.' Guilder had had the exit sealed off. After all that struggling, I was still trapped. I felt my way to where the bars joined the rock wall and tugged as hard as I could. I felt pretty sure that my fingers were bleeding, but the metalwork hadn't budged even a fraction of an inch. Maybe if I had days to tug at it something might work free, but I doubted I had even half an hour. Without a crowbar I had no hope.

I sat back with a sob of frustration, head against the rock, muddy, dangerously cold, and deeply terrified.

It took several minutes and three deep breaths before it finally struck me that if I survived this and did manage to continue being Demus, then that was *me* back in the cave heading towards the 1980s. In which case I would have come this way years ago and would have remembered to leave a crowbar somewhere useful. I started to pat about the walls for a place where I might have concealed a handy pair of bolt cutters or something similar.

As the minutes went by in fruitless search, my desperation increased. It seemed more and more likely that I wouldn't survive this. That I had somehow forked from the timeline where I was Demus and I was no longer making his memories for him . . .

'But then how would Demus even be in there with the others?'

I went to the grill again and began a fingertip search of the whole perimeter. Somewhere near the bottom on the right I found broken stone and rough metal.

'Thank God!' Even atheist scientists are apt to praise the local deity at such moments. The bars had been worked free of the tunnel wall for several feet. It felt as if the grill had been bent up and then forced back so that the damage would be less conspicuous. Then I got it: the traveller or travellers who had departed recently, since Guilder had found the cave! Demus would have arranged for a crowbar or something similar to be waiting for them and given them instructions on finding it before they left. He would have remembered how I found the area that they'd loosened and managed to pull it back, thereby escaping.

So I did just that. It was buggery hard. The bars absolutely did not want to bend, even a little bit, and when they did they presented a small gap between the rock wall and a fringe of stiff metal fingers all eager to impale me. I struggled under them, tearing my clothes and my skin, and stumbled on, convinced that I must be bleeding to death from all my wounds.

Sixty seconds later I staggered, muddy, torn and bloody, from a narrow mossy crack into what felt like blinding daylight. I pushed on through a large holly bush, discovering by dint of stepping on the spikes of a million dead leaves that I had managed to abandon one of my shoes in the tunnels.

The first thing I had to do, other than lose myself in a manner such that Rust or Guilder's other men couldn't find me, was to find a phone and warn Mia.

I hobble-hopped through the woodland, turning my head this way and that for signs of pursuit. I could hear an occasional car, indicating a road ahead, but instead left the trees via open fields and hurried through acres of ripening wheat to climb a gate into another large field. There aren't many places in England where you can walk very far in a straight line without hitting a road, and this wasn't one of them. I soon found a country lane that wouldn't be top of the search list, and set off along it in my single shoe.

Hitchhiking is easiest when you are young, female and clean. I had only one of those things going for me, so it was a while before anyone took pity on me. And by a while, I mean that I'd walked most of the way to Bristol and the entire sole of my right foot felt like a single huge blister.

The large black vehicle that crunched up on to the gravel verge behind me looked disturbingly familiar. A Land Rover Discovery with tinted windows. The driver flashed the headlights and waited for me, anonymous behind dark glass.

CHAPTER 10

2007

I had, over the years since Guilder vanished into the future, made extensive efforts to find out where he had hidden himself to do it. His instinct in finding that first cave was a sound one. His enemies would have worked against him if they knew where his time trail was. If I found him, I was just going to seal him in with a motion sensor to alert me to his arrival if it happened to fall within my lifetime. I guess less charitable souls would have entombed him in concrete and left him to a short, painful life in whatever future he arrived at.

My efforts to find Guilder's hideaway had been unsuccessful, but my work in dismantling his business affairs, using all the legal avenues available to me and a few less savoury ones, mainly involving hacking, had borne considerable fruit. And when the land under which the traveller-filled cave hid came back on the open market, I bought it. I say I bought it, but scientists are never well paid, so I did depend on a little help from a moderately successful merchant banker and a very successful accountant who I happened to know from way back when.

Friendship is one thing, but to sink a considerable fraction of one's wealth into a Somerset field usually requires rather better motivation than merely being asked to by a mad scientist. John especially had other calls on his money, having three children all of whom his wife expected to be sent to private schools, and rather more expensive schools than the one we had gone to. And Simon, of course, had his extensive hoard of *Star Wars* collectables to enlarge. He also had his eyes on a bigger house to allow expansion of his model railway, which now comprised over five scale miles of track.

I gave them the *Field of Dreams* speech. I told them, 'If you build it, they will come.' And when asked how I was so sure, I pointed out that in many senses our customers were already there, down in that cave. Furthermore, I noted that if they didn't come, then the paradox shock to the timeline would probably tear the fabric of time and space apart, rendering the issue of whether or not the scheme made its money back somewhat moot. And so, I concluded, it was our duty as responsible citizens to facilitate the passage of these various billionaires back into the year, month and day of their choosing. And if we happened to grow fabulously rich in the process, then so be it.

Since Guilder's disappearance back in 1992, forward time travel had become common knowledge. The public were perhaps less impressed with it than the science merited, most seeing it only as an incremental advance on cryogenics. I really think that if the subjects had just vanished and reappeared in the future then the public would have been far more wowed by it all. In any event, Halligan, Creed and I had shared the Nobel Prize in physics for the work. In my humble opinion it was me who did 99% of the heavy lifting, but the Nobel Prize has always been about experimental discovery, and to be fair to Ian Creed, he was the one who got his hands dirty and made it happen. Also, my willingness to share the credit and to keep feeding them the breadcrumbs they needed to continue making progress was the unspoken price for their silence concerning the cave of travellers heading back into the past. They were both clever men – they understood that my presence among that crowd of time trails was significant, and potentially granted me boundless power over them. I think that knowledge damaged our friendship, but it also proved remarkably effective at sealing lips.

In consequence, there were now government-regulated warehouses all across the world where the terminally ill or the merely curious stood frozen in time, bound for the future.

I continued my own work into unlocking the secrets of travelling back in time largely in secret while earning my living as director of the National Institute for Temporal Studies, where I leaked out old results at as slow a rate as I felt I could get away with.

Once the whole world's scientific community saw the early results – especially in forward travel – and began to focus on the problem, they started to catch up with me at an alarming speed. I'd been arrogant to assume that without my genius there would be no progress for decades to come. Though, to be fair, that was the impression I'd had from Demus.

Using some of my Noble Prize money and contributions from John, Simon and Mia, who was now a fairly successful actress with significant parts in several quite big movies, I built a house over the cave.

The house started small but with grand designs. Getting planning permission was the hardest part, but by parcelling the development up with plans to build an extensive solar and wind farm where until now the main crop had been wheat, I was able to get away with murder.

In February of 2000 I solved the theoretical side of traveling backward in time. It took another seven years of secret experimentation in the caves below the new house before, with the aid of a vast reservoir of power from the wind and solar energy farms above, I was able to turn that theory into practice. I did this on my own, employing contractors who had no idea what they were building. My fifteen years watching Ian Creed at work had furnished me with the technical skills needed, though I still counted myself a theoretician despite the best part of a decade spent cursing electromagnets and capacitor banks just yards from 113 silent witnesses to the fact that I must ultimately succeed.

Since I knew the names of most of the travellers by now, having been hunting the internet for them for years, I made discreet overtures to the first few, hinting at the possibility of returning to the past. I entreated them to secrecy, and of course my reputation and position ensured that I was taken seriously.

It might seem like a rather weak plan, but these were people I had seen in the cave for nearly twenty years now. They clearly had strong reasons for wanting to go back. The fact that others in the cave went back after they did strongly implied that everyone managed to keep the secret, or at least not spread it to anyone the world would take seriously. There had, of course, been rumours and conspiracy theories about me and my work for decades. Many of them were started by me, so that when the time eventually came where I actually did start to clandestinely send people back into the past, nobody would give credence to any fresh round of rumours.

Melissa Reede was the first to approach me, which was a good thing because she was the first in line. At my invitation she came to the house where Mia and I lived on the edge of Cambridge. I opened the door to an immaculately groomed middle-aged woman who I of course recognised immediately. She was in fact fifty-four, but money made her look under forty. She stood about five six, her hair descending in a thick black sheath over one shoulder; a broad, generous mouth, eyes dark and guarded. To her credit, she managed to hide most of her astonishment at how small our modest suburban home was: nothing like the mansions she and her friends inhabited in California.

'Please, come in,' I said, taking her coat.

'Can I get you tea?' Mia asked. 'Coffee?'

'Thank you, no.' She followed us to the living room.

Melissa Reede had made her hundreds of millions in the dot-com bubble, securing lucrative domain names, starting retail websites and selling them on for silly money before the world realised that plenty of hard work and luck were required after that stage and that profits might be longer in coming than first thought.

She sat on our sofa, uncomfortable despite the mounds of superfluous cushions. Mia soon unwound her, though. Mia had a rare talent for that, and I, sadly, had none. Within a few minutes of small talk, she cracked a filthy joke and had Melissa and me smirking. After that it wasn't too hard to get to the point.

'I want to go back in time. To the summer of 1980,' she said. 'I don't care about the cost.'

'That's good,' I said. 'Because it's going to be expensive! Just remember that you can't take anything with you. So whatever money you don't spend on this will be left behind.'

'Are you sure it will work?' She frowned. 'And why is this secret?'

'Two good questions. If we proceed then I have something to show you which should convince you that it works. And the secrecy is because if the government knew about this, I believe they would swiftly pass laws prohibiting it for a variety of reasons, one being fear – a groundless fear I should point out – of being somehow manipulated by what you might do "upstream" in the timeline.' I bit my lip and studied her. She sat calmly, hands folded over knees that were hidden beneath a cashmere skirt. Everything about her was tastefully understated. The silver bracelet and necklace had a slight dullness to them that suggested they were platinum rather than silver. Her watch looked merely elegant, but doubtless cost more than our house. 'I have to ask why you want to do this, Ms Reede. You need to understand that if you try to change anything in 1980 or do so inadvertently, then you will create a new fork in the timeline and make no difference to the reality you've left behind.'

'I understand.' She nodded. She sipped at the black coffee I'd brought her despite her declining the offer. Sipped again, as if buying time to gather herself before plunging in. And then she told us.

Like many very rich people, Melissa had come to understand that her wants were actually fairly simple, and while yachts and helicopters were fun, they were not in fact the stuff that happiness is made of.

'I had a child when I was very young. A son. Julian.' Her expression hardly changed through the Botox and the make-up, but her eyes grew bright, and in her lap one hand wrestled the other. 'He drowned in the neighbour's pool when he was three years old. Found a way through the fence. I've missed him every day for twenty-seven years. I never had another baby. If I could go back, it would be so easy to stop him.'

'You understand that the Julian you knew would still drown? If you stop him, the timeline forks and the child you save goes on to lead a different life.'

She nodded. 'I've done my homework, Dr Hayes. But I will carry back from that yard a Julian who was mine until that very instant and who will still have his whole life ahead of him.'

'You'll carry him back to a mother who may not let you share in that life,' Mia said.

'Oh, I think I know how to deal with myself.' Melissa smiled. 'I hope the young me will understand what I've done for her and let me be a part of Julian's future. My own parents were dead by 1980 so perhaps I can stand in as a second grandma.'

We agreed to send Melissa Reede back. If we didn't send back someone who already stood in the cave there were dangers of paradox fields growing out of control, but even so it still wasn't a clear-cut decision. Yes, the new timelines that would be started if anyone we sent back changed history felt abstract and less important than our own, but we had to remind ourselves that they were in fact just as real as ours and filled with real people. If we sent back someone who wanted to exploit their future knowledge to harm others, then we were complicit. With knowledge of the market trends, anyone we sent back could become vastly rich. A sadistic murderer with unlimited funds could inflict untold horror on the world. They could literally build a torture palace in some suitable nation and spend their life killing innocents. Thus, some measure of vetting was required, if only so we could sleep at night.

Having our travellers try to change their pasts, and thereby splitting off new timelines where different pasts unfolded, was not a problem. New timelines are a billion a penny. Every choice makes them.

What had happened with my almost-daughter Eva concerned a choice that should have created two timelines from one. Special circumstances had led to those two timelines not separating properly and building up a growing contradiction between them, such that the mounting paradox energy threatened to destroy both. My understanding of Eva's analysis was that the chances of that happening again were incredibly remote, and that the effect was linked to both me and her. In science it is unwise to think of yourself as the centre of the universe. We once thought Earth was the centre, then the sun. But in this case, it really did seem that both Eva and I had become important temporal nexuses: the foci of the weird event that had given our timelines their almost unique properties. Most likely it was because we had invented the technology, and as such all other travel was inextricably linked to us.

In short, I could send back the 113 travellers without worrying that saving this child or marrying that man would doom the Earth, or several Earths.

We took Melissa to the house in Somerset and accessed the cave from the spiral staircase that led through all three storeys and down into the traveller cave. There was an elevator, too, but the stairs felt more reliable and I had never quite recovered from my own brief experience of being lost in the dark.

Melissa had set her affairs in order and said her goodbyes. She understood that the dreams of those who might follow her were as precious to them as hers were to her, and that any failure to keep this secret could ruin them.

She came incognito, following the numerous steps that I had prescribed in order to prevent her disappearance leading the police to our doorstep with a search warrant. She knew that she would arrive naked in 1980, standing in an undiscovered cave, and that she would have to extricate herself from it before somehow establishing herself in the UK and eventually flying to California to save her boy.

Before she left, I insisted that she make the escape five times. I remembered how terrifying it was. The first three times, she did it in suitable clothing with a powerful torch; the last two times in a thin jumpsuit and bare feet with no light at all. I made sure she could orient herself in the dark and locate the correct exit tunnel.

'We've found no human remains in the cave system, so it seems pretty sure that everyone gets out,' I told her.

That was a lie. We had found one partial skeleton half a mile from the cave in completely the wrong direction, wedged in a narrow fissure. But we'd taken Melissa's DNA from her coffee cup and knew it wasn't her. If we did find a match among our travellers then we would have a thorny decision to make. We would have to weigh the certainty of that person's unpleasant death against the small but significant possibility that the paradox damage caused by them not going would kill everyone in our timeline, including them. The mathematics of it suggested that sending them to their doom was by far the best option, but if I came face to face with the person I just didn't think I could do it. My own terror in those tunnels had been fifteen years ago, but I still had nightmares.

Mia and I led the way down into the cave of travellers for the final show, all rehearsals complete. Until that point, all the travellers had been standing within the plastic tubes we had set over them, both for their privacy in their state of undress and to keep any one traveller from knowing the identities of their fellow travellers. I'd chosen to have the tubes silver. It just made things seem more space age. Mia had sighed the first time she saw them and shaken her head sadly. 'You could have just thrown sheets over them, you know?'

This time we had already removed the tube from around Melissa's time trail so she could access it. The electromagnet array almost completely hid the trail it had been erected around. It was larger than that used for forward travel and was held on a robust titanium framework. The power cables were thick copper rods descending along conduits through the rock that led to the main capacitor banks up by the energy storage facility for the solar and wind farms. For a few seconds, I could pump as much electricity into the cave as a state-of-the-art nuclear power station could manage. I really wanted to have a big lever to throw, like Dr Frankenstein bringing his monster to life, but that might freak out the travellers; so instead I had a button. A button that caused a big lever somewhere upstairs to be thrown!

Mia led Melissa around to the narrow slot clear of cables and magnets through which she would be able to approach her waiting time trail, now fully revealed.

'So, I guess I really have nothing to hide from you two.' She glanced from her time trail to Mia and then a flick of her eyes at me. We had warned her, but there's warning and there's seeing.

'I've been looking at all of them for years and years,' I said. 'You're all still life to me, Melissa. Impersonal works of art.'

She approached her trail, frowning. 'Do I have to . . .' She mimed taking her clothes off.

'No,' I said.

'And when should I?' She took another step towards her motionless doppelganger. 'You know. Do the deed?'

'At the time you choose,' Mia said, setting a hand to Melissa's shoulder. 'We don't know when the trails start but we assume everything works out so that the moment you choose is the right moment.' A smile. 'Take your time. Just not so much that you start looking older than she does.'

'Well.' Melissa looked around again, her poise eroding at last as she faced the finality of her decision. 'I guess I should get on with it then. Bite the bullet, as it were.'

'It won't hurt.' At least I didn't think it would.

'Go, then.' A hug from Mia. 'You've got a little boy to save.'

She had six months to make it to her old home in California. Hopefully long enough to establish herself, but not so long that some random disaster might befall her.

'Good luck,' I said. 'Enjoy your second chance together.'

Melissa nodded, wiped at her eyes with both knuckles and stepped back into her time trail. It looked as if the solid and immovable figure behind her just became a projection and that she stepped into it, mascara smeared, hands lowering, and suddenly froze into exactly the same pose it had held for all these years. In the next heartbeat she was gone, simply vanished into nothing. Her jewellery hit the ground first, followed by her clothes, falling down to cover her shoes.

'That's more like it!' I said.

With the many millions that Melissa Reede paid for her ticket to the past we began to build the castle in earnest. Described as an English folly, the castle was aimed squarely at that faux-medieval style generations of fantasy artists had refined on the covers of books, D&D modules and album covers. Ours, having to comply with the laws of physics and local building regulations, was somewhat more conservative in design, but still damn cool. Over the great stone arch of the gatehouse the legend 'The Tower of Tricks' was carved beneath a set of gargoyle heads loosely modelled on all the members of our D&D group over the years. Elton was the centrepiece, the founding father of our group. The Tower of Tricks had been his invention, after all, rising about us deep in that wilderness all those years ago in our hour of need. A double-edged sword that could cut us free or cut our throats with equal ease.

The years passed and travellers came to us in a steady stream, in ones, twos, and once four together. We never did have to turn anyone away. Their reasons for wanting to return were always rooted in some missed opportunity which, like Melissa Reede's, was deeply personal rather than based on a desire to harm or exploit. We did what we could to check these stories out, but mostly I relied on Mia's instinct. An actor knows better than anyone else when someone is sincere. Mia had a way of drawing emotion and honesty out of strangers after just a few minutes' chatting.

One rich woman dying of cancer remembered cruel words spoken as one child to another, words that hit harder than she could have imagined. 'I broke her life. It still haunts me. I want to see it whole.'

An old man with a trucking empire only wished he had asked that girl in 1958 to dance with him. He just wanted to speak to the boy he had been and give him the courage to act.

A middle-aged film star, whose time in Hollywood had come to an end, had been too far away and perhaps too busy waiting LA tables, hoping for her big break, to visit her mother on her deathbed. She wanted to know that she had visited and that she had told her mother that she loved her one last time, face to face. She wanted to tell her mother that her little girl had made her crazy dreams come true, and found them both more and less than she had imagined.

So many decisions to be reversed, missed chances taken, words unspoken now given voice, words that could not be retracted now rethought. I let them know that if they wanted the younger them to change their mind then they would literally have to change it for them: to convince their younger selves to act, just as Demus had convinced me. And even if they succeeded, perhaps the girl would say no to the invitation to dance, perhaps the baby they decided to keep would die the next year in its crib. I sold them no guarantees, only a ticket. I wished them all well and let them step back into their time trails, back into their lives.

And all the time, my eyes would stray to those last two silver tubes that hid me and Mia from view. Would we step back into ours? Mia was never supposed to do that, though the evidence that she had done so or would do so had been standing here since the previous century. Would I really take that final step and become Demus, instruct my younger self, then die in some manner that I'd made myself forget? I didn't want to die. Not at all. Once, I had thought that by forty I would be old, my ambitions over, my journey complete. As the years between me and 2011 frittered themselves away, those teenage thoughts revealed themselves for the nonsense they had always been. I was scared. Terrified. But the trail that would take me to my death stood before me, just where it had stood for decades, and the reason to take it stood beside me, reassuring each traveller that everything would be OK, setting them at ease as only Mia could.

And that's how it went, with the travellers coming in order to the castle gates without further prompts, and going at their appointed time, vanishing from the world. First a handful, then dozens, then scores. The newspapers began to refer to them as 'the disappeared'. You can't remove so many of the super-rich from society without someone noticing. Investigators eventually called at our doors, but by that point our shell companies controlled billions, and billions count. Without proof – and there was none – nobody ever came uninvited into the Tower of Tricks; there was nothing for the investigators to do but leave again.

After that, of course, the ways in which our clients arrived became still more covert. The methods we used could have taught people smugglers across the globe a thing or two.

Everything went smoothly up until the day in 2009 when Ellery Elmwood, British supermarket magnate and man who had spent a lifetime regretting turning his back on a music career arrived at the Tower of Tricks. In the cave he took a step back towards his timeline, took another, then stopped and said those five fateful words: 'I'm not sure about this.'

CHAPTER 11

1992

The black SUV crunched up on to the gravel verge and I froze in its metaphorical headlights. Guilder's men had me cold. I had nowhere to run to. The passenger door opened. Nobody came out. I stood there, muddy, missing a shoe, body frozen, mind racing. Rust had tried to kill me. These men would take me straight to him, if he wasn't already in the car, that was. I couldn't see anything past the tinted windscreen.

The driver's window lowered smoothly, and unexpectedly a woman leaned out of it. A young blonde woman. A startlingly attractive young blonde woman.

'You're Dr Hayes, right?'

I nodded.

'Get in. We've got to go!'

Call it sexism or plain stupidity, but I limped around to the passenger side and got in. There's no reason why a young blonde woman couldn't be one of Guilder's enforcers. It wouldn't take many years of karate training for her to be able to beat me up, and a few minutes spent on the basics of aiming and firing a handgun would give her the upper hand even more quickly. But even so, something about her put me at ease. I'm going to say it was the worry in her voice.

She was alone in the car, and the moment I closed the door we were off with a squeal of wheels and the sound of gravel pinging off the paintwork.

'You said you'd be muddy and hard to recognise.' She took her eyes from the road ahead for a second to glance my way. 'It's so weird. You look so young.'

'I said?'

She swerved round a tight corner too fast, hedges scraping across the doors. 'Yes. When you sent me back you asked if I could stop by and give you a lift.'

'How long have you been out?' I gripped the door handle to steady myself.

'Of the cave? Nearly six months now.'

'You've done well to stay on the timeline then.'

She didn't respond to that, focusing on the road instead, which at least let me let go of the door. 'I am Natasha. Natasha Volkov.'

'From Russia?' I'd noticed an accent but there had been a lot going on.

'Moscow, originally.' She flashed me a perfect white smile.

We drove into Bristol. I turned several times to check for any pursuit, but saw no signs. Natasha seemed to know the city, parking a little way from the centre and suggesting we got some lunch and had a chat.

'I know a nice restaurant near here . . .'

She really was unreasonably beautiful. The sort of unreal kind that you might see in magazines but never sitting right next to you.

I looked down at my torn and muddy shirt. My trousers weren't in a much better state and were still damp. 'I doubt they'd let me in.'

'We will get some food from the market, then, and eat it by the river,' Natasha said. 'It is a sunny day, no?'

'I need to call Mia.' Not even the spell Natasha was putting over me could erase the horror of my escape or of what I had been running from. I needed to contact Mia and let her know to get the hell out of Dodge.

'We will find a phone,' Natasha agreed. She set a crimson-nailed hand on my shoulder. 'Don't worry, Nick.' The way she said it, my name sounded like Neek.

I opened the car door and shuffled out. She smiled knowingly after me. 'You were not so shy when we last met, Nicky.'

I walked slowly around the front of the car to join her, trying to process what she had just said. Did Demus have some sort of . . . thing . . . with Natasha? It seemed at odds with the idea of giving his life to save Mia.

Natasha, who I now saw was wearing a tight white dress that ended just below her knees and which looked to have been sprayed on to her, came quickly to my side. In her heels she was just a few inches shorter than me. She took my hand and led me down the sunny street.

'I . . . Uh.' I struggled to find the words. 'Did we . . .'

Natasha turned to face me, her Russian accent suddenly more pronounced and seductive. 'We did, Nicky. And I like you even better this way.'

We passed a telephone box, one of the older red ones, and, remembering Mia again, I stopped, pulling free of Natasha's hand. 'I have to call my . . . Mia.'

'You told me to tell you there's no rush,' Natasha said, following me to the door. 'Mia is fine. Mr Guilder . . . that is right, is it? Guilder? Anyway, he takes his trip to the future tomorrow and leaves you both alone. So unless you want to chase him to the twenty-second century there is nothing to worry about.' She set one hand to the phone box door and walked two fingers of the other hand up across my chest. 'You told me to tell you that we get away with it. Nobody ever finds out. So why don't we just go to a hotel and have room service send us some food afterwards?'

'I . . . uh . . . really need to make this call.' I pulled the door open against her push, not roughly but firmly, and slipped inside, escaping her heady scent of flowers and musk to discover the familiar aroma of stale urine. Though why anyone ever chooses to relieve themselves in a glass box I have never figured out. Perhaps the other party just won't get off the phone and they get desperate . . . Anyway, the phone was out of order so I had to emerge again, rather shamefacedly, into the dazzling light of Natasha's 500-watt smile.

'You're not planning to chase Mr Guilder, are you?' Natasha walked by my side, close enough to show she had no qualms about getting her little white dress muddy.

I walked along, scanning the road ahead for another phone box and trying not to let Natasha's proximity distract me from my quest. The pavement felt hot beneath my bare foot. 'I didn't ask you to bring me some new clothes, or a shoe?'

'Maybe you forgot?' Her hand closed around mine again. 'Maybe we made better memories?'

Almost every passer-by looked at Natasha, half of the men turning to check her out as she walked away from them, and not a few eyeing me up in mild astonishment as if to ask what a skinny one-shoed geek like me was doing with a supermodel on his arm.

'So, will you go after him?'

'Sorry?' Despite my efforts I was finding her very distracting.

'Guilder,' she said. 'Or will that barrier you talked about stop him?'

'I guess so . . .'

Natasha squeezed my hand and held it close to her hip. 'You guess the barrier will stop him?'

'Well, I should think it w—'

A figure loomed up in front of us and punched Natasha squarely on the nose.

'Come on!' It was a woman in a business jacket, about fifty years old, stout, with greying hair. 'Up there!' She pointed up the alley she'd been waiting in, too narrow for a car even if it hadn't been a thirty-yard flight of worn stone steps.

'What?' I glanced back at Natasha, who had staggered back a few paces, both hands over her nose, blood leaking between her fingers.

The older woman strode past me towards Natasha, shouting at her, 'That was from Mia!' She turned back to me. 'Quick! They're coming!'

A big black car with dark-tinted windows *was* accelerating towards us.

'I don't understand.' I moved to help Natasha.

The new woman grabbed my shoulder, speaking quickly and urgently. 'Demus told me to say you should trust me. He said to tell you he remembered both Evas – the one from the hospital that you watched die, and the one from the future you had with Helen.'

It wasn't an explanation, but it was enough to know I'd sent her. Bewildered, I turned and followed her up the steps. She was quick, despite her age. I was winded by the top and, turning, I saw two men in dark jackets already halfway up and running.

The steps connected the road we'd been on to another higher up the steep hill that eventually takes you to the Clifton Downs and the suspension bridge over the Avon Gorge.

'Quick!' The woman got into a small green Ford covered in parking tickets. I scrambled into the passenger seat and she accelerated away before I could even get the door closed.

'I'm Anna Mazur. The woman you were speaking to is employed by Miles Guilder.'

'She's not from the future?'

'No.' Anna checked her rear-view mirror, then took a sharp left up a ridiculously steep road. 'She's what we call a honey-trap, honey.' She gave a grim smile. 'Rust scared you out of the cave and she was waiting to offer you sanctuary. Guilder set it up and told her what to say. It's an easier way of learning secrets than old-fashioned torture. This way, the victim is more likely to be truthful.'

'Crap. I think I said too much. I should go back and wipe her memory.'

'You can do that? *Men in Black* style?' Anna asked.

'Men in black?'

'Too soon?' She shook her head. 'I'll get the hang of the nineties again in a while.' She took another turn and drew up at the curb in a narrow street of tall dingy townhouses. 'Come in. You can use my phone.'

'But the girl . . .'

'She was wired. Guilder already knows everything you said to her.'

Anna opened the street door to one of the terraced houses and led me up several flights of communal stairs to a flat on the third floor. 'This would have been a lot easier if you . . . I mean Demus . . . had let me pick you up from the cave before she got to you.'

'Yeah. A lot of things would be so much easier if it worked like that.' I followed her into the flat. 'It's kinda hard to explain, but a knot—'

'A knot got tied into the timeline, allowing us to go back without starting new timelines. And if we stick to the script and keep to what you and we remember went down, we get to stay in our own past,' she recited. 'But it means we have to play the cards we were dealt when it happened. All the double-guessing got baked in when "the event" happened.'

'I see we've had this conversation before.' I sat on the leather sofa she aimed me at.

'I've had it. You will have it.' Anna passed me the phone from a side table. 'Guilder and Rust vanish, probably tomorrow. You and I last spoke in 2010 when you sent me back, and at that point you had never seen either of them again. Dr Hayes . . . Demus, I mean . . . he told me to call him that with you . . . Demus is sure they both went forward, but he doesn't know when they're aiming at or where they're hiding while they travel.'

It made sense that Guilder would take Rust with him. He would need help when he got to the year he'd targeted, and, whatever else you might say about him, Charles Rust was very capable. My finger hesitated above the number buttons on the handset. 'So . . .'

Anna shrugged. 'Call her anyway. Demus said he didn't entirely trust me when I came back. So he and Mia went into hiding for a week before they were convinced it was safe to return to Cambridge.'

I still hesitated. Anna had handed me my first chance in years not to be Demus. To break the chain that linked me to him, all I had to do was *not do* something that I knew for sure that he did. If I didn't call, if we didn't go into hiding, then Mia and I wouldn't be Demus and his Mia any more. And, really, what did I owe the man? My cancer had been in remission for five years now. I didn't need to be him in order to stand a decent chance that it was gone for good.

But . . . it was true that even if I trusted Anna, I didn't trust the whole situation sufficiently to not want to take me and Mia out of Guilder's firing line for long enough to make sure he was gone. The look in Rust's eyes and the gleam of his knife were still front and centre in my mind. I made the call.

After all, if I didn't want to be Demus, all I had to do was not send the message with Anna when my turn came to dispatch her to the past.

CHAPTER 12

1992

'Well, at least you didn't burn to death!'

Simon and John had come to join Mia and me at the holiday cottage we'd rented to hide out in. It stood beside two others on a lonely country road just outside Lyme Regis on the Dorset coast. The English summer had decided to really go for it and was currently doing a passable impression of a Mediterranean one, and had even managed to heat the Channel waters to a few degrees above 'Fuck that!' Miles of shingle coast stretched out between crumbling cliffs and wild waves, offering the very best of the Jurassic Coast, a fossil hunter's paradise. Ammonites littered the beaches in gleaming iron pyrites, or fools' gold as it's better known. Belemnites lay like scattered stalactites in lustrous flint-like stone, intermingled with shells galore . . . So, of course, we were all indoors playing D&D.

Simon had claimed to be worried that Guilder's men might find him and hurt him to get our location, though the game was the real reason he had left his mother's house for the first time in an age for any reason other than to go to university. John hadn't been worried, but his girlfriend was on the warpath about something . . . most likely another girlfriend, and so he had decided that a short vacation might be good for his health.

It was true that my mage Nicodemus's possibly foolhardy insistence on disbelieving the inferno in the tunnel leading to the outside world had eventually succeeded. The flames finally gave up existing just moments before his hair would otherwise have ignited. Sadly, the exit to the surface was also an illusion, linked to the first one, and that too vanished with the flames.

'So, let's have a standing order not to believe anything we see, and soldier on up this damn tower,' I said. 'We'll just take the nearest stairs.'

I glanced out of the window into the cottage's sun-dazzled grounds, looking for Rust as usual.

'He's gone,' Mia said. 'And even if he wasn't, he wouldn't find us here.'

Mia and I had formulated our escape plan long ago. I'd told her about the way Guilder used threats against her to keep me from running off, and as soon as I accumulated enough money we had sorted out our escape should things ever reach a point where I could no longer tolerate the man's control. We would simply mail all our evidence to the police and hop aboard a plane to somewhere hot and cheap, the particular destination being of far less importance than the ready availability of the flight. I reckoned we could last six months on my savings before I had to think of new ways to make money. Mother was also in Rust's crosshairs and I had broached the subject with her, too. That had been a more difficult talk, especially when it came to stopping her going to the police immediately with her two handfuls of hearsay. In the end, though, I had managed to persuade her to agree to take immediate sick leave if I told her she really needed to. The plan was for her to take one of a score of rental cottages I'd identified in places that she enjoyed. I didn't think Rust would go after any of the small number of other family members I had out there. If he'd done enough homework to find them, he would also have figured out that I didn't much care for any of them anyway and hadn't seen them in years.

In the end, we'd opted for a cottage, too. England seemed hot enough this summer, and our reserves of cash were more than adequate to keep us going for the planned week. Besides, I'd already assured myself, albeit via a woman I didn't know, that Rust wasn't even looking for us. He was in some dark place staring fixedly at the future, and would likely be doing nothing else for many years to come. At least until he hit my barrier. And by that point, if I was Demus, I would have been dead for decades.

I found myself unable to take much comfort in that last part.

'Well, *Fineous* doesn't disbelieve in the existence of the Tower of Illusion as a whole,' Simon qualified. 'It would be rather inconvenient to have the entire thing vanish while we were on the tenth floor.'

'Inconvenient for you,' I said. 'Nicodemus has a feather fall spell. He'd just waft down after you.'

'Boris notes that only Fineous would fall if Fineous disbelieved the tower, and it was actually an illusion,' Mia said.

I shook my head. 'I disbelieve Boris. I can't believe you guys are keeping up this Boris shit.'

Mia rolled behind her screen. 'Boris doesn't vanish.'

John swigged his Coke and burped before commenting, 'I still think it's your own fault. You've done one of those time tricks. Like where we've all experienced different realities reaching this point. Maybe one of your explosions mixed things up somehow.'

'They weren't *my* explosions! There was only one, as far as I know, and I was trying to stop it.' I shook my head and decided to play along with the Boris nonsense. Sooner or later one of them would slip up and admit that either Simon and John invented him to mess with me, or Mia introduced him as part of the tower's illusions.

'OK, so we ignore the dead end formerly known as fiery tunnel and head up the spiral stairs we found instead. It's time we got into the tower proper. We've spent too long messing about in the basement. Onward and upward, lads. All we need is one measly time crystal and then I can get the lovely Sharia back.'

'Hooray . . .' Simon and John cheered half-heartedly. Neither of them shared my attachment to Mia's old character, though they both agreed that having a cleric in the party to cure our wounds with spells was a lot cheaper than buying healing potions in bulk.

I picked up the barbarian's figure and advanced him to the stairs. 'Boris can go first, of course, since he's illusionary anyway.'

And so we made our way up through the levels of the Tower of Illusion and the sun headed down towards the sea. The hour hand spun while imagination wrought its own version of time travel on us, unravelling another day double-quick.

Some monsters we disbelieved, consigning them to memory without so much as raising a sword. Others, still less believable, stubbornly resisted our doubt and had to be slain the old-fashioned way. Sir Hacknslay was almost killed by a levitating pink dolphin in a sparkling blue top hat, but unless we all made a series of spectacularly bad saving throws, the damn thing was as real as we were.

We found new cunningly linked illusions, too: illusions where two or more things were connected, like the flame-filled tunnel and the distant exit; where by disbelieving the flames I had made the way out vanish, too. That was an eye-opener in terms of just how powerful the Grand Illusionist who dwelt at the top of the tower was. If you believed his illusion of a passage through solid rock, then it would take you into one side of a mountain and out the other.

In one room we were confronted by a three-headed ogre wielding a burning club longer than I was tall. Since it seemed more likely that the illusionist had made the thing up with a spell rather than found and employed such a monstrosity with all the additional housekeeping bills such a recruit entails, we all tried to disbelieve it. Against the odds, it was Sir Hacknslay and Boris who made their saving throws whereas Fineous and Nicodemus failed. Since the floor of the room was a linked illusion, it also vanished for both warriors and they fell through into a spike-filled sub-chamber, while the thief and the mage remained suspended high above them on illusionary floorboards being attacked by an illusionary three-headed ogre that they were poorly equipped to deal with on their own.

On other levels of the tower, Hoodeeny, the Grand Illusionist, had gone to vast efforts to populate the place with real monsters and other genuine threats so bizarre that it was hardly possible to believe they were real. And of course, to give yourself a really good chance to disbelieve an illusion, you had to demonstrate your belief through faith. If you really don't believe that this oversized glowing green pixie with the bright pink sword is real, then let it swing at your neck. If you make a move to defend yourself, then clearly you *do* believe it. That was the whole story of how Boris got stabbed in the gut with a bright pink sword and had to guzzle half our healing potions: something I considered a great waste given that he was the actual illusion.

Another time, we reasoned that the icicles hanging high above us couldn't possibly be real because the room was as warm as the rest of the tower and the floor beneath them hadn't so much as a drip on it. Rather than advance cowering beneath shields and risk being injured by a particularly heavy blow we advanced boldly; Fineous even whistled, showing our faith that the icicles were illusionary. Sadly, the ice only vanished when we were below the area of ceiling festooned with the things, and although it disappeared, the very real stalactites beneath the ice did not. And they fell on us. Fineous, despite his extravagant and swift display of acrobatics, was struck a glancing blow that broke three of his ribs.

Nicodemus was able to banish some of the illusions with 'dispel magic' spells and identify others with 'detect magic' spells, but the scrolls of 'dispel illusion' were the tools best suited to the task, and without using those my mage was really just trying to knock in screws with a hammer.

'How far up this damn tower are we?' John asked. Outside the cottage windows, the shadows had started to stretch themselves out.

'I reckon we're about halfway, judging by the estimate of its height and the number of steps we've climbed.' Simon didn't take any notes or write down any sums, but we all trusted his accuracy.

'That's based on the assumption that the first floor of the tower that we encountered was at ground level,' I said. 'For all we know there are ten basement levels.'

'So let's poke a hole in the outer wall and find out!' John grumbled.

All of us were a bit rattled, as our map of the tower's thirteenth storey had started to sprawl into an ugly maze of intersecting corridors extending well beyond the twelve previous maps that had all fitted into neat, albeit mysteriously expanding, circles.

I glanced back at the cottage windows to see the sun dipping towards the horizon. Normally it would be the rooftops of Putney waiting to receive it, the sunset gilding an array of satellite TV dishes, but here only treetops waited. Reality pushed its way rudely into my thoughts, reminding me we were on the run.

I leaned back in my chair, the game forgotten for a moment. Had Guilder and Rust already started their journey to the future? Were they even now frozen into a time trail that would keep hold of them for many years to come? I thought about how easily Natasha, if that even was her name, had fooled me. Demus had lied to me, too, though I couldn't see why he would. His lie had painted a picture of his journey back as something from the sci-fi shows, a Terminator-esque appearance out of nowhere that had him standing in the middle of London. Perhaps the other woman traveller, Anna, who had punched the delicious if duplicitous Natasha on the nose, had also not told the whole truth, or any of it.

'Lies!' I said, startling the others from discussion of some finer point of cartography. 'Illusions are basically elaborate lies.'

'Well, yes,' said John.

'A cleric would be useful, then,' Simon said. 'Clerics have the "detect lie" spell.'

'See, I told you clerics are useful,' I said. 'This is why we need Sharia back.'

Mia smiled at me across the table and brushed her foot along my calf.

'If we wanted a cleric that badly we could have just hired that priest of Suckit back in town,' John snorted.

'Sobek,' Simon said.

'What?'

'Sobek, the crocodile-headed god.'

'Sobek, Suckit, same thing.'

'Sobek is one of only two gods to feature on the front cover of the early D&D expansion *Gods, Demi-Gods & Heroes*,' Simon continued relentlessly, 'though oddly he is not one of the twenty-three Egyptian gods detailed inside—'

'A quarter-share of treasure was all the Suckit priest wanted, and we could have been adventuring somewhere real with real treasure rather than all this smoke and mirrors shit!' John said.

I coughed pointedly. 'So, here we are questing to save our *beloved* and beautiful Sharia and not bitching about it at all. But, returning to my point about lies' – I found my character sheet and tapped my pencil on the entry in my equipment section – 'Nicodemus happens to have a potion of truth. Anyone who drinks it is unable to lie while the effects last.'

'Great.' Simon slumped over the table. 'So all we have to do is get every monster we encounter to take a sip and then ask them whether they're real. And if they say "no" we can easily disbelieve them. I do hope they're feeling cooperative!'

'Not for monsters, micro-brain!' I set my finger to the lead figure with the furs and the big axe. 'Boris can have some, then try to tell me that he's not an illusion. Let's settle this once and for all!'

John and Simon sat up at that and exchanged glances.

'That's a waste of a valuable potion!' Simon made a poor case, since Fineous had campaigned vigorously for us to sell it at the first opportunity. Enforced truthfulness was not the friend of any thief. He scribbled something on a piece of paper and passed it to Mia.

John pushed his warrior's figure up to Nicodemus's. 'Sir Hacknslay throws a friendly arm around Nicodemus's shoulders and begins to slowly recount the details of the last three times Boris saved the life of one or other of us.'

Simon pushed Fineous up close, too. 'And Fineous looks Nicodemus squarely in the eye, then says, "And let's say for a moment that this ridiculous allegation of yours is true. Let's think about that. Then, instead of wasting a valuable magic potion, you would have wasted a valuable magic potion *and* got rid of half of our fighting force, leaving us with just one overly muscled idiot to hide behind when the next bunch of monsters charge at us."'

I sat and chewed on that one as the sun vanished behind the treeline. I was a seeker of truth. By nature and by profession. Lies, falsehood, ignorance. These were my enemies. The idea that a lie could be a saviour . . . that was a new and alien concept to me.

'But you're both missing something,' I said. 'The real question is, WHY is Boris with us? If he's an illusion—'

'He's not!' said Simon.

'Not Boris.' John laughed. 'No way.'

'If he's an illusion,' I continued, 'then even if he has helped us on occasion, that can't be the reason he's with us. And I want to know why he's here. I'm sorry. I just can't let this go.'

'Alright then,' Simon said. 'Waste the potion then!'

'Alright then!' I said, my conviction waning.

'Alright then!' Simon repeated.

'Nicodemus asks Boris if he will drink the potion,' I said.

'Fineous suggests he does,' Simon said.

Mia looked up from some mysterious dice rolling and shrugged. 'He isn't pleased, but he booms out, "I drink it. I drink it all if it shuts up stupid whiney magic-man!"' She mimed him taking the flask from me, pulling out the cork in his teeth, spitting it aside, then throwing back his head and consuming it in a series of glugs.

'Nicodemus asks Boris if he is an illusion!' I said triumphantly.

'No,' Mia said in the Northman's growl. 'I'm as real as you are, magic-man!'

CHAPTER 13

2009

Flamboyant supermarket magnate Ellery Elmwood came incognito to the Tower of Tricks towards the close of 2009. Actually, he was hidden inside a triple-seater sofa, since we were under observation by at least one police force regarding the disappearance of several billionaires. We were running down our operation at that point, both because of the growing surveillance and because there were only nine travellers left in the cave. Though of course those two facts were inextricably linked in a mind-twisting causal loop.

I picked Ellery up myself as arranged on an anonymous stretch of B-road running through rural Somerset, and oversaw his conceal-ment before setting off once again in the delivery truck. I drove him through our many acres of solar farm, beneath the slowly turning rotors of several dozen of the tallest land-based wind turbines in the UK, and into the courtyard of our faux medieval castle. The portcullises closed behind us: one, two, three, lowered by their own motors, the last word in automatic garage doors.

We had met several times before, entering into discreet negotiations over his long-anticipated – at least on our side – travel plans. On those first occasions, Ellery had lived up to his reputation and had talked the proverbial hind legs off all our non-existent donkeys. Today, though, he seemed a shadow of that man, tight-lipped and nervous.

Mia made him some tea before we went down and tried to set him at his ease. She spoke again about the reasons he wanted to return to 1979. She talked about the band he'd been the vocalist for. Somehow she'd managed to dig up an actual poster for one of their gigs, and there in glossy technicolour was a young Ellery in uncomfortable transition from something that looked half glam rock, half punk, towards the New Romantic vibe that the band had come to dominate with their new singer after Ellery quit.

'Of course, it won't be me that gets to make a different choice.' Ellery raised his voice over the rattle of the descending elevator.

'No.' I had told him this the first time he explained his plan. I wasn't sure why he was telling it back to me now. 'It may not even be the younger version of you if you aren't sufficiently persuasive. And even if he does choose music over a business career, there is no guarantee that the band will experience the same success with him as they did with the vocalist they hired after you.'

'They bloody well should! They should be even bigger. Massive. I was much better than Ray Donovan. His falsetto sounded like he was in pain.'

This was more like the Ellery Elmwood we first met. Even so, I had no clue why crawling naked, cold and muddy from a cave in 1979 to set a different version of himself on a different path had ever seemed like a good idea. The Ellery beside me wouldn't get to sing to those crowds. He wouldn't get the groupies backstage, and he already had the money here and now. Did his ego really need that success so badly he would give up what he had now to live it vicariously through a younger incarnation of himself? It had always seemed like a flawed plan, but he had been insistent, generous with his money, and, most importantly, he had been there in the cave all these years, waiting.

We stepped from the elevator into the well-lit cave. Most of the travellers were gone now, just a dozen silver tubes standing to conceal those still to leave, and of course Mr Elmwood himself, now deep in the clutches of the electromagnet array that had been constructed around his time trail. Somewhere in among the towering magnets and forest of cables he stood waiting in his birthday suit, a sheet wrapped around his hips for modesty's sake.

We said our goodbyes and good lucks, tugged away the sheet, then guided Ellery to the spot from where he could step back and join his time trail; at which point he and his trail would fuse and vanish, leaving just the clothes he now stood in, slumping to the bare stone floor.

Then he said it. Those five fateful words.

'I'm not sure about this.'

Clearly the choice had rested on a knife edge all along, and some tiny current in the time stream, some random eddy, had nudged him to come down on the wrong side of the decision.

Perhaps we could have talked him round. Maybe I should have just shoved him into position. After all, his time trail had always looked rather shocked, and slightly off balance, as if the first thing he might do on arrival in the dying months of the seventies was to fall on his bare arse.

But the decision was taken from all of us. The time trail vanished without Ellery. His moment to join it had come and gone.

The entire cave shuddered as if there had been some detonation impossibly far beneath us. The lights flickered, dimmed, died, and surged back to life.

'What happens now?' Mia stepped back towards the elevator, gazing at the ceiling as though unsure it would hold.

'I don't know.' I knew that Ellery had just hit the world with a paradox bomb. My daughter, Eva, who now existed only on another fork of the timeline, would have been able to calculate the impact but she was, though it pains me to admit it, much cleverer than I am.

'You don't know?'

'Nothing good.' My best efforts at analysis indicated that the effect would either fade away or grow without limit until it tore the world apart. Well, actually it would tear the universe apart, though only at the speed of light, so it would be a slow end. And frankly I wasn't that bothered about the universe past the borders of our solar system. In fact, my compassion didn't really extend beyond the atmosphere.

While unable to calculate whether we were safe this time or not, I was able to show that the effect was cumulative, so that each hit of paradox took us all closer to that tipping point where it became a chain reaction.

◆　◆　◆

We climbed the spiral stairs back up into the departure lounge within the castle, not trusting the electrics of the elevator. Ellery seemed almost pleased with himself, as though he had just dodged a bullet. I guess some decisions are balanced on such a sharp edge that you just don't know until that very last moment what you are going to end up doing.

I left him to witter on earnestly to Mia about how it was all for the best, and that he was sorry to have wasted our time and was still sworn to secrecy, of course. I wasn't setting any store by his promises of discretion. I was going to get my memory erasing device. My friend from Cambridge, Helen Wilson, had worked with me and Ian Creed to develop the idea. That particular secret hadn't lasted long, and the government soon impounded the technology, making Helen and Ian rich in the process. I guessed that, by now, MI5, the CIA and a whole bunch of other agencies had their own versions, and that state secrets were better kept these days than they had been for quite a while. But the important thing was that I had mine.

By the time I reached the end of the corridor I felt sick to my stomach. For the few minutes since that detonation deep below us when the time trail vanished without its passenger, I had been experiencing that same disorienting nausea I used to feel when Eva or Demus were trying to approach me for the first time.

I reached my study door and stopped. Ghosts bled from me, dozens of them, scores, replicas of me, turning back, striding on, opening the door, pausing, coughing, looking around . . . All of them might have been me's streaming away into alternate futures, separated one from another by hundreds of small choices, each of them branching out into new timelines on which I would live alternative lives, many very similar, some spiralling away to wholly different ends.

Suddenly the whole castle shook as if struck a blow. Plaster dust sifted down, and from my odd new perspective I deduced that somehow I was on my back, lying on the floor. I rolled over and scrambled to my feet, ricocheting from the walls as I made an uncoordinated dash back to the room I'd left Mia in.

'Nick!' She rose from behind a toppled sofa as I burst in.

'Mia!' I reached her side in five quick strides, catching her as she stumbled. The room was a mess, mirrors fallen from the walls, furniture thrown left and right, parts of the ceiling down and the dust making it hard to see from one doorway to the other. 'Are you alright?' Her hair was in disarray and blood trickled from one nostril.

'I . . . I think so.' She looked around. 'Where's Ellery?'

'I don't know.' I coughed, then lifted my T-shirt over my mouth to keep the dust from my lungs.

'He was right here!' She looked around. 'Help m—' And she froze. 'Oh.'

The chunk of ceiling moulding that had struck Ellery Elmwood was no larger than my fist, but it would have hit him considerably harder than any fist ever could, and the side of his head had a bloody dent in it of the kind that says you should call a funeral director rather than an ambulance.

'What just happened?' Mia looked more bewildered than upset. I guessed she was in shock. Perhaps I was, too.

'I think the universe just killed him.' That had been the universe's go-to response when I was the cause of a paradox. That paradox, like Ellery's, had been a minor one, nowhere in the league of killing your own father before he meets your mother; more of an accounting error, really. Not many people had ever seen Ellery's time trail back through the years to 1979, but the point was *how* had they seen it at all, given that Ellery did in fact opt not to go at the last moment? Or to put it another way, how was Ellery still here when he had gone back to redirect his younger self into pop stardom? That was the accounting error that had been eased by a lump of plaster that set us passing on into a future that Ellery was no longer active in.

Sam Robson was the next traveller to come to our doors, early in the new year. I'd known his face for years and wondered many times who he was. We knew all the rest of them now. They were wealthy, famous, easy enough to track down in the information age. But not Sam Robson. He remained a mystery until the moment he pressed our doorbell button and caused the automaton in the main courtyard to strike the huge gong that you see in the introduction to Rank films. Simon had insisted on that one.

Sam wasn't rich. He was a hacker. He seemed a nice enough guy, about my age, fortyish, solid build; he looked the sporty type rather than the bedroom-haunting teenage nerd usually associated with the hacking fraternity, at least in the papers. He'd pieced together what was going on, or at least the bones of it, from small mentions in the email accounts of several of our previous clients who had been less careful in what they said to their friends than they should have been.

Surprisingly, Sam hadn't come to blackmail us. At least not for money. What he wanted was to go back nineteen years in order to tell a series of whopping lies. It turned out that Sam's mother had died when he was in his early twenties and that, wrapped in the selfishness of the young, he had missed the chance to say his goodbyes. I felt there might have been more to that story, but since he had us on the back foot I didn't press him.

What he wanted to do was go back, visit her at the hospice where she died, and make her happy by telling her about the fabulous, and fictitious, success he'd had in the future.

'You think she'll believe you've come back through time?' Mia wanted to know.

'I do. She wasn't thinking too clearly on those painkillers at the end. And, if need be, I'll find the younger me and haul him over there to make my point. I just want her to die happy. I want to see her. To have her believe her boy got all the good things she wanted for him. After that I can use what I know now to make millions and live the life of Riley, so I won't even be lying to her really, because I will be rich just a few months after her death.'

Sam's plan was perfectly sound. He could fork into a new timeline in which he would be wealthy beyond measure if he played his cards right. It was, however, the sort of thing Mia and I had decided was the main argument against travelling to the past. We had thus far sent only those who already had wealth and power and had grown tired of it, wanting instead to revisit deeply personal moments in their past for the kind of catharsis we never usually get to have. Sam's ambitions, though, could put into his hands the lives of millions, and we really didn't know anything about him. He could turn out to be a new Hitler for all we knew. The mother story could be entirely fake.

On the other hand, his time trail was there in the cave, and if we didn't let him go then reality would have to withstand a second para-dox bomb, plus the universe would try to kill him even if space-time withstood the shock and the rest of us got to carry on living. Finally, if we rejected him and sent him back into the world, he might make good on his threats, expose our work and possibly end the process, leading to another seven paradox explosions as the remaining travellers failed to meet their schedules.

We made the right noises and sent him on his way, saying we had to get things ready for him. 'I can tell you one thing for certain, Sam,' I said at the castle gates, 'if you don't keep this to yourself there is no way you'll get what you want. There's no profit in this for you in the here and now.'

He turned back at that, still smiling, still pleasant. 'I wouldn't say that was strictly true, Nick. I mean, you're clearly a wealthy man. How much would you pay to keep this quiet?'

I had no answer to that and stood frozen at my gates, seeing him as if he were something new, though he had been extorting us from the first moment we met.

'So really, I get paid whether I take your trip or not. But I do want to see my old mum, so sort it out, Doctor Who, there's a good chap.' He clapped a hand to my shoulder as if we were best buddies, then strode off towards the visitors' parking.

I went back to the reception room where Mia was lifting Sam's DNA from the glass he'd had a Coke in. She was quite the expert at it by now.

'He's going to blackmail us either way,' I announced. 'Either he travels or we pay him to stay.'

Mia shrugged and bagged her sample. 'You want I should kill him, boss?'

I grinned. 'It would be quite easy to turn into Guilder, wouldn't it, if we had no morals?'

'Life's simpler without them. But if we didn't have morals, we wouldn't care about whatever timeline we were going to saddle with a Sam Robson – if that's even his name – who knows the future.' Mia pressed her lips together in a flat line. 'I'd better send this to the lab.'

A horrible thought occurred to me. Mia was sending Sam's DNA to be tested against the DNA taken from the bones we'd discovered wedged in one of the tunnels connected to the cave. 'We have to find the one who didn't make it out of there soon,' I said. 'We know it isn't you or me, and there are only six other possibilities.'

'If it really *is* one of the travellers. It's always possible someone else—'

'You don't believe that for a moment.' The bones weren't old and yet there hadn't been a shred of clothing found with them. No shoes, no spare change, nothing. 'And if it has to be someone, then maybe we are the reason it was whoever it was.'

'I don't . . .' But she did. I could see it in her face.

'Maybe we didn't train him how to get out. Maybe we only showed him once, with a torch. Or just said, "Follow this tunnel and it's a straight shot." Maybe—'

'Don't, just don't.' Mia turned away.

So I didn't. I still remembered my own nightmare in those tunnels and I wouldn't wish it on anyone. Even though it had to be someone. Instead I sat back and waited for the results.

Mia brought them to the breakfast table two days later. Not in an envelope – she'd received them by email – but written in her expression.

'So it's him,' I said.

And she nodded.

I took a deep breath and asked the question I had never expected to find on my lips outside of a D&D game. 'How are we going to kill him?'

CHAPTER 14

2010

Whatever we did, it seemed very likely that we were going to end up killing the man who had introduced himself as Sam Robson. If we sent him back to 1991, he was going to die alone in the dark, lost in the tunnels. If we told him and he didn't go, then the resulting paradox would set the universe to trying to kill him and might very well rip the planet apart, too. Along with all the other planets, in due course.

It seemed strange and rather abstract to hold in my hands the power of life and death not only over one man, but all humanity, and not only over humanity but potentially over distant alien races who had never even looked twice at our star in their night sky. Establishing the barrier to further travel was clearly a moral imperative. Without it, anyone with a time-rig could imperil existence.

I wondered how many foolish scientists had already triggered the end of time and space in separate incidents across the cloth of our expanding universe. Each would be a hole in the fabric of reality, racing out in all directions at the speed of light. Clearly it didn't happen often or we wouldn't be here, but the universe is a big enough place for these things to have happened many times and still to have left us with millions or billions of years before we suddenly find out and simultaneously cease to care.

In the end, we did kill him.

We gave him the full training and sent him back. I felt sick about it, but I did it anyway. He didn't look the sort to panic and lose his way where so many others had not, but even so the evidence said that he did, and I watched him as he stepped back into the timeline that had been waiting for him all these years, and I said nothing.

I think that was the point at which I first realised that whether I ended up going back to 1986 or not, I was no longer the Nick Hayes who first met Demus a few streets from Simon's mum's house. I had left that boy behind in my wake, just as we all abandon the children we were. Slow or fast, the years pull us apart from them, sometimes in one savage yank, sometimes by degrees, like the hour hand of the clock, too stealthy for us to perceive its motion and yet when you look again it is no longer where you left it. That night I looked in the mirror, not wanting to meet my own gaze, and it was Demus who looked back at me and smiled a bitter little smile.

It wasn't until a year later, over another breakfast, that Mia stopped with a piece of toast raised halfway to her mouth and said, '1992!'

'What about it?' I looked up from my laptop and sipped my coffee.

'We've sent six travellers back to the years between 1992 and this one.' She looked slightly sick.

'Something like that. One of them was Anna, who we have yet to send back and who we need to have warn me about Natasha. None of them were Sam.' I winced as I always did when I said his name. 'He went to 1991.'

'For the cleverest man in the world you can be very stupid,' she said softly.

I frowned. 'So help me out.'

'When did Guilder discover the cave?'

'1992. You and I both went to see it.'

'And then he sealed the exit at the base of the cliff to stop anyone discovering it.'

'I know.'

'And have you arranged the hiding of that crowbar down by the exit yet? The one Anna is going to need to break her way out shortly before you run from Rust in the traveller cavern?' Mia asked.

'Not yet. There's still plenty of time.' I brushed the question off with the casual defensiveness I normally reserved for questions about whether I had put the rubbish out or loaded the dishwasher, but a cold finger ran up my spine. 'All I need to do is get one of the travellers we saw when we first went into the cave to promise to come back to the tunnel later and place a crowbar for Anna. They're all headed pre-1992 so they won't have any issue with blocked exits.'

'And you'll need to tell Anna that the crowbar is there and where to look for it.' Mia spoke slowly as if leading me through a mathematical proof.

'Of course. And we know it all works because the crowbar was there and we got out. I've told all the travellers to 1992 onwards about the crowbar just in case they need it, even though they won't, because by then Anna will already have worked the corner of the grill free.'

Mia kept looking at me but said nothing.

'What?' I asked. 'The next traveller . . . Angus McDonald . . . I'll get him to do it.'

'But Guilder didn't discover the cave in 1992. His men found it in November '91 and he just didn't tell us about it for months.'

'So?'

Mia kept looking, mouth closed.

'Oh,' I said. We *had* killed Sam Robson, after all. It hadn't just been some random moment of panic. When we sent Sam back to December 1991, I'd forgotten that Guilder's metal grill might already be in place. In my mind, any date before '92 was safe. The crowbar had been there, hidden by the exit, but I hadn't told him about it. He must have exhausted himself at the metal grill and finally gone back, looking for some other way out. He must have died hating me. 'Oh.'

From then on, we improved security both online and off. The months came and went, bringing the remaining travellers to our gates just as fate dictated, and we sent them on their way. Angus McDonald came, and when I sent him back to his childhood in 1959 I explained that part of the price of his ticket was that he return to the exit tunnel and hide a crowbar on the ledge high on the right side. I took him there and showed him the crowbar and how to place it. I explained the consequences of not doing so and he shuddered and swore that he would. I explained that he must do this swiftly and before pursuing the reason for his journey, or time would branch and the crowbar would never reach the woman for whom it was intended.

Anna Mazur came, and I told her that the price for her included punching a Russian called Natasha and explaining to a young Nick Hayes that he was being fooled by a beautiful woman, something which on this particular occasion he should avoid. I let her know that the way would be blocked, told her how to escape, and let her know that I remembered that she already had.

Slowly the cavern emptied, its travellers all departed with only two remaining. Mia and me. We both stood there in the winter of 2010, gazing at our dimly warped reflections on the two silvery tubes that hid our trails. By our feet lay the clothes of a rich old man, our last customer, piled before us on the shoes he had so recently stood in.

'So that's that then,' I said.

'Seems to be,' she said.

I took her hand. 'I don't want to go back.'

'I don't want you to.' She made a smile for me. 'I forbid it.' We had run around the circles of this conversation too often. It made us both sad. 'By this time next year we'll only be a few weeks from being free of all this. You just have to stay safe until then.' Without the accident, there would be no point in going back. I wouldn't need the recordings of Mia's memories in order to restore her.

'If we don't go,' Mia said, 'then the paradox might destroy, well, everything.'

I said nothing as we made a slow retreat towards the elevator.

'And the universe will try to kill us if we don't go,' Mia said. 'Us personally. Like it did that man who didn't want to go back and be a singer.'

'Ellery,' I said.

'Yes, him. Killed in the room above us with a lump of the ceiling!'

'The universe has tried that on me before. You learn to live with it.' I'd explained to her how it worked, how when it had happened to me there always seemed to be a way to step around the threat into one of the timelines where I survived. 'Also, once the travel barrier is in place, my calculations show it will help shield us from those effects. Ellery was just unlucky to die before he understood what was happening to him.'

'Hmmm.' Mia seemed unconvinced.

'The main thing for now is to see you safely through into 2012.' I walked on, frowning. 'I just wish I could put you in a box out of harm's way.'

Mia dug her nails into my hand as we stepped through the doors. 'Just try it.'

'I could send you forward!' I stopped halfway in, the elevator doors unable to close. 'Just a year. You'd be in transit. Nothing could hurt you. I could send you into 2012 and it would all be over! It's genius!'

Mia frowned. 'Unless Demus lied about it happening in 2011.' She always called him Demus, never 'you'.

'Why would I lie?' I asked.

Mia shrugged. 'Demus lied about just appearing in front of that police station. Why would his lies end there?'

I stepped into the elevator and pushed the button. 'Why would I lie to myself?' That bit had never made sense to me.

The plan was too perfect, too simple, for Mia to resist in the long run. I would send her forward into 2012. She'd be out of action for a year, but she had no major roles coming up for a while anyway and it wasn't as if she needed the money. I would miss her, of course, but a lost year compared to her suffering a massive injury and brain trauma in 2011 seemed an easy choice. Ideally, I would have just travelled with her, but it seemed safer to have one of us still active, and I wasn't the one in danger.

I set her travelling in the cave beneath the Tower of Tricks, since I had all the right equipment there and didn't want her stuck in one of those government-approved warehouses. The nearest one, down in London, was actually closer to our Cambridge home, but having her travel at the Tower of Tricks meant I could visit her whenever I wanted and in private, rather than on scheduled appointments with a crowd of relatives strolling around the frozen ranks in London like it was a waxwork museum.

Everything was fine until the call I got on my landline at work in late October 2011.

'Nick?' A woman's voice.

'Hello, yes?' I was sitting at my desk, avoiding administration niff-naff in favour of a tricky bit of paradoxical algebra requiring the use of not only imaginary numbers but hypothetical ones, too.

'It's me,' she said.

I looked up from my calculations at that, shaking the equations from my head. 'Mia?'

'You've forgotten my voice already?' A hint of amusement.

'But . . . it's too early. I sent you forward a year.'

'Yet, here I am.' Something rattled. 'Making breakfast at four in the afternoon.' A clatter of spoon in bowl. 'Did you miss me?'

'Of course I did . . . but—'

'If you set off now you could be here in time for bed,' she said. 'And you could show me how much.'

'I'm putting my coat on as we speak,' I lied. I had missed her, though. 'I'll be there as soon as I can. Do. Not. Go. Anywhere.'

'Yes, Master.'

'Seriously. This shouldn't have happened. I need to find out why and you need to stay safe. Lock everything! Don't go near anything sharp or hot or—'

She hung up on me.

I drove at unsafe speeds and got speeding tickets from two different police forces. But it wasn't me who was in danger of a massive head trauma, it was Mia, who had mysteriously emerged from her time trail, where she would have been safe from a close-proximity nuclear explosion, into a castle where not so very long ago a man had been killed by two kilos of ceiling plaster.

It had been dark for hours by the time I reached the castle. It stood unlit, a black fist among the silent fields of solar arrays. Behind it the great blades of wind turbines turned at their leisure in a gentle breeze. I activated the portcullises at a distance and roared through in my BMW, coming to a screeching halt in the main courtyard. From there I could see lights burning in the kitchen.

'Mia!' I pounded on the main door, heart thudding. She'd set the bolts, so at least she had listened to something I said.

A few moments later the bolts were drawn, the door opened, and there she was, her face a mixture of pleased and cautious.

'Mia!' It felt good to hold her in my arms again. I'd known that I had missed her: a dull ache on which I piled endless work to distract me. But pulling her to me, the relief was something physical, as if her absence had been a slowly increasing weight now removed in one instant.

'Whoa there, stallion.' She pushed herself free, grinning. 'I should go on these trips more often.'

I grinned back. 'Don't.'

I knew that to Mia we had said goodbye a few hours ago, so I wasn't hurt by her more reserved greeting. And since I had some serious investigation to do, it was probably for the best that she wasn't feeling the separation the same way I did, or we'd have both headed for the bedroom and the night would have been wasted. Well, not wasted, but not productive when it came to answering the most important question: what the hell was going on?

We went back to the traveller cave where the equipment that had sent Mia forward still stood, enclosing the space she had until so recently occupied.

'The easiest test to run is just to repeat the exercise,' I said.

'I'm game.' Mia started towards the towering magnets.

'Not you. This could be how you get injured, for all we know.'

'Well, we can't send you!' Mia said. 'If it went wrong, who would figure out how to fix it?'

'This is why we should keep guinea pigs,' I said.

'Nuh-uh. That's vivisection. Besides, we don't visit often enough. They'd starve.'

'I think vivisection means you have to cut the animals up afterwards rather than just experiment on them. But' – I raised my hand, seeing that she was about to argue – 'this will do.' I bent to scoop up a woodlouse I'd just spotted crawling across nearby cabling. The lights had given the cave a whole new ecosystem over the years.

I put the bug in an abandoned coffee mug and set it where Mia had stood. The readouts on my shielded computer indicated that the capacitor banks above ground held sufficient charge for a forward journey, so I initiated the sequence.

The magnets emitted their normal creaks and groans as huge currents flowed around them. The resulting magnetic fields fluctuated in a swift but complex three-dimensional pattern, building a resonance within the fabric of space-time, pouring in more and more energy until the vibrations grew so large that a bubble of space-time should detach itself from the rest – just as the surface of a body of water may throw up a single droplet, breaking free of the surface tension, if the right frequency of sound is played through it at sufficient volume.

Stray magnetic fields escaped the array as usual, giving me a momentary trippy feeling, as if I were larger than my body, a god with boundless power who could step outside the universe and behold it all as a gem containing time within it, all the years from the Big Bang onward held as a single vision. The sensation passed, leaving me back in my own flesh with that familiar disappointment at having something glorious snatched from my grasp.

Mia went forward as the creaking died away and peered into the mug. 'Nope. Ol' crawly is still crawling.' She frowned. 'Should it work on bugs, anyhow? I thought it was about consciousness, not just life.'

'Maybe . . .' I hadn't ever tested it. I examined the read-outs. 'Doesn't matter, though. No completion . . .' The necessary power had been delivered, the components all seemed to be working, but the resonance hadn't reached the levels required to break free the bubble of space-time that was supposed to be the vehicle in which our woodlouse would speed into the future. The complex pattern of reinforcing feedback cycles feeding energy in at a rate calibrated to the elasticity of local space-time should have built relentlessly to reach the target level. But they hadn't even come close. 'I don't understand.'

'Maybe someone blocked it,' Mia said.

'Don't be silly, how could th—' But then I saw it. There in the background readings. It shouldn't have been possible, but she was right. Exactly right. Someone had discovered my barrier theory and made their own.

CHAPTER 15

2011

When you are going to disbelieve an illusion, you need some kind of act of faith to strengthen you, to show your resolve and commit you to your course. Standing there with Mia in the travellers' cave facing the only two remaining time trails, mine and hers, I already had my act of faith in hand, or rather, 'on hand'. While Mia had been safe, speeding into 2012, I'd had my first ever tattoo done, a closed integral, , set across the back of my right hand. I actually asked for an infinity sign, ∞, but when the tattooist asked what it was and I showed him and he said, 'Eight?', I thought better of it. The point was that I now had a tattoo and Demus, both the one standing there before me and the one in my memory, did not.

'Shit.' I flicked through more screens of data in the vain hope they would suggest a different answer. They didn't. 'Someone has set up a barrier.'

'I thought nobody was that close yet,' Mia said.

'So did I.' I opened an internet browser and hit the BBC News website. 'Nothing in the headlines, and it's been hours now.'

'Headlines?' Mia blinked.

'If this was a decent attempt, it would have covered the whole country. All the government facilities where they keep the forward travellers would be full of rather confused people right now making angry noises. The lack of news suggests they're all still statues. Which in turn suggests that this is a localised effect. Whoever is causing it may not fully realise what they are doing. I'm guessing it's one of the universities nearby. All the physics departments have their own research rigs now.'

'So, we can't go back now? Even if we wanted to?' Mia's gaze returned to her time trail. We had removed the covers, since nobody else would be coming into the cave again. At least not before the trails had vanished. 'What will happen? You know, about the paradox, if we don't go?'

'I'm not worried about that,' I said. Though I was. 'I'm worried that they'll boost the power and block the whole country before they know what they're doing.'

'Why would that be a problem?'

'Rust and Guilder would hit it. And Guilder would see me as his best chance to fix the problem.' Even as I said it, I wondered just how large an area was blocked right now and whether Guilder's hideout was affected. 'We need to get you some security.'

Mia shook her head. 'I don't need a bodyguard. Some beetle-browed thug following me everywhere.'

'You do, and more than one,' I said. And seeing her mouth opening to protest I added, 'No Neanderthals, I promise. Jason Stathams, all of them. Two hundred and fifty pounds of hard muscle packed into a suit.'

She pursed her lips and pretended to consider it.

In the end, I hired the men and had them trail her covertly. Relationships should be based on trust, but until 2012 had been sung in on New Year's Eve and the clock had struck midnight, my relationship with Mia was based on fear: the fear that she would meet her long-prophesied accident and the competing fear that Charles Rust would find her and steal her, holding her a prisoner against my solving an impossible problem for his boss.

I spent the days after Mia's return to our time stream hunting down the source of the barrier. Rather than wander the countryside with the heavy gear necessary to detect it, I delegated that task to hired hands and organised the effort from my office as director of the National Institute for Temporal Studies, or NITS as it was more commonly referred to.

Unfortunately, no matter how much money you happen to have, some specialist equipment just can't be had on demand, so I could only muster four trucks, which I sent out to hunt the edges of the barrier and map its strength in an attempt to estimate the source. I felt pretty sure I would only have to locate it with sufficient accuracy to say which university city it was nearest to. At that point I would know where to find the equipment and could hopefully buy off whoever was experimenting with it.

It was important for the researcher not to extend the area, as that would increase the risk of bringing Guilder and Rust's journey to an end – though the current barrier might have already done so. My plan would bring their forward trip to an end soon anyway, but I wanted it to be next year at the very earliest. Additionally, if the barrier did reach London and bring all the travellers there to a halt, it would be very hard to hush up the technology, and if Mia *did* get hurt I still needed the option to go back to 1986 to ensure her recovery.

My mind whirled around all these competing desires, needs and possibilities, and, as they did so often at such times, my eyes returned to the closed integral tattoo on the back of my hand. Barrier or no barrier, that was an act I had taken myself to put a wall between me and Demus. At the time it had felt like a bold move; a brave one, even. But with Mia in jeopardy once more, it suddenly seemed like a very selfish decision.

Six days after the barrier went up, I was still at my desk in the NITS head office. On the screen in front of me a map of the UK glowed in glorious technicolour, shaded to indicate the likelihood of any given point being the source for the barrier. My software updated it each time new measurements were sent from the mobile units that I had out criss-crossing the country. I divided my time between refining the algorithms that calculated the probabilities and staring moodily at the screen. The latest data had shifted the bulk of certainty towards the Midlands, centred on Coventry, with Birmingham and Warwick almost as likely. I'd phoned to order a car to drive me to Warwick and had annoyingly been put on hold before I could protest. Instead of just calling a different company, I let my eyes return to staring at the hypnotic colours of the map, and found myself once more pondering my connection with Demus. I was still on hold and daydreaming when someone shook my shoulder.

'Nick?' The hand shook me again. 'Nick! Did you hear anything I said?'

I looked up. Neil Watkins, my assistant director. 'They've been trying to reach you. Mia's been in an accident. You need to get to the hospital.'

And that's how Mia and I ended up trying to escape Addenbrookes Hospital covertly, expecting that at any minute Charles Rust might come limping out of the shadows with murder in his eye and a silenced pistol in his hand.

Fortunately, the hospital had been surgically attached to a Burger House, perhaps so those overdosing on triple-decked layers of beef with double cheese could have their obese bodies wheeled directly to the coronary ward. In any event, it meant that along with the obligatory link in a chain of coffee franchises, there were plenty of ways in and out of the place with a steady flow of people.

We mingled with the burger munchers and left keeping our heads down. We abandoned my car in favour of a taxi summoned while still inside the hospital.

'I should call the police,' I said.

'And tell them what?' Mia asked.

'Rust has a string of charges outstanding after the investigation.'

'So I tell them I might have been attacked by a man nobody has seen for twenty years and who should be fifty now, but isn't?' Mia shook her head. 'Turn left at the next lights,' she called out to our driver.

'We shouldn't go home,' I said.

'Where, then?'

'The castle.' I nodded to myself. 'It's secure and we can see him coming. In town he can just ghost up on us out of any crowd.'

And so the rather surprised taxi driver found himself being offered a large sum of money to drive two lunatics across the width of the country.

We left Cambridge on the A428 heading west and were soon driving through rural England, free and clear; or at least we would be until the next time Rust – it had to be him, nothing else made sense – tracked us down again. I wasn't sure what the long-term solution was. Perhaps that's why Mia and I still had time trails standing in the cave: we said to hell with paradox and ran to the past together to escape Rust once and for all. Maybe I decided not to show up for my death scene and just dared the universe to do its worst. At least Mia would be with me. It wasn't the worst plan in the world, though I would miss some of the folks we'd have to leave behind. Also, I wasn't sure how long I could survive without the internet.

I called John and Simon just to let them know what the situation was and got their voicemails in both cases. I left word for them, then turned round to give my phone to Mia on the back seat so she could call her mother, who against all predictions was still alive, and still consuming cigarettes and whiskey at a frankly scary rate of knots.

My thoughts returned to the cave. We wouldn't be running anywhere, future or past, unless I got that barrier down. I was pretty sure I could knock out the generator causing the disruption and open a window for me and Mia to get away into the past. Rust, however, would want more than that. He would want me to knock out all barriers ever, or at least until he and Guilder had got as far into the future as they wanted. And that I could not do. The cat was out of the bag now. Whoever was generating the current barrier would be busy telling the planet about the technology soon enough. It wouldn't take so very long before the world's scientific community managed collectively to solve the reverse travel problem. I'd been edging them slowly towards it, more out of pride than need; I'll admit it stung me to think someone else would be credited with the discovery. Once that particular can of worms was opened, and the dangers of paradox identified, then governments everywhere would ban it. And once governments started operating their own temporal barriers, the shutters would come down on the whole technology. There was nothing I could do about it. Only, Rust wouldn't see it that way. He'd taken Guilder's money, accepted an obligation, and from what I knew about the man he wouldn't give up on that, no matter who he had to cut into pieces trying to make it happen.

'Bloody hell!' The driver, a small bald man with an improbably deep voice, waved his fist as a white van overtook us with the barest of margins in the face of oncoming traffic. 'Idiot!'

We drove on a quarter of a mile, staring at the back of the van, which, having got in front of us, seemed in no particular hurry to get anywhere.

'Jesus please us!' our driver rumbled, stepping on his brake.

'What the—?' In my seat beside him I found myself straining against my seatbelt in a momentum-induced attempt to headbutt the dashboard. All around me loose objects migrated towards the windscreen.

We left a lot of rubber on the road but to the driver's credit we managed, albeit by millimetres, not to hit the van in front of us as it came to a grinding halt. The car behind us did a far less good job of it, but had five times the space and came to a smoking halt a yard or two behind us.

I looked round to see if Mia was alright.

'Ow!' She rubbed at her collarbone where the seatbelt had dug in. Without it she would have joined the loose change and tissues on the dashboard.

'Fucking maniac.' The driver unbuckled himself and set a hand to the door.

That's when I saw Charles Rust limping round from the passenger side of the van, a predatory grin on his face. He hadn't changed since the day I last saw him, holding that knife on me in the cave. Not one hair. I reached over the driver to pull his hand from the door. 'He really *is* a fucking maniac. That's exactly what he is. Get us out of here and there's ten grand in it for you.'

The man didn't have to be told twice. As fortune had it, we'd come to a halt beside a turning off the main road and, with a deft bit of reversing and hauling on the steering wheel, our driver had us pulling away as Rust reached for the nearest door. I craned my neck along with Mia, both of us watching out the rear window while our old nemesis dwindled into the distance. He appeared to be waving rather than shaking his fist.

'Where does this go?' I asked as we bumped along the increasingly narrow lane, hemmed in between high hedges.

'I don't know, mate.' The man tapped his satnav. 'I wasn't planning on coming this way.'

The satnav spoke into the pause. 'In one hundred yards, slow down and make a U-turn.'

'It's a dead end!' Mia said. 'He forced us down here so there wouldn't be witnesses.'

Looking back along the winding road I could just make out the top of a white van speeding along between the hedgerows. 'Shit. Call the police!'

'I lost your phone. I think it went under the seat.' Mia started to unbuckle her seatbelt so she could hunt for it.

'Control. Control!' The driver was talking into his radio. 'Control?'

We were out of range, though. Cambridge lay over twenty miles behind us.

Farm buildings loomed ahead, a gate sealing the rutted track.

'We'll go in there,' I said as the driver slowed. 'He's only after us, so he should leave you alone. Once he's gone by, call the police and then run for the road.'

'Right . . .' The driver came to a halt before the gate and started hunting in his pockets for his phone. The momentary road rage he'd shown back on the main route was well and truly gone, and his hands were now shaking so much I wondered if he would be able to dial, if he ever managed to extract the thing from his jeans.

Mia and I scrambled out as Rust's van sped into view. We ran for the gate and I was still fumbling with the chain when Mia vaulted over.

'Run!' I shouted, somewhat redundantly since she was doing just that, and followed her through the yard, aiming for the end of a long cow barn. We rounded the corner, spattering mud with each step.

Mia turned, wide-eyed. 'He's coming!'

'We should hide.' The driver would be calling the police and nobody on the farm could handle Rust. We needed time for help to arrive.

'Over there!' Mia pointed to a machine shed, a tall barn through whose huge doors I could make out at least two tractors standing in the shadows. She took off again and I followed in her wake, slipping and sliding around the turn.

The farm seemed deserted. Perhaps they were all out doing . . . agriculture . . . in the fields. I'll admit that my knowledge of farm life is pretty sketchy. I couldn't, for example, name any of the dangerous-looking equipment facing me as I came to a halt in the barn entrance. The walls seemed to be hung with torture devices made of sharp metal. The rational part of my mind was telling me that they were the sort of things tractors drag behind them to break up the soil, but the rest of it was screaming that we were about to walk into some kind of Bedfordshire version of *The Texas Chain Saw Massacre* where Charles Rust would be the least of our worries.

'C'mon!' Mia beckoned me forward and ran on between the two tractors, both of which were far larger than I had imagined they were from a distance.

In the movies, barns are full of hay, great piles of the stuff ideal for hiding in. This barn seemed to favour sacks of fertiliser pellets, bales of wire fencing and, for some unknown reason, bitumen in metal barrels. The wild thought that a half-decent chemist could make an excellent bomb out of this stuff crossed my mind. I quickly opted to leave hastily constructed weaponry to MacGyver and looked for somewhere to hide instead.

Mia lay down behind three 500 kilo bags of Carrs Fertiliser and pulled some discarded sacking over her. She waved me away to find my own spot. It proved maddeningly hard to find somewhere. Suddenly my body seemed too enormous to fit into any likely hole, and all the time I knew that Rust was limping inexorably towards us. Any moment now he would be standing silhouetted in the doorway, sniffing the air like a fox.

I hurried up the ladder to the split level and settled for crouching between a big plastic barrel, contents unknown, and a large filing cabinet that had been co-opted into some sort of service. It was pretty gloomy up there, and I felt fairly inconspicuous. Fairly inconspicuous, that was, until Rust rattled one of the main doors open a little wider and then turned the lights on.

'Miiiiaaaa!' He called her name out just like his younger brother had all those years ago, and the chill of it ran through my bones. 'Miiiiaaaaa!'

I realised that I was actually very easy to find if he decided to come up and search for me. I crept forward, looking for a better alternative. Down below I could hear Rust moving about, starting to poke around. Terror had my hands shaking, a cold sweat sheathing my body. Maybe this was where I finally split away from Demus. Maybe he and his Mia made a different decision on the road. One that saved them. And now me and my Mia were going to die.

'Mia?' Rust rattled an oil drum. 'Where aaaaare you?'

Up above I was failing to find anywhere better to hide. It seems easy when you're a kid; hard when you're six foot two and trying to hide from a grown-up. But also, I was growing increasingly concerned by Rust's fixation on finding Mia. Perhaps he thought that if he kidnapped her, I would do what he said. Or that going after her would bring me out into the open. He was right on both counts.

My hands were trembling like the taxi driver's and no part of me wanted to move in any direction but 'away'. Even so, I focused on Mia and inched towards the ladder on my hands and knees, hoping to get a view of Rust's progress as he hunted for her. I almost reached it, but must have scraped the floorboards too loudly or something, because Rust suddenly went quiet; and just as I was expecting to hear an 'Aha!' as he pulled Mia from her hiding place, I heard instead the sounds of someone climbing the ladder at speed.

Without thinking, I rolled on to my back and swivelled so my feet faced the ladder. Then, trying to dig my nails into the boards to anchor me, I struck out at the ladder with both heels. The effect was less impressive than I had hoped, but I did knock it back about a yard. It was still a fair way shy of the tipping point where the whole thing would fall over in the other direction, but even so, when it jolted back the base must have slipped some and now only six inches of the ladder poked over the edge.

I got to my feet and saw that Rust was already starting to continue his climb, his single black eye fixed on me, teeth showing in a snarl. I had time for one more kick before he reached me and I took it, shoving the ladder violently to the side. The base slipped back a little more and the top end lost contact with my level of the barn. Rust and the ladder slammed forward into the floor. If his fingers had been in the wrong place they would have been pulped, but instead he rolled away, seemingly unharmed. I know if it had been me, the only way I would have left the barn would have been on a stretcher.

'Nick.' Rust looked up at me, blood running from the corner of his mouth. 'Long time no see.'

'I can't do anything for Guilder,' I called down, trying not to let my voice shake. 'I didn't make the barrier and I can't unmake it. But I can pay you triple whatever he's paying you. I'm rich now, and Guilder's money is gone.'

Rust wiped his mouth and spat out something that looked worryingly like half a tooth. 'It doesn't work like that, Nick. Not once I've been paid. This isn't about money. It's about obligation.'

'Well, I still can't help Guilder.'

'You can do anything, Nicky-boy. You're the wunderkind.' His cold eye slid over me. 'Or rather, you were. Now you look like the man in the cave.'

He turned his gaze back to the ground floor, scanning the sacks and barrels. 'You stay there for now. I'll just check down here for Miss Jones and if I don't find her I'll be up to join you presently.'

'The police will be here any—'

'Even if I had let your little taxi driver make his call – which I didn't – it would still take an age before anyone showed up. This is the real world. Nobody arrives in the nick of time to save you. The authorities arrive after the event, tag the bodies, photograph the blood spatters. It's always been that way. Always will be.'

Rust looked away and walked out of sight beneath the split level in a direction that would take him to Mia's hiding place.

'Wait!' I shouted after him. 'I'll do it. Whatever you want! I'll go with you.'

I heard Mia's shout as he found her. More anger in it than fear. I threw myself down on my chest and hung over to see, the blood immediately running to my head, making my eyes prickle. Upside down it was hard to make sense of the scene; the lights revealed so much machinery along with the sacks and barrels that my eyes had difficulty separating one thing from the next. Then Mia screamed, this time in pain, and I saw them both, Rust emerging from behind some kind of wheeled hopper with Mia before him, her arm twisted up beneath her shoulder blades.

'Get off her!' I looked around wildly for some way down. Another ladder, a rope, anything. I even considered jumping and I am not in any sense good with heights.

Rust flicked his gaze towards me, that familiar malicious amusement on his face, but the smile was short-lived. Mia stamped on his foot and managed the seemingly impossible feat of twisting free without breaking her arm. She ran for the exit, but Rust seized a fence post from a stack of them and with a roar threw it after her like an overweight javelin. It struck the back of her leg and she went down below my position, sprawling across the floor with a tooth-rattling impact. Rust was on her moments later, despite his bad leg. Something had broken inside his mind, the veneer of reserved professionalism gone along with any thought of using Mia to compel me to do his master's bidding, and in its place was a wild dog's naked aggression. In a fury he threw her over with one hand, grabbing up the fence post in the other, a good four feet long and thicker than my arm. I lay paralysed in the moment as he hammered it down at her face as if pounding grain.

Some instants, though they offer no time in which to act, somehow refuse to let you go. I hung between heartbeats, watching the woman I loved sprawled across a concrete floor as the fence post drove down towards her face. A face I knew every line of. A face I'd seen nearly every day for a quarter of a century. Mia Jones. The need for her still ran through me like a fever after all these years.

Terror filled me to overflowing. Terror at what that savagely driven piece of timber would do to the fragile bones of her face, at what it would do to the brain behind it.

And in the next moment the post smashed down on to concrete, missing her by millimetres as she snapped her head aside. Rust drew back for a second thrust, but by then I was already falling.

I hit across his shoulders and back with horrific force. I'd slithered over the edge without any thought for the consequences and fallen head first, arms out before me. If I'd missed, then the impact with the floor would definitely have killed me. As it was there was a crunching thud, a cry of agony, possibly from me, and I rolled away, blacking out with pain.

The next time I saw anything it was through one eye with my head lying on the barn floor, looking out towards the too-bright day through the main doors. Mia was up and running again, and somehow Rust was giving chase. He threw himself after her, catching her ankle like a rugby player tap-tackling an opponent. I saw Mia stumbling on, unbalanced and predestined to fall, arms pin-wheeling. Hanging on the wall she was careening towards was something resembling a bead curtain, except instead of beads, it was chain links, and large metal spikes jutted out at regular intervals. I prayed to a god I didn't believe in for her to miss it, but the only gift I got was that the thing's name popped into my head. A chain harrow. And then she hit it, side on, arms still flailing.

The air had yet to return to my lungs and the loudest shout I could muster came out as an agonised hiss. But still I managed to start crawling towards her. Rust stood a good ten yards ahead of me, though, fence post in hand again, drawing back for the swing like a baseball player as she hung on the spikes. He lined the blow up against the base of her skull. I tried to stand, but only reached my knees, watching helplessly again as Mia waited for an impact that if it didn't kill her must surely be the one that would rob her of her memories and leave her drooling and broken.

I tried. With everything I had in me I tried to get to my feet. But the strength had left me. The horrible finality of it all twisted inside me like a fist that had closed around my heart and lungs. And in that moment of pain and desperation, just like the young men lying torn by shrapnel in no man's land, crying out for all to hear, it was, for reasons I could never explain in words, my mother who I wanted.

Time decelerated again as though wanting to draw out the cruelty and make the moment last an eternity. With aching slowness Rust began to lean into his swing. At the same time some dark, unexplained shape detached from the shadows behind the door at his back. Fragments of a second stole by and with each one's passing the shape behind Rust seemed more human. It held something out before it. Some kind of stick or pole. The pole struck Rust below his shoulder blades and he lost his grip on the post, which went spinning through the air in a lazy arc that had it smashing into the cab of the nearest tractor.

Rust turned my way, staggering. The daylight streaming through the doorway behind reduced him to a silhouette, stealing away details. He took three more paces and fell forward. The pitchfork that had been driven through him stood proud from his back, swaying to and fro.

Finally, spitting blood from my mouth, I made it to my feet and stumbled towards Mia. She, in turn, pushed away from the chain harrow seeming miraculously unhurt, as if somehow she had contrived to evade every one of the four-inch spikes standing ready to receive her.

'I'm OK.' She spluttered a laugh. 'I think I am . . .' She patted herself to make sure.

Then, together, Mia seeing for the first time that we weren't alone and me recalling it with sudden surprise, we turned towards the figure standing empty-handed by the door.

'Mother?' I took a step towards her, astounded. 'Mother?' My sixty-four-year-old grey-haired mother, standing there in her outdoor coat and a sensible pair of wellingtons. 'What . . . How . . . I don't understand.'

Her eyes flickered towards Rust, still lying where he fell, the pitchfork standing from his back, blood spreading out beneath him. 'You asked me to come here and save your life,' she said. 'So I did.'

CHAPTER 16

2011

'I did what?' I doubt that many people ever expect their elderly mother to kill someone. Still less to do it in front of them and then claim that you were the one who told them to do it.

'You asked me to come here and save Mia,' Mother said. She glanced again at the body. 'I wasn't sure I would do it in the end, but I came anyway. I mean, he was going to kill her, so I shan't get into trouble for it. I shouldn't think.'

Mia stood at my side supporting me, or maybe I was supporting her. Both of us were rather stuck for words, but it was Mia who asked the important question. 'When was it that Nick asked you to come here?'

'In the hospital.'

I frowned. '. . . Addenbrookes?'

Mother's face softened. 'No, of course not. In the hospital that night when you went in for your first chemotherapy session.'

Mia turned to stare at me in confusion.

'Demus!' I said. 'I saw him talking to you. And when I asked you, you pretended not to know who I was talking about and then changed the subject. I always wondered what he said.'

'What *you* are *going* to say to me,' Mother corrected. 'You said a lot of things that a fifteen-year-old Nicholas would never tell his mother. You told me enough about your father and our life together to convince me you were telling me the truth, or at least that it was worth allowing the possibility that you were. You told me that I had to carry on as if we had never had the conversation. That was the hardest part. Knowing that you were going to get better and not being able to tell you that you were. Not knowing how to act. That was a very difficult year, Nicholas.'

Mia, knowing instinctively what to do, dragged me forward and put her arm around my mother's shoulders, becoming the filling in that most unusual of things, a Hayes hug. And then, by gently extracting herself, she left Mother and me with our arms about each other, a position that, crippled by our own particular version of unbending upper-middle-class Englishness, we could never have reached by ourselves.

'You told me that I had to come here, to Owlscroft Farm, and hide myself behind the left-hand door of the machine shed, and that whatever happened I had to wait until the man who was hurting you and the woman you were married to had his back to me.' Mother looked up at me reprovingly and wiped something from my face – blood, I think. 'I told you then that it would be a lot easier if I just had the police here waiting to help you when you arrived.'

'And I told you that wasn't how I remembered it happening, and that if you did that you would help a Nick Hayes, but not the one standing in front of you.'

'Yes. Yes, you did. I still find it very odd, but you've explained the basics of it to me so often over the years that I have to accept it.'

I smiled at that. I'd explained more than the basics. Mother was an exceptionally clever woman. I squeezed her in my arms and stepped back. We both needed the hug, but we were also both relieved when we were allowed to finish with it. I guess that while 'British reserve' is one possible diagnosis, another reasonable one is that, like many clever people, we were both on the autistic spectrum at the Asperger's end.

Two new thoughts occurred to me at that point, the first being that I really did need to stop standing up because I had definitely hurt myself falling on to Rust. The second thought occurred to me on my way to the floor. In my last desperate moment I had thought of Mother, and suddenly there she'd been, saving the day. While I still didn't understand the crazy process that had baked into our strangely knotted timeline the events Demus remembered and brought back with him on his return trip, I felt that somehow I had been offered an inkling. The whole thing was some kind of insane paradoxical feedback loop spiralling around itself, and when the 'event' had happened and our timeline had uniquely tied itself into a Gordian knot, this just turned out to be what was frozen in. It didn't have to make sense. It was what we were given. Like life itself. The parameters within which we had to operate. We had to stick to the letter of that law, but the spirit could be whatever we chose.

'Quick! Call an ambulance.' Mia was at my side.

'I'll go to the farmhouse,' Mother said.

'You don't have a phone?' Mia sounded amazed, even as she cradled my head.

'Of course she doesn't.' I managed a laugh, and it really hurt. Mother still believed telephones should be anchored to the wall and sit in the hall. I beckoned Mother closer so I wouldn't have to raise my voice. She got down on her knees, first brushing fussily at the grimy floor. 'You have to go home now,' I told her.

'I will do no such thing!'

'There's a dead body, and you have absolutely no explanation for why you are here. No believable explanation.' I winced. It felt as if I had broken glass inside my chest, but perhaps it was just my ribs.

'If I leave then that's just an admission of guilt,' Mother said. 'And someone at the farm must have seen something, or will when I try to leave.'

'I think if I didn't want . . .' I hitched in a painful breath. '. . . want you to follow my advice then I would have told you not to back in 1986. I wouldn't send you to prison back then any more than I would now. So please go, Mother.'

Mother bit the side of her mouth, uncharacteristically unsure. She gave a curt nod, patted my hand, and stood to go.

'You were never here,' I hissed after her.

By the time she'd left, the world was growing dim around me. 'I'll be needing that ambulance,' I whispered.

I woke in a hospital bed in a small room with a policeman outside the door. Fragments of being blue-lighted back to Cambridge returned to me. I remembered the paramedics coming into the barn, pulling back my eyelids, asking me stupid questions.

I summoned a nurse with the call button. My chest had been strapped, and my ankle, too. I had a line feeding fluids into my hand. Internal bleeding, I guessed.

The pretty young nurse who bustled in a few minutes later sported the name tag 'Lisa' and put me in mind of the nurse who tended to me on that first chemo night long ago. I think that one was also a Lisa, about the same age as this one, and too old for me, just as this one was too young for me. I might have spent a life studying time, but it still had the capacity to surprise me. Years crawl by but once they get behind you in a big old stack, it's amazing how they seem to have done it in the blink of an eye.

'Where's my wife?' I asked her before she could roll out any pleasantries.

The nurse's face clouded. 'The police asked her to go with them to answer their questions. She said to tell you she was fine and would be in to see you as soon as—' She reached out to interrupt my attempt to get out of bed. An unnecessary intervention, as it turned out, since the agonising pain in my side had me collapsing back on to the mattress before she could so much as lay a hand on me. 'As soon as she can.'

I sighed and lay back. I would let them fix me. The police would come and do their thing. They did have a corpse with two holes in it that needed explaining, after all. I would say I was the one to stick him with the pitchfork to save Mia's life, and with no witnesses save me and Mia, along with Rust's nineteen-year absence and the list of ageing charges against him, it should be enough to close the matter.

The irony of it all was that having been stopped unceremoniously in his tracks on his journey through time, Guilder had clearly decided that landing in 2011 was insufficient to meet his needs. He had almost certainly failed to investigate the current state of medical science in any detail, on the reasonable assumption that the sort of cure he was looking for would take more like a century. What he didn't know was that over the last twenty years, medical science had seen an incredible revolution, and that the technology that now allowed us to regrow and repair injured brains might very well also allow for the cure of whatever neurological condition was killing him. But no, he had just sent his snake out after us.

I had no way of knowing for sure, but I strongly suspected that Demus might have had something to do with the stunning advances in medicine, neuroscience in particular. Not that I was claiming any genius for medicine; simply that if I were to want to ensure that medical science really would be in a position to heal Mia in 2011, then what I would have done was to take the foundations of the existing technology back to 1986 and seed it in the right places for it to grow.

The whole thing was another example of the mystery of how you could lift yourself up by tugging on your own bootstraps. Was Demus so confident that his trip wasn't the cause of the advances Mia needed that he didn't do anything to make sure it happened? Or had he acted, and risked that he would start a new timeline, screwing up his plans?

I relaxed into my pillow. It wasn't my problem. I didn't have to go back. Rust was dead; the year was nearly at an end. All we had to do was wait a little longer and those two time trails beneath the Tower of Tricks would simply vanish. We would be taking a gamble on the resulting paradox not getting out of hand, yes. But right then it was a gamble I felt willing to take. Both the Rust brothers were dead. I had no desire to go back to a time where they were both alive and to let the younger one kill me.

Even with all the wonders of modern medicine, it still took three days to get me out of the hospital bed and hobbling through the front doors on crutches. Despite my injuries, I felt good. The police had seemed largely satisfied with our almost true account of the incident at Owlscroft Farm, and the world was minus one Charles Rust again after a brief addition. Mia was at my side and the sun was shining.

I crutch-walked my way towards the car park where Mia had her Clio parked. John always ribbed us about our cars. In fact, he ribbed us about our lifestyle in general. With his return on the investment into the time travel project, he had upgraded his three already ridiculously expensive cars into a collection of supercars, the insurance on any one of which was more than most people could earn in a lifetime. But the truth was that money was never something that interested me, and simply having a lot of it didn't change the fact that I really couldn't be arsed to spend it. The castle over the cave was my only indulgence and we hardly ever got to spend time there. There had been a plan for the four of us to get together at the Tower of Tricks once a month for a weekend of D&D; Mia would write a new campaign and we would recapture the old days. But I think we managed it more like once a year. All of us were always too busy. Even Simon!

The joke now was that we would arrange to all go into the same retirement home where we could Zimmer-frame our way to the communal hall and catch up on lost gaming time. I told Mia that this had been the time I was going to allocate to catching up on all those great fantasy books I never managed to get round to reading. She told me that they were still publishing great fantasy books, with more coming out each week than I could read in a year. I told her to shut up.

Plans for better ways to spend my time continued to flow through my mind as we crossed the road to the car park. The vehicle that hit us seemed to come out of nowhere, accelerating rapidly. I thought maybe it was another attack. I thought that Guilder hadn't given up on us after all.

They told me later that the driver was a little old lady, eighty-six years old, her foot pressed to the metal, too confused to be able to reconcile the car's violent acceleration with her strong but incorrect belief that her foot was on the brake.

The car struck me a glancing blow and sent me spinning to the side of the road. Mia it hit head on, throwing her over the bonnet and windscreen. She bounced once on the roof of the car and then hit the tarmac with her head.

CHAPTER 17

2011

There was never any doubt about what I was going to do. The idea that I wasn't going back had always been a daydream. A selfish one at that. A lie I told myself to keep from thinking about the day when I would have to do it.

I had sent Sam Robson back to die a lonely death in the dark rather than risk the world-destroying paradox of having him not go. I was never seriously going to run that risk for the world on my own account. Sure, the world had a lot of shitty stuff in it that wasn't worth saving, but it also had Mia in it, and my mother, too, I guess, and then there were baby turtles, rainforests, John, Simon, Elton, little children in playgrounds. Not necessarily in that order, but you get the picture. I was just scared, that's all. Now, though, I was more angry than scared. Angry with time itself, perhaps, and its stubborn refusal to let go of this future in which I now found myself. Its relentless demand that Mia should end up where she was now, in an intensive care bed in hospital, having vital sections of her brain slowly regrown with stem cell technology.

I sat by her bedside for a week, talking to her, telling her my plan, telling her goodbye. A week where every day the rain beat on the windows without pause, as if the heavens were being wrung out between two great hands. I spent a lot of that time staring into space while my

mind turned inward. Boredom, like hunger and the necessary consequences of feeding that hunger, is one of reality's ways of nailing us
down. It's nature's way of telling us that however much we aspire to
be spiritual beings, and even the atheists among us seek to be in some
way greater than the biomechanics that supports them, our efforts are
doomed to fail. We imagine ourselves creatures of deep emotion and
grand gestures. I had thought that my sorrow would be some vast thing
that I would wrestle with, that I would be locked in battle with it as I
sat by Mia's bed, unblinking. But the truth was that boredom soon took
over, relegating my grief to a hollow ache that wouldn't let me go, but
wouldn't occupy my mind either. I sat not seeing Mia, her bandaged
head, the tubes and lines and monitors, the nurses and doctors who
came and went. I looked inward instead, back along the years, back at
the life we'd had and the future I'd reached for just as a falling man will
reach for the rung that has already slipped his grasp.

I think a lot of us dream about a life we know we'll never have,
but we hold it out there as a light to follow, even so. Mine had been a
dream about a life with Mia that carried on past my fortieth birthday
and ended with us growing old together. Disgracefully old, perhaps. It
seemed insane that I had ever thought of forty as old. That at fifteen
I had considered Demus, if not ready to give up on life, then at least
having had a good bite out of it and in no position to complain too
much about facing the end.

I sat by Mia's bed as dawn came fingering its way through the
slatted blinds, her hand in mine. John and Simon had come and gone
several times over the past few days. They didn't talk about Demus but
I knew that they saw him sitting in my chair. They knew where I was
going, and when they said their goodbyes it was me rather than Mia
who got the full force of them. John shook my hand too hard and
pressed his mouth into a flat line with the desperation of a man not
wanting to cry.

Simon and I sat side by side, not speaking, watching Mia, the only sound the slow rise and fall of the respirator. We sat like that a whole morning.

'What were those numbers again?' I asked.

He didn't ask which numbers. '4, 17, 17, 6, 1, 2, 11, 3, 5, 3.'

'Thanks.' I'd forgotten them long ago. Simon never forgot anything. That's a blessing and a curse.

'You have to wait for John to say "batter up".' He took a napkin from his pocket. 'Here, I'll write them down for you.' And in his laborious handwriting, so at odds with his deft touch with the paintbrush, he wrote the words in capitals and then the numbers.

He handed me the napkin. The numbers were the dice rolls that Demus predicted in order to start convincing us of his story. I'd tried to forget them so as to break the chain between me and him, and eventually I'd managed it. Maybe there was a note of them somewhere in my things. Some scrap of paper that my subconscious had refused to let me throw away, but this was easier. Also, it was a goodbye that Simon and I could share.

I had other questions, lots of them, and he answered them all, pulling the facts from the vast and incorruptible store of his eidetic memory. Finally, when at last I had run out of things I suddenly needed to know about the past, Simon dug into his pocket and brought out a steel watch. It had an understated elegance to it that hinted at a considerable cost.

'For you,' he said.

'Thanks!' I took it from him. 'It's . . . great.'

It seemed an odd gift, given that neither of us had ever cared about fashion or statements of wealth or, in fact, watches.

'It's kind of antique. It lights up, too.' He leaned forward and pressed the button that made the dial glow in the dimness of the room.

'Cool.' I was still a bit lost for words. 'You just thought a man who travels through time should have a watch?'

He quoted Galadriel's line from *The Lord of the Rings* when she gives Frodo her gift, the one about a light to save him in the dark. Now it was a proper Simon present.

I grinned and frowned. 'You know this is just going to end up on the cave floor with everything else I'm wearing?'

'That's why I chose an antique,' Simon answered without a hint of a smile. 'I want you to buy the same one in 1986.'

'I will.' I nodded solemnly. Now it really was a Simon present. I had to go and get it myself. And pay for it. 'Thanks, man.' I stood and set a hand to his shoulder as he got up beside me, ready to go.

Simon surprised me then. He broke the habit of a lifetime and, as though trying to speak an alien language for which his tongue had not been designed, he opened his arms and clamped me in a hug that felt more like an act of violence, but which was obviously well intentioned. He left with a cryptic quote that I was still nerdy enough to identify as coming from *The Search for Spock*. The one about weighing an individual's needs against those of everyone else.

As he went through the door, I replied with the line from *The Wrath of Khan* that Spock begins and Kirk completes. A quote that basically says the exact opposite. Irreconcilable logic. A paradox.

The room was crowded with flowers and cards, many from fans who only knew Mia through her acting, but many from friends too, of whom she had a ridiculous number. The hospital was a private one, a neurological centre that we had funded over the years with a sizeable portion of the money our billionaires had paid us for their tickets back into the past. The cash had also paid for a fair bit of the research behind the techniques that were now reconstructing the damaged portions of Mia's brain.

When I presented her consultant, Mr Briars, with a memory stick containing, appropriately enough, recordings of Mia's memories, he was astonished at our foresight and asked how far back they went. I lied and told him that the earliest recording was from 2002, and that floored him since the technology had been in its infancy at that point. The fact was that I had been recording Mia's memories since 1986, when Demus came back and gave us the necessary devices. This meant that she should be able to remember her whole life. Her childhood memories would be as fresh to her now as they had been to her when she was fifteen. I had transcribed the early recordings from where they had been stored in my own brain into the data matrix held on the memory stick, a 2048-terabyte monster of a thing closer to the size of a Snickers bar than the normal model.

Not once had any of Mia's memories leaked from the store in my mind into my consciousness, but even so, having removed them from my head, I felt an emptiness; a lack of something that I hadn't even known was there. The memories were no more open to exploration in the memory stick than they had been in my mind. The technology was an ultimate form of encryption: the data and the brain were two halves of the puzzle, each useless without the other. Only when imprinted on to the unique and regrown structure of Mia's brain would the memories make any sense.

I could have stayed to help her recover. Perhaps I should have. But I never claimed to be a hero or even to be brave, and I knew that if I held her whole again in my arms, I would lack the courage to do what needed to be done. Also, if I tried, Mia would demand to come with me.

So I sat for a week holding her hand, and then I got ready to go. I stood and I kissed her cheek. I thought my goodbye rather than spoke it, because I'm a Hayes, dammit, and we don't say stuff like that even when the other party is unconscious. I told her that when some hearts break the world breaks with them, and although mine had broken the day that her accident finally caught up with her, I wasn't going to let the world suffer, too. I would go back as Demus and close the circle. And by doing so the data on the memory stick would be her memory, free of paradox, and she would be well again.

I kissed her forehead. Love had come into my world unexpected, unannounced, like a gentle breeze, hardly noticed at first, yet where it wandered it moved everything. Now there was no end to where I would let it carry me.

I straightened up and watched her for a moment, seemingly sleeping. I left with a sigh so deep that it hurt something inside me that I would like to imagine was more metaphysical than just my slowly healing ribs. I left knowing that I wasn't ever coming back.

The data coming in from the researchers I still had out in the field had narrowed down the source of the intermittent barrier to Birmingham. Which meant that, barring the unlikely event of a mad scientist experimenting in his mother's basement, all I had to do to find those responsible for it was to call in at the University of Birmingham's physics department and make some discreet enquiries.

I walked from Mia's hospital to my car, put the satnav on and drove to Birmingham. Bizarrely, now that my fate was sealed, a weight seemed to have lifted from me. Perhaps it was the burden of having to fight the inevitable. Maybe I just needed to be doing something, making progress, rather than sitting helpless at Mia's bedside, just waiting.

I didn't know whether months from now, when her brain was ready to accept the reimplanted memories, it would work. The technology was still new, and nobody had ever had so long a period of their life restored to them. So, I didn't know whether it would be successful. But I damn well knew that if it wasn't then it would not be my fault for lack of trying. If Mia could remember again, then she would remember why I had abandoned her. She would know that I'd given time its due and gone back to play the part written out for me when I was still a child.

I drove through the afternoon, hardly noticing the towns pass by. I remember Kettering, Coventry, and suddenly the urban sprawl of

Birmingham. The university, contrary to expectation based on the city's grimy industrial heritage, sits in green acres, and while it may be a far remove from the dreaming Gothic spires of Cambridge, the red-brick buildings, most of them scattered among the fields and woods of the campus in the 1960s, are pleasant enough to look at.

I drove smartly up to the School of Physics and Astronomy and asked for the first of the staff members whose name showed in my list of those having applied to the Institute of Temporal Studies for a research grant in the last eighteen months.

Dr Root appeared in the foyer minutes later, somewhat breathless and straightening his jacket. At first I thought he was a schoolboy stuffed into an interview suit. Very young, painfully thin, a quick, nervous way about him, long-fingered hands always busy. He appeared somewhat star-struck. 'Professor Hayes!'

'Dr Root.' I shook his hand. 'Call me Nick.'

'I . . . uh. I didn't know we were expecting you.'

I understood his confusion. It's not often that a world-famous Nobel Prize winner who happens to direct a major scientific institute turns up on your doorstep. 'Sorry. I should have called ahead—'

'No, no! You're more than welcome, Professor!' He looked suddenly horrified, realising he'd interrupted me.

'Call me Nick.' I grinned then cut to the chase. 'Someone here has been running a time-rig for most of the last fortnight. Who would that be?'

Dr Root blinked, looked rather guilty, and then rallied himself. 'That would be me.'

'Direct hit, first time.' I gestured to the doors into the main building. 'I'd consider it a great favour if you were to show me what you're up to, Elias. It is Elias, isn't it?'

'I . . . uh. Eli,' he said. 'But Elias is fine.'

'Eli it is.' I took his elbow and steered him towards the doors.

Eli finally took the hint and started to lead me in. He paused by the elevator. 'The lab's on the third floor.'

'Let's take the stairs.' I thought it best to keep him moving. He didn't actually have to show me anything if he didn't want to. I wasn't the time police.

'How . . .' He turned to look back at me as we climbed the steps. 'How did you know I was running my experiment? I mean, if you don't mind me asking.'

I smiled what I hoped was a reassuring smile. 'Doctor Who. Isn't that what they call me?'

'I . . . uh.' He tripped on the next step and sprawled on to the landing.

I helped him up. 'You're throwing out temporal micro-disturbance over ten thousand square miles.'

'Well, I don't know . . . Ten thousand?' He rubbed his knees and looked up at me in shock. 'Are you sure?'

'Very.'

'But that would mean . . .' The look of horror that stole over his face let me know just how much he understood what he was doing.

'Fortunately, the affected area is an ellipse,' I said.

'So London . . .'

'Has not been affected.' I followed him out of the stairwell and along a corridor. He was practically sprinting now. Clearly, he understood that the disturbance his experiment was propagating would interfere with time travel, but he had not anticipated the range of the phenomenon. Right now, he was beginning to realise that if he simply rotated his equipment he would sweep the barrier across the designated travelling sites in London and bring to a stumbling, possibly fatal, halt the journeys of the many hundreds of travellers housed there.

Eli Root unlocked a side room, flicked on the lights, and there before us was a fairly standard time-rig, the towering electromagnets almost hidden from view behind the bulky moderators that had been crowded around them.

'I never thought it would require so many moderators.' I'd never actually built a barrier generator before. 'Have you tried sympathetic generators at the L2 and L5 points?'

Eli blinked at me again and pulled a pair of glasses from his inner pocket. 'Sympathetic? At . . . But that's just . . .' – he frowned and considered it for a moment before the slow dawning of realisation across his face – '. . . genius.'

'Just a suggestion,' I said.

Eli's face suddenly fell, as though something precious had been snatched away from him. 'You've discovered this already, haven't you? But why isn't it in the literature? I mean . . . How long have you known?'

'A while.' I hadn't the heart to tell him that I'd finalised the necessary proofs as a teenager, almost certainly before he was even born. 'Don't worry. I'll let you tell everyone.'

'W . . . what do you mean?'

'I need you to do me a favour, Eli. A big favour. Only unlike most favours, I'm going to pay for it. I'm going to privately match all your public research funding for the next ten years. Sound good?'

Dr Root spluttered a laugh. 'Do you want both my kidneys or just the one?'

'I want you to turn this machine off for a week. And after that I want you to turn it back on and keep it running no matter what anyone else says to you.'

'For how long?' he asked.

'Until the government institute their own barrier across the entire country.'

'I don't . . . but why would they do that?'

'To stop people going back.' I reached into my pocket. 'I can write you a cheque for the first instalment. Let's call it two hundred and fifty thousand pounds.'

The excitement that suddenly lit Doctor Elias Root up was nothing to do with the quarter of a million. I don't think that even registered with him. 'You've done it! Haven't you? You've bloody done it!' He reached for me, then thinking better of it hugged himself fiercely. 'How? I mean the Hayes Conundrum . . . How could you— How *did* you solve it? And then even with that, it would take . . .' He ran long fingers up into his dark locks, tugging at his hair.

'Focus, Eli.' I waved my hand in front of his face to get his attention. 'Money. Lots of lovely money. And really all I'm asking is for you to switch off for a week. I mean, failing that I can pretty much buy the university and switch it off for you.' I couldn't, but I wanted to get the message across. What I would do instead would be to pay someone unscrupulous to total the building's power supply, but I wanted to keep the man's attention on the money.

'Couldn't you just tell me how you did it instead?' He was almost begging.

I shook my head, trying not to smile. 'You'll find out soon enough. The international community really have their teeth into the theory now. Pieces of the puzzle are being assembled all across the world. The dam's bursting at the seams.' I slapped his arm. 'You're a bright fellow. This barrier business proves it. So why don't I just leave the rest as an exercise for the student? That way you can still get a piece of the action. Have your name on part of it.' I paused. 'Look, what you really need to be thinking about is why your barrier is so efficient. You should look at n-spaces on high-order manifolds of the zeta-mapping. Collaborate with a topologist in your maths department if the equations get away from you. Those guys are all looking for experimentalist partners. Susan Pichencko is here, isn't she? Go talk to her about it.'

Young Eli looked as if I'd given him the biggest present ever in the history of Christmas. He still didn't seem to have registered the huge financial bribe I'd shoved in his face.

'Thank you, Professor Hayes! Thank you so much!' He continued to tug his hair with one hand while seizing mine for vigorous shaking in the other. 'My God! The zeta-mapping! I know Susan . . . I just never— I have *so* much to do!'

'Nick. Call me Nick, Eli. I'm just some guy at the end of the day. We all are.'

'Tap.' He nodded, still distracted. 'My friends call me Tap. A joke on my surname.'

'Just remember the bit about turning the rig off for a week, Tap. Starting today. And then back on forever after. Yes?'

'Yes.' He nodded.

'I'll have my solicitor send you a contract for the funding.' I escaped from the handshake and started towards the door.

'You're leaving?' He looked bereft.

'Very much so.' I opened the door. '*Tempus fugit!*' And with that I was striding away towards the stairs.

By evening I was approaching the castle through the fields of dozing solar cells. The Tower of Tricks hulked before me, a black fist against the paling sky. I had arranged Elias Root's funding with my solicitor on the phone as I drove.

For the last time, I raised the portcullises and decelerated beneath their metal-shod teeth into the courtyard beyond. In my office I took from my wall safe the letters I'd made ready for the people I cared about. It's hard to write anything with that sort of finality. They weren't quite suicide notes, but they almost were. Where do you start? How do you finish? What will the person be thinking by the time they reach the last word and know that they can never respond? I wrote them in the hope they would somehow release the people reading them. I told my mother that I had always loved her but never found the words to say it.

I reminded John of the good times we'd had and asked him to be there for Mia even if she was angry. I told Simon that the adventure never ended – I was merely changing game systems. Mia I told that I would see her again, and that all she had to do was remember. I told her it wasn't a sacrifice or a gift, it was just who I had always been. I was going back to write those memories and to ensure they were returned to her. Memory is all we are, I said. So don't forget me.

Events seemed to be accelerating now, time running away from me like sand between my fingers. I knew I could wait until the next day, the next week, if I wanted to, but some convictions have to be acted on. Any delay dilutes the certainty, allows stray thoughts to worm their way into your mind and cloud that clarity with doubt. I didn't want to die. I didn't want to go back and fulfil the prophecy I'd lived with all my life: the one Demus delivered into my hands when I was still a boy. He'd taken away one death sentence and replaced it with another, but that second one had offered me twenty-five more years.

'Twenty-five years.' I said it out loud as I descended the spiral staircase into the travellers' cave. 'Twenty-five years.' At first they had crawled by so slowly and so sweetly that it felt as though I had been given an eternity. Lately, though, the months had zipped past, blurred by the speed of their passage, like trees seen from a train. And now, with them stacked behind me, with their weight against my shoulders, I felt no more ready to go than I had at fifteen.

Perhaps it would be the same even if I lived to be eighty. Perhaps it's the same for everyone, no matter how many years they're trailing behind them. Always the child standing there wearing an old man's clothes, an old skin hanging from old bones, and wondering where the days went, remembering how marvellous it had been to fritter away so many slow and sunny days. And wanting more.

Demus and Mia were waiting for me, just as they had been all my life. I would go. She would stay. If her time trail persisted until after her recovery, then the barrier would keep her here in the present. The world would have to take its chances with whatever paradox resulted. I wasn't going to let her try to stop me. My calculations indicated that the time barrier would dilute the effect that had killed Ellery Elmwood. The universe would want to kill Mia for not going back as her time trail demanded, but the barrier would help hide her from that retribution. She should be fine. She would rebuild her life just as the doctors had rebuilt her body. I didn't know why she would choose to come back after me. To stop me, I guessed. But the fact was that I had an important job to do in 1986, and she did not. And so I would close the door behind me and leave it in place forever to shield her.

The instrumentation in the traveller cave indicated that Dr Root had done what I asked and turned his rig off, stopping the temporal micro-disruptions propagating across the country. All set. Ready to go.

It wasn't until I approached my time trail that I noticed the tattoo on my hand, the closed integral, black and irrefutable across the skin on my right wrist. I hadn't even had it for six months yet and already my gaze flowed over it as though it wasn't there, just part of me, as much a piece of the design as the pattern of my moles. It had been its absence on the wrist of my time trail that drew my eyes.

I had had time to go and have it removed. The treatments weren't perfect, but they were pretty decent. But I had written my letters, set things in motion, prepared my mind. I was ready to go. Now. Not in a few weeks, after multiple sessions under the laser to remove one detail.

Mia's make-up! I sprinted back up the stairs. We seldom came to the castle, but our room had all the stuff we needed; clothes mainly, but also make-up for Mia. She had left her Goth days behind her and I never felt she needed make-up, but an actress without war paint draws the paparazzi and invites magazine pieces commenting on how she's ageing and speculating on whether she might be ill – all the sort of nonsense I thought society might have outgrown in the new millennium but that we somehow trailed after us like chains linking us to the bad old days. Bad old days I needed to head back to.

I found her collection of flesh-tone foundations and tried brushing some over the tattoo. It actually did a decent job. I mean, it wouldn't last long, but for short periods when nobody was looking for the tattoo, I very much doubted they would notice. I pocketed a bunch of the powders and foams then realised I was being an idiot. They would be left behind when I went. Would the make-up, though? I mean, we took our hair with us and that was dead; so was the outer layer of our skin. It was, after all, hard to say where the living body ended. The time travellers didn't leave their fingernails lying on the clothes left behind. Technically the tattoo ink was dead. Maybe it would settle to the floor as dust. Or perhaps the body's own bio-generated fields enveloped anything sufficiently close to it and allowed that to be transported, too. Maybe this was what Eva had exploited to bring back the Lewis Carroll book, not to mention her imbedded technology, and to travel clothed.

Either way, it would work or it wouldn't. I masked the tattoo beneath a layer of foundation then returned to the cave.

It was good that Mia was there to watch me, albeit in the form of the frozen trail through time. A journey that I had taken measures to prevent. I kissed her forehead once, my lips meeting the slickness of the discontinuity that wrapped her time trail. And then, with a last look around and a sigh of resignation, I stepped back into my own long-awaited return.

CHAPTER 18

1985

Dark.

Technically the journey back had taken me no time, but inside it felt as long as it was, it felt as if I had been travelling backwards most of my life. Always in darkness. And so the cold was the thing that alerted me to the fact that I had arrived. The cold and a tiny jolt as I fell the centimetre or so to the floor, the drop occasioned by the fact that my shoes had opted to remain in 2011 and head on into Christmas in the usual way.

I reached out to the side and found Mia's slick, touch-defying curves readily to hand. That was good. She grounded me. Still in the cave. And gave me orientation in case I lost my own. Her time trail would always be present in the cave in the years between the date of her destination and the date of her departure, whether she used it or not. Part of me felt I had abandoned her, locked her in the future behind Elias Root's barrier. But if she came back, she would try to stop me. If she succeeded in stopping my sacrifice, she would create a much more dangerous paradox than the one caused by simply not returning along her time trail. If she failed, she would have to watch me die and be stranded in the past with the aftermath.

I started to shiver. The warm clothing I'd been wearing had been left . . . or would one day be left . . . as a shapeless heap resting on top of the shoes I had been standing in. If I had arrived on time then the cave would currently be undiscovered, and none of the elevators or stairs that first Guilder and later myself had installed would be present. I knew the way out. Long ago, or in a few years' time, depending on your point of view, I'd done it blind and panicking on the basis of a quick look at the map. Now, having shown each of over a hundred travellers through the tunnels several times, it was second nature.

I made my way back to the rear wall and set off, trailing my fingers over the familiar contours of the rock. The damp stone was chilly underfoot, the occasional drips a shudderingly cold surprise. I knew that Matthew Hartinger had been this way just a few weeks before me and that Giselle LeJeune was due to follow later in the year. I wished them both luck as I made my way towards the as yet unseen daylight.

Somehow, despite the number of times I had previously navigated the way in the dark, I still managed to bang my elbow, graze my forehead and lose some skin from my hip. I squelched barefoot through the mud and, remembering at the last moment the plaster cast footprint Ian Creed had discovered, I took care to make one deep impression right in the corner of a turn where nobody else was likely to step on it, at least not for the next seven years.

The numbing coldness of the mud made me very glad not to have to wallow through the half-flooded passages I'd used on my first escape. A wider, drier tunnel paralleled that particular section and brought me at last to the exit where the grey light of dawn splintered in through the fissure in the cliff.

Late December in England is not a good time for nudists. I had considered arriving in the summer of '85 to a warm afternoon and living the high life for a while, but the longer I left between arriving and my appointment with Rust and the others at the microchip factory the harder it would be to do, and the greater the chance that I would somehow slip from the timeline by doing something that had never happened in my past.

Naked and shivering I eased out into the forest. It was ridiculously cold. The oh-I'm-going-to-die kind of cold that thankfully very few of us ever get to experience. On the bright side, I doubted that I could be done for indecent exposure. Freezing weather is never flattering to a man and my power to offend appeared to have retreated inside my body, leaving a reminder so shrivelled that it was more likely to provoke hilarity than outrage.

I knew where the nearest farmhouses lay, but Mia and I had long ago decided that the regular arrival of naked, mud-smeared strangers at the homes scattered among these particular Somerset fields would create not only suspicion but a significant amount of press coverage that was singularly absent in the historical record.

Instead of trekking through the forest barefoot, I went to one of several locations where I knew that with a degree of random poking about with a stick I would find, buried in a shallow grave, a large plastic box containing an array of clothing and a modest amount of money.

There were more than one such caches, since we hadn't known in advance how far back the furthest traveller would go. It turned out to be 1957 in the end, but to start with all we knew was that if Demus went – and that was a big if – there would be a cache placed in 1985. So when Melissa Reede, the world's first reverse time traveller, went back to 1980 she really did have to make her way to the nearest farmhouse and throw herself on the mercy of whoever lived there. We did make some efforts to establish which farms had housed families at the time, rather than potential serial killers living on their own.

Melissa had been asked to return and bury clothes and money for later travellers at a pre-agreed location close to the exit. It turned out that after four more customers we got Hector King, a grey-haired and rather rotund multi-millionaire who very much wanted to return to 1968; so Melissa had unknowingly walked right past the cache he'd buried in the swinging sixties. But of course, there was no helping that, just as there was no helping the fact that Hector had hobbled his way barefoot and naked in a February gale right past the cache of clothes buried in 1957. But the arrangement did drastically cut down on the number of nude arrivals in family homes around the area.

To my great delight, I struck plastic after only a few minutes' digging around, and had soon unearthed a box from which I was able to dress myself in a curious but warm assembly of garments. I pocketed half of the £100 available and reinterred the box as best I could. Making a mental note to return and restock the box as soon as possible, I walked off, relishing my warm stripy socks and ill-fitting brown shoes.

The date remained unclear. I trudged along the country roads accompanied by the raucous dawn chorus, wishing that I had my smartphone so I could summon a taxi.

Depending on your side of the equation, Demus had turned up first in the January of '86, then again in the summer of '86, or vice versa. The events of the upcoming summer were more than a little confused owing to the fact that they arose from a paradox that had been destructively anchored into two timelines, and that we had successfully resolved with the judicious application of a time bomb.

The resolved paradox left a confused jumble of partial memories and the strong conviction that none of it had actually 'happened', at least not in the accepted way, which involved it becoming part of the history of our timelines. It had *happened*, but in a time and space uniquely its own.

All of which left me very confused as to whether I really needed to go back to the summer first, act out the parts where I recalled Demus and then build another time-rig to bring me back to January. Eva would have been able to do the sums to resolve the issue, but Eva had vanished with the paradox, as if she had never been, which technically she hadn't. And that paradox, which in my timeline had never happened since we shook it free with our bomb . . . was the only reason Demus had accidentally arrived in that summer in the first place.

In the end I had concluded that my fractured memories of that summer were not memories from my own timeline and therefore did not need my cooperation in order to be formed. I recalled Demus being fatally irradiated in Bradwell nuclear power station. I recalled him being stabbed by Charles Rust. I recalled him dying. I really had no desire to experience any of those things, especially not to let Charles Rust, who I had seen my mother kill, stab me and . . . kinda . . . kill me before I had to come back six months later and let his little brother finish the job.

No, it was sufficient that I play Demus in January and let a paradox-free timeline run its course thereafter without me.

The only niggling worry was that I had, after that summer, always assumed that Demus's baldness and apparent ill health the first time I saw him were the result of his radiation poisoning at Bradwell.

I walked on amid the shortening shadows, starting to limp as I got my first blister from the too-small shoes, and wondering what strange stroke of fate was going to make me go bald over the course of the next few weeks before letting young Nick catch his first sight of me.

I spent the next few weeks over the Christmas period getting rich again. I got a lift into Bristol town centre and hit the first betting shop I saw. I'd memorised appropriate horse race results, along with some more general sporting results spread out across quite a few years, just in case I hadn't arrived at my destination time. I mean, I would have been rather stuck if I'd arrived pre-1970, but my technical knowledge could have been converted into money, albeit on a slower timescale. I was fairly confident of arriving when planned, especially since I remembered doing it, but you never know with science. A decimal point can always be missed, and who knows if I had accidentally slung a few of our travellers back into the Jurassic? The twentieth century I felt equipped to deal with. Before that, no, I wasn't going to last long. And had I emerged from the cliff face to find a primordial swamp, I would have just gone looking for a T-Rex to make a quick end of it.

I spent the week before Christmas mailing carefully worded letters to medical researchers all across the globe. Not to the most prominent figures, but to the men and women who were the stars of neurological regeneration in 2011. I guess in some way I might be seen as having stolen from them the chance of independently making the discoveries I was steering them towards. But I didn't tell them everything, just as I wasn't going to tell young Nick everything. I just pointed them in good directions and hoped that the rest would take care of itself.

For Christmas I bought myself a black BMW, and on the day itself I sat back with a bottle of tequila, a mound of snacks and a tower of VHS cassettes to watch on my new, state-of-the-art video recorder.

On New Year's Eve I went to hear the chimes of Big Ben and see in 1986 with the crowds. I missed all twelve strikes of the clock beneath the roaring of my fellow Londoners, but it felt good to be part of that throng. The weeks before had been a rush of getting established, getting ready, setting up a lab to make the memory eraser and storage device. I'd been too busy to dwell on the strangeness of it all, but it *had* been strange. I was walking about in my own past. I knew what was going to happen next. Not when each person opened their mouth or when any given casino dice were rolled, but I knew the headlines, I knew the fates of film stars, sportsmen, politicians. I knew that in four days Phil Lynott, the Thin Lizzy singer, would die. That in nine days the secretary of state for defence would resign his position. That on the last but one day of the year Ellie Goulding, whose songs I had listened to on my drive from Birmingham University to the castle, would be born, and that two days earlier a former prime minister would shuffle off this mortal coil. I'd felt that knowledge sitting there between me and everyone else, a kind of distance that couldn't be breached no matter how many hands I shook.

In that New Year's crowd, though, for the first time since my return, I felt a part of the world. And I didn't want to leave it.

CHAPTER 19

1986

It is a curiously distressing thing to meet your own mother and to be older than her when you do so. It's an upsetting of the natural order of things, and I hadn't come prepared for just how unnerving it was going to be.

I stood waiting for her in the hospital foyer. I knew the time and the place. I knew the outcome. I knew all the facts. I just had no idea what to say or do.

She looked so goddamned young. Hair long and dark and thick. The lines of her age fallen away, the delicacy of her movements, shaped over the years by arthritis, replaced with a determined certainty. Surely my mother had never been so . . . fresh. She had been for my entire life perpetually twenty-four years my senior, burdened with additional decades of life, weighed down with responsibility for me, unable to step clear of the shadow cast by a dead husband who she never stopped loving even though he left her. And now I had left her, too. Abandoned her in a suicide not so different from my father's.

She walked towards me, unseeing, head high, her face a trembling mask that had to hold only long enough for her to reach the privacy of her car. I could see that in her now. She was one kind word away from crying. For me. She was walking away from her son, leaving him with his cancer, both of them caught in the straitjackets of their lives, of who they were.

Suddenly I knew what to say. I stepped into her path and, before she could protest, I took her hands in mine. 'Nick is going to be fine.'

She tried to pull away, until she saw my face. Even then, her body kept on struggling, left on autopilot while her eyes widened and widened again and her mind went into free fall.

She knew me. Even with my shiny scalp and a quarter of a century wrapped around me. I had worried that she might mistake me for my father resurrected, but a mother knows her son. She set one hand to my face, covering my mouth as if unable to let me speak, and the other to her own.

Of course, knowing and accepting are not the same thing.

'Who *are* you?'

She was crying. We both were. I led her to a row of chairs by the exit and we sat without words.

It took a while to explain. I hadn't known what to say, but instead of trying to prove my story I suddenly knew how to start. At the end.

'When I left it was the year 2011 and I wrote you a letter to say goodbye. I put in it all the things I couldn't ever say because of the way we are. Both of us a little broken. Some of it because of how my father left us, but mostly just because not everyone is good at this stuff. Me and you, we're good at a lot of other things. But, if you'll let me, I think I can tell you what was in the letter.'

She nodded.

'Only you can't ever tell Nick that you know, or I'll never be able to write it.'

Another nod.

'And it can't change how you are together. Not too much, anyway. It's complicated. I'll get to that later.'

And so I told her. I read the letter that I still had right there in my mind. And because it was already written and I was just reading, I found I could do it; my tongue let me.

'You have questions,' I said when at last I was done with the letter, with the explanation. I glanced up the clock. 'You can ask as we walk. We need to go back to the ward.'

'We do?' Mother stood up with me.

'Nick sees us talking in the corridor. I remember it. We have to make that memory.' I set off for the stairs and she followed.

'First question,' she said behind me. 'What happened to your hair?'

The truth was that I had shaved my head. I'd grown bored of waiting for whatever mysterious event was supposed to come along and suddenly rob me of my locks, so I took matters into my own hands. On New Year's Day I'd shaved my head in the mirror of my bathroom. A final act of capitulation. I'd watched as the dark locks fell into the sink, and from behind them the Demus of my memory emerged looking vaguely surprised.

I had a role to play, after all; and actors don't just deliver lines, they shape themselves to the part. They put on the appropriate costumes. They accessorise. And when necessary they slap on a false moustache, gain twenty pounds, plaster a 'broken' arm, whatever is required. I'd learned this from Mia, who chameleoned her way from one role to the next with a magical ability to become new people as easily as change wigs. You'd think a talent like that would make me doubt who she really was, but somehow it never did. I think she gave me everything she was within the first seven days of us meeting beneath that street lamp, and I had loved her for it ever since.

After the meeting at the hospital I turned up for my date as 'vampire' in Richmond Park, and then lurked around the back of Simon's house towards the end of D&D the next day, waiting to be seen.

I stood in the cold, staring up at the window of Simon's bedroom. Occasionally I saw movement. Once I glimpsed Mia. The urge to go up there was a physical tug, pulling at my chest. Simon's mother had moved after his little sister went to university. I hadn't been in that house for decades, but it still felt like home. I knew what they were doing up there and how safe it had felt, even after the cancer arrived. How that sense of belonging had felt, of discovering that there were in the world people whose minds were like mine, open to something more than reality, ready to follow imagination wherever it went.

I wanted that back. I wanted those days back. And even though I was standing in them, letting them flow by me hour after hour, I knew that could never happen. We get one shot. However you play it out. Fast forward it, rewind, it's still the same: a single shot.

I saw my own face at the window. The first real look I'd got at young Nick. A wave of déjà vu came over me, a memory of standing at that window and seeing me as I was now, looking up. Young Nick turned away to report the sighting and I hurried away, fighting to keep to a straight line as temporal distortions continued to mess with me.

I had a week to kill before our next encounter, and while I may have spent it poorly, I did enjoy myself. I was on death row, waiting to die, only I was on the outside and my pockets were stuffed with money. I drank too much. I took up smoking and liked it enough not to stop. I ate the wrong food in expensive restaurants and cheap kebab shops. I took up residence in an arcade and dropped endless ten-pence pieces into Defender, Robotron, Joust, Galaxian, Gorf, you name it. I got asked to move on from the arcade before I grew tired of the games. I guess they assumed I was a paedophile, which was harsh but understandable.

People often speculate as to what they might do with the last month, week, or day remaining to them, given that they are in good health and know what's coming. The truth is that even though I'd had plenty of time to think about it, I didn't really know what I wanted to do. In an awful way, I just wanted it to hurry up and happen. There's a certain pain associated with doing even things you love and knowing that it is for the last time.

Mostly I felt lonely, and wished that Mia was with me.

A week passed and I turned up on schedule to punch Michael Devis in the mouth. Now *that* I really did enjoy. I arrived as he loomed over young Nick, who was doubled up over a pool of chemo vomit, and I just unloaded on him and watched him fall on his arse clutching his face.

'You better run, because I enjoyed that and want to do it again.' I kicked his outstretched foot. 'Scram!'

Devis got unsteadily to his feet, swore at me and ran off, saying he was going to call the police.

I turned back and found myself facing . . . me. Impossibly young, a couple of inches shorter, a lot skinnier, mouth hanging wide open, hair at all angles.

'Wow, that felt good!' Though now the adrenaline was dying away my hand felt kinda broken. 'I've been waiting twenty-five years to do that. Hurt like fuck, though!'

I wasn't remembering my script and speaking my lines; the words were the ones I wanted to speak – they came naturally. All I had to do was watch myself and make sure I didn't stray from the preordained path.

We both spoke our lines. I gave him the numbers that Simon had scribbled down for me in Mia's hospital room. It amused me that Simon had been the one to give me the numbers that would now drive him to distraction over the next few nights.

I told him I was Demus. It felt like a big thing, coming right out and saying it. Another nail in my coffin. I told him a bunch of other stuff, but the kid was hurting and didn't seem to take it all in. The temporal resonance was still strong, though not as bad as over the previous weeks, and it was messing with me so I knew that with the chemo as well, Young Nick wasn't in a fit state to talk to. In the end I sent him on his way with the numbers on the napkin and a promise to meet again in a week.

It was only after I'd left him there that I properly remembered that I had a script to stick to, but it seemed that I'd said everything I needed to and nothing I shouldn't.

Meeting Mia again was . . . weird. Very weird. Let's just say that I kept my mind strictly on what had to be done. Sticking to the script was hard now; there were a million things I wanted to say, but the fact that she was the girl I remembered from more than half a lifetime ago rather than the woman I had left behind made it easier.

I had to tell them both the lie about my time travel from 2011 causing me to appear outside the police station on Watkins Street at three in the morning of January the first. I didn't understand why I was lying, but before Mia and I blanked our memories of the two weeks that followed, Mia had told John about it, and after the memory blanking he had told me. So either Demus told that story and lied to us then, or John lied to me later. Neither of which made much sense.

Shortly after that, Mia fled the car and I let Young Nick chase after her with the money to pay her debt to the drug dealer Sacks, who she'd been getting the resin from to help with the chemo.

I sat in my BMW, tapping distractedly at the wheel, and watched my young self running into the distance. The stupid lie bothered me. Had it just been frozen into the timeline like so many of the seemingly silly decisions that I now had to work around, including the need for a not-yet-on-the-market microchip, the hunt for which was going to get me killed?

And yet I could see a mechanism at work behind those choices. The lie just seemed senseless. Was there a message in it? Some kind of message to myself? If so, I wish I'd been less cryptic.

Events rolled on just as they had before. All I needed to do was pop up and play my parts. All of the time since picking up Young Nick and Mia in my BMW by the Miller blocks was a blank in my own memory, so I felt both freer and more vulnerable. I no longer had to watch every word, but similarly I no longer had the tight guidelines I'd started with. I had nothing to ensure that I was staying on the timeline, and a mis-step would fork us on to another reality, leaving everything that was to come in jeopardy.

In many ways it would have been great to step off. If I just did something noteworthy that wasn't in the news record of the 2011 I'd left behind, then I would know I was free and clear of my date with death. But I couldn't do it. It would remove the guarantee that the memory stick I had left with Mia's doctors would work. It might even lace her timeline with so much paradox that it collapsed. And so I stuck not to my absent memories but to what John and, more importantly, Simon had remembered about Demus's appearances. Which meant that I knew exactly what to do and say after 'dance lessons' at John's house.

I predicted the Space Shuttle Challenger disaster, then showed it to them on live TV. I also got to see young Elton, which was bittersweet, since what I was doing was going to see his father killed. I truly understood then for the first time quite why he had withdrawn from our friendship. It was my fault. My choice. Even now, I was prepared to trade his father's life for Mia's. In one sense it had already happened, but that was splitting hairs. The father he had right now, the man he knew, could be saved.

I said what I could to him.

Before I left, I had a word with myself. I told Young Nick that Mia would save him in the end. There was truth there, and I spoke those words with conviction. Mia may never have saved me in the sense of pulling me from a burning building, but the man who stood there carrying the name Demus was a very different person to the one who might have stood there had she never entered his life. She kept me from vanishing into the weird world of mathematics that called to me constantly. She kept me real, in contact with other humans and what it meant to be human. In a small but very real way, she saved me every day.

I had two final appointments with Young Nick. The first was outside the hospital as he went in for his last chemo session. I was glad to have forgotten some of the chemo. It was still, after all these years, the absolute worst thing I'd had to endure physically. I felt bad for the kid.

I sat there waiting for him, smoking. I didn't know if it was in the script or not. It was just me and him. He would blank the memory soon, and he'd never told anyone about the meeting. Not that I knew of. So I smoked. I wondered idly about trying some harder drugs. It hardly mattered if I got addicted now, and why not experience what

183

the big deal was before I kicked the bucket? I blew smoke and laughed at myself. I doubted I really would. It just wasn't . . . me . . . somehow.

Young Nick turned up and gave me a holier-than-thou sermon on smoking. I went easy on him, knowing what he had to come. In the note he would write to himself before he wiped these weeks from his memory, he said not to forget that he had been to see Eva, the girl he met on the chemo ward, and that she was dying. He wrote that she couldn't have lasted more than a few days, and that he stayed with her and did his best to say something useful, but couldn't. Perhaps while he was in there speaking to her, he would think that I might do a better job of it with a few more decades under my belt. But really, I wouldn't, and I didn't envy the kid. A dying child is a mirror. What you find to say to them is a truer reflection of who you are than anything you'll see over your toothbrush.

I left him with wise words and told him I had things to do. I left him with half a lie, saying I didn't know if I would see him again. But I knew enough to say, if I had wanted to, that both of us would soon be in the staff canteen at the microchip research and fabrication plant where John's father worked. I also knew that only one of us would be leaving. But what point was there in telling him that? Sometimes knowledge isn't power. Sometimes it's just a burden.

I walked away feeling seven kinds of maudlin and musing on the difference, if any, between lying to yourself in your own head and me telling Young Nick untruths.

I was so deep in thought that an ambulance nearly ran me over in the street outside, which would have been ironic on several levels. But instead of walking on in the customary cloud of embarrassment, I actually just stepped to one side and stood there with a foot in the gutter and a foot on the curb, frowning furiously. Before I'd left 2011 I'd had the edge of an idea. Just the edge, mind. Not even a corner. But I'd had the edge, and it was a big one. Now I tugged the idea free of the murk and saw how it might just work. It would be a long shot, and it was all about lies.

CHAPTER 20

1992

On the last day of our self-imposed exile on the Dorset coast, Simon, John and I – plus Boris – finally reached the top level of the Tower of Illusion.

I was pretty sure that Guilder and Rust had absented themselves from our timeline. I was happy with the notion that I would never see either of them again, Rust in particular. Guilder was a son of a bitch, but if he managed to get cured in the future, then good luck to him. I knew from what Demus said about Mia that medical science had accelerated beyond all expectations, and I had a suspicion that Demus had something to do with that. Maybe it would pay off for Guilder, and they would be able to help him in whatever year he ran into the inevitable barrier.

'So, the final flight of stairs is before you,' Mia said, marking a spiral staircase on our map.

'We've heard that one before,' said John.

'But this time it's actually written above the archway into the stair-well,' Mia said, lifting and spreading her hands to sketch out the banner for us: '"The Final Flight".'

'That,' Simon remarked, 'sounds decidedly ominous. As if they might vanish suddenly and our final flight might be straight down three hundred yards on to rocks.' He frowned. 'I disbelieve the stairs.'

Mia rolled. 'They vanish.'

'Aha!'

'And all that remains is a round vertical shaft going down about fifteen storeys and up one. A rope hangs right at the centre.'

'I disbelieve the rope,' we all chorused.

Mia made a bunch of rolls. 'It's still there, but Boris says it's vanished for him.'

I poked Simon. 'Fineous, leap out, grab the rope and shin up for a look-see.'

He shook his head. 'Boris says—'

'BORIS,' I pinched the top of my nose, just between the eyebrows, to drive off the spiking pain of a headache, 'is a freaking illusion. I'm not taking his word for it!'

'Cast "dispel illusion" on the rope. If you tell me it's real then I'll go for it,' Simon said.

'Nicodemus takes out his *last* scroll of "dispel illusion".' The other precious copy of the spell had been read from its scrolls and the words had vanished as my mage enunciated them. The information had probably saved lives, but I still wished I'd kept it. 'I'm going to cast it on Boris!'

'No!' Simon protested.

'Are you crazy!' John actually got up from his chair.

'Why must you hate Boris so?' Mia asked, smiling.

'Don't do it!' Simon said. 'You'll waste our last spell.'

'It won't be a waste if it makes him vanish and tells me he's an illusion.' I tapped my character sheet where the last scroll had yet to be crossed off. 'I read the spell.'

'Wait,' John said. 'So, if things go your way then you've got rid of Boris, half our fighting team, and we still don't know if we can trust the rope.'

'We can't trust the rope even if it's real, and I'm not going to meet Hoodeeny, the Grand Illusionist, with one of his fakes standing at my back with an axe in hand.'

'Leave Boris alone and Fineous will climb the wall of the shaft, then let down a rope we can definitely trust,' said John.

'Hey!' Simon squeaked.

'What? You've got like a ninety-nine per cent chance of doing it.' John kept his eyes on me while addressing Simon.

'But . . . Boris isn't . . . real.' I couldn't let go of it. He was a lie, an error. I spent my days building proofs. They needed concrete foundations. 'Why is this so important to you guys?'

John and Simon both looked down, studying their character sheets, gathering dice, doing anything but looking my way.

'Oh.' I pursed my lips. I'd spent the whole week looking at Boris from my point of view. I'd questioned everything about him. Except why my friends were so invested in lying to me. I still didn't know, but it suddenly struck me that it didn't really matter. The fact was that it was something they were doing, and if I trusted them then that should be enough. I let my shoulders slump. 'Onward and upward, then. Go for it, climby thief-man.'

And so it was that Nicodemus arrived in the hall of the Grand Illusionist, Hoodeeny, on the end of a rope, being dragged up the wall of a nearly bottomless shaft by Boris and Sir Hacknslay.

'Nicodemus unties himself and brushes himself down,' Mia told us, placing the mage's figure behind that of his friends. 'Hoodeeny's hall is like a cathedral, a tall vaulted roof, thick stone pillars marching away—'

'Not circular then?' Simon paused his pencil above the map.

Mia drew in a huge rectangular hall, completely at odds with the idea that we were at the top of a slender spire. '—pillars marching away, narrow windows many times taller than they are broad and set high in the walls, sunlight streaming in to pattern the floor. All along the hall are marvels: some bigger than a man and standing alone, others smaller than an egg and resting on velvet cushions on stone plinths. There's a mechanical giant built from bronze and silver with its workings visible through windows set all across it. A black sphere hovering in the air, a great clock with multicoloured clockwork jesters juggling amid the swirl of cogs and the swing of the pendulum. A burning horse that seems to be made of water, a flower larger than a man with petals whose iridescence shades into colours never seen before, a pillar of electric blue stone from which a voice sings songs in unknown tongues that would break your heart if you listened too long, a golden pool, a bolt of lightning. On it goes, stretching the whole length of the hall.'

Hoodeeny sat resplendent on a throne of gold and silver resembling a great lily unfurling its petals. The man himself bore an uncanny resemblance to Dr Strange from the *Marvel* comics, with the collar of his luxurious red cape rising behind his head, extending fang-like projections. On his tunic of deepest crushed blue velvet a rayed amulet hung, and at its centre a single pearl, big as an eye. In fact, given that Hoodeeny had only blank skin where his eyes should be, maybe it *was* an eye and was watching us even as we looked in awe at the treasures arrayed around us.

'He says, "Welcome!"' Mia told us, placing a figure on a throne to represent the illusionist.

'Would it be rude to kill him at this point?' I asked.

Simon and John frowned at me.

'What?' I blinked at them. 'He's not going to just give us the time crystal, is he?' After our troubles reaching him, I wasn't the least bit confident that we could actually defeat the Grand Illusionist, but it was what we had come to do, and beyond asking nicely with a pretty please at the end I wasn't convinced we had any other options.

'"I have greatly enjoyed watching your ascent!"' Mia said in her booming Hoodeeny voice, which rather reminded me of the Wizard of Oz from the film.

'"Thank you, O Grand Illusionist,"' Simon said. 'Fineous makes a sweeping bow and goes down on one knee, then thanks Hoodeeny for granting us this audience.'

'He does what now?' My eyes widened in surprise.

'Sir Hacknslay follows suit,' John said. 'One knee with sword across his leg.'

'What's going on?' I looked between them.

'It was the price of the audience with Hoodeeny,' John explained. 'He spoke to Fineous and Hacknslay while you were bargaining for those scrolls back in the city. Well, it was a little old man, but he said he had a message from the Grand Illusionist. He said we could only come before him if we managed to bring Boris with us, and that meant making you believe in him.'

'But I don't,' I said. 'I never did.'

'Well, by "believe" he meant you had to have not dispelled him before we got to the top. Fineous and I knew he was an illusion from the start. The illusionist told us that. So, for us, Boris vanished almost as soon as we first saw him. But we had to keep you doubting enough in-game for you not to make your saving throw. And if we just came out and told you outside the game, that'd be cheating, and Boris would have vanished.'

'But I gave him that truth potion and he said he was real!' I protested.

'Fineous pickpocketed you while Hacknslay kept you talking, and replaced the contents of the potion bottle with water.' Mia grinned.

'Fine,' I said, somewhat exasperated. 'How come Boris is still . . .' But the barbarian figure had somehow been snuck away while we were talking. I looked at Mia. 'Nicodemus tells the Grand Illusionist that he wants the time crystal and hopes that he will be prepared to trade for it. Otherwise things may have to get ugly.'

Mia grinned at me, then stiffened her face into Hoodeeny mode. '"Little mage, you have been most amusing, but do not presume to threaten me. I am the great and marvellous Hoodeeny. I am the alpha and omega. All the world is paint upon my canvas. I decide what is real, what is true; it is me that says what is up and what is down, what is black and what is white."' Mia delivered the lines with incredible intensity, staring only at me. Call it acting skill, but somehow she imbued those lines with more weight than any others ever spoken across our D&D table. She moved the throne closer to us. '"Your friends' efforts have earned you one chance. It is easy to fool an audience. Harder to deceive a friend. Hardest of all to trick yourself. You have one chance to find the crystal. Do it and it's yours. Fail and you will be gone from my sight, never to return."'

'How many treasures are there in the hall?' I asked. 'Any chests, coffers, large urns? How big is this crystal supposed to be anyway?'

Mia consulted her notes. 'Thirty-one curios stand between the pillars along the two sides of the hall. There are no boxes, sacks, jars, etc. And your studies indicated that the crystal was between one and two feet long, octagonal in cross-section, and of a thickness that you might just get your hand around. Also, it is said to glow with a curious blue radiance.'

'Well, it's hidden by illusion,' Simon said. 'That's obvious.'

'It could be sitting on a shelf on the wall and illusioned to look like plain stone,' John said.

I shook my head. 'This guy likes to play games. Where's the fun in hiding it like that?'

'So it has to be disguised as one of the treasures,' Simon said. 'One chance in thirty-one if you make a random guess.'

'I reckon it's the clock.' John stood his warrior in front of the circle marked with the 'Cl'. Most of the treasures remained unlabelled, but the eight Mia had specifically mentioned had very brief notes beside them. A one in eight chance, if it was one of them. 'It stands to reason. That one's about time. So it's hiding the time crystal.'

'I don't know. It seems a bit on the nose.' I looked at my character sheet for inspiration. 'There must be some clues. What are we missing?'

'The clock,' John said stubbornly.

'We didn't spend months climbing sixteen levels of the Tower of Illusion to decide that the Crystal of TIME was hidden in the CLOCK,' I said. 'I have more faith in Mia than that.' I glanced at her and grinned. 'Apologies in advance if Mr Merchant Banker here is right.'

'OK . . .' John spread his hands. 'If there are clues, what are they? Nothing he said sounded like a clue.'

'What did he even say?' It had run through my mind like water through a sieve.

Simon promptly repeated Mia verbatim, without the theatrics. 'It is easy to fool an audience. Harder to deceive a friend. Hardest of all to trick yourself. You have one chance to find the crystal. Do it and it's yours. Fail and you will be gone from my sight, never to return,' he concluded.

'Hmmmm.' I really had no clue. 'I take out the last scroll of "dispel illusion" and read the spell.'

'What?' John cried. 'You don't know what to cast it on yet.'

'It's late. It's our last day at the cottage. We're back to our lives tomorrow. I say let me go with my hunch,' I said.

'But we don't even know what it is yet.' John scowled at me.

'If I tell you, you'll talk me out of it. Sometimes you just need to rip the bandage off, right?' I had the edge of an idea, but it was the nebulous sort of idea that words would undermine. Logical examination would reduce it to meaningless corners.

'If we can talk you out of it then it's not much of an idea,' John said.

'See! You're doing it already. One more word and I won't trust it either, and then what will we have?'

191

'Simon, tell him.' John set a hand to Simon's round shoulder.

Simon looked up. 'I think he should do it.'

'What?' John sounded as surprised as I felt.

'Go on.' Simon nodded.

Quickly, before the conviction left me, I set my finger to Hoodeeny's figure. 'I cast the spell on him.'

John threw up his arms in disgust. Simon bit his lip. Mia rolled dice behind her screen.

'He shivers,' Mia said, 'Like someone walked over his grave. His face twists up and very slowly, like he absolutely does not want to say the words, he says, "Stoic fretwork".'

John snorted. 'What the hell?'

'Nicodemus tells him to say it again,' I said.

Mia rolled some more. 'He's really trying to clamp his jaw shut. He's shaking with the effort, and this time the words are much quieter. "Firework Scott".'

'Again!' I said.

Mia shook her head. 'He presses his lips together and says nothing.'

I turned to the others. 'Stoic fretwork, firework Scott? Some kind of code?'

John shrugged.

Simon frowned and then smiled. 'Fineous approaches the throne and says, "Two sicker fort."'

Mia smiled back. 'He grates out an answer through gritted teeth. "Woof trickster."'

'Will someone tell me what the *fuck* is going on!' John banged the table in frustration. All the figures wobbled, but only Sir Hacknslay fell over.

'Anagrams,' I said. And suddenly it hit me. 'Nicodemus takes another step forward and says in a loud clear voice, "Tower of Tricks."'

Mia took the throne and its occupant from the table and replaced them with an old man in a white robe. 'He has a long white beard,' she said. 'And he's holding a crystal about eighteen inches long. It's emitting a curious flat blue light.'

'It's that man from the Tower of Tricks!' John sat up straight, finally catching on. 'But we got out of that ages ago!'

'You're still in the Tower.' Mia took on the tone of a querulous old man. In fact, she sounded like *Elton* taking on the voice. The Tower of Tricks had been his masterpiece, the last campaign he ran for us before his dad was killed and he withdrew from our little circle. Well, from me. 'You never left.'

'What?' John edged his warrior back from the man.

Mia croaked out her startlingly accurate impression of Elton's impression of an old man. 'We are all still in the Tower. We were born in it and nobody ever gets out of it alive.'

'You've been working on this with Elton all these years?' I boggled at Mia as if seeing a whole new woman sitting there behind the dungeon master's screen.

Mia just smiled. 'All good stories come full circle in the end. You should know that, Nick.'

'How did you know?' Simon asked. 'To cast the spell on him?'

'Well . . . I kinda guessed,' I confessed. 'Only . . . what kind of number is thirty-one? Everything else was powers of two: one chance, two scrolls of "dispel illusion", four adventurers, eight ways into the Tower, sixteen storeys to the Tower, thirty-one objects to choose from to cast my spell on? Thirty-one? It didn't make sense. So I guessed Hoodeeny was the thirty-second and most likely to be concealing the time crystal.'

Mia laughed. 'Most of that was just chance! There were ways to get more "dispel illusion" scrolls. But yes, I did think the number of wonders would bug you.'

'So what now? Can we get Sharia back and get out of here?' John asked.

He had a point. The time crystal was never the end game. Going back and saving Mia's cleric, Sharia, was. 'Nicodemus bows to the old man and asks if he may now have the time crystal?'

'The old man nods and hands it to you.' Mia looked me straight in the eyes. 'He tells you that you have won the means to find your love. All you have to do now is take her.'

And if that wasn't an invitation to end the game and go to bed, I don't know what is.

CHAPTER 21

1986

My final destination loomed ahead of me in the frosty air: the squat research centre and fabrication lab where John's father worked and where they had the only example in Europe of the prototype processor chip that I needed to make my memory bands work. The building in which I was destined to die.

The night had wrapped itself around London hours earlier, and very few people found they had a need to be walking the streets of what was essentially an urban industrial estate. Young Nick and the others wouldn't be here for a good ninety minutes. I had the place pretty much to myself. Elton's father was the sole security guard. There were supposed to be three, but one had quit two weeks earlier and had not yet been replaced, and the other had called in sick.

The van I had purchased was parked in a nearby street. I would bring it to the front entrance if I needed it later.

I'd had the place bugged by a shady-looking fellow who I met in the early 2000s and who told me the sorts of things he used to get up to. I'd been looking for people like him at the time. It turned out he also liked to exaggerate about his past exploits, but he was still handy enough to furnish me with keys to the place, security codes for the alarms, a staff roster and, of course, access to their phone conversations.

Yes, it was cheating, but there I was with my head half-frozen because I'd shaved off my own hair to fit the memory, and a wrist covered in make-up that I had to keep checking to ensure that my tattoo wasn't showing because I sure as hell didn't remember Demus having a tattoo there any time I met him. So, yes, I was playing to the letter of the law, but not the spirit.

A few days earlier I had been brooding on the fact that I had lied to myself about where I arrived at the end of my time travels, and implicitly about the very mechanics of the travelling itself. Why, I asked myself, would I have told myself such a stupid lie? One that would easily be found out as the years went by? Bizarrely, I found myself remembering our marathon D&D session way back in 1992 – that week we spent holed up in a cottage ignoring the glorious countryside in favour of more or less continuous gaming. I remembered how Simon and John had lied to me about Boris, and that despite it being a bald-faced stupid lie they had skilfully maintained it through sixteen nightmare levels of the Tower of Illusion, or Tower of Tricks as it was revealed to be. And at the last, just when I had been about to undo their good work, dispel Boris and expose the lie, thereby denying all of us access to Hoodeeny, they had managed without cheating to make me think about the message behind the lie.

While thinking on those good old days, a moment of epiphany had struck me, perhaps belatedly; but, in my defence, I am a man dedicated to uncovering secrets, exposing flaws, shining a light on the mechanics behind the magician's tricks. I have never been an actor, a deceiver, a liar. But I realised that, somehow, just as all manner of highly inconvenient nonsense had been baked into our timeline – this business with the microprocessor, for example: I could just have come back to 1988 and avoided the whole mess – this lie was the baked-in remains of some message, something I was trying to tell myself. I was trying to tell myself to lie, to cheat, to deceive, to do anything and everything I could to have things my way just so long as I didn't break the fundamental rules. Young Nick had to live the life I had lived. He had to see and remember what I'd seen and remembered. Everything else was open to interpretation.

◆ ◆ ◆

I checked the street and went on past the security barrier, crossing the car park and making my way to a side door around the side of the building.

'This is it. The final show.' My breath plumed into the night. I sounded about as confident as I felt. Which was not very.

The key my fixer had secured fitted the lock. The door opened without any alarms sounding and I had been assured that the small red light, which should now be blinking on and off on the security guard station, would remain unblinking.

I had the official timings of Mr Arnot's rounds and planned my route through the building accordingly. Elton's dad remained my biggest regret. He was going to die tonight and I wished I could save him. But if I stopped Rust killing him, then I would just start another timeline. Mr Arnot would still die on the timeline that I remembered, and all that would have changed was that I could no longer affect the future that I'd left behind. In my 2011, my Mia would be lying there in that hospital bed, still attached to all those machines, and whatever was on that memory stick I had left with the doctors seemed unlikely to be her memories. In fact, a possible outcome would be that the building paradox shredded her reality and everyone in it.

The dark corridors lay oppressively silent. I made my way with utmost caution, inching along the walls. I knew Rust was coming. I assumed he followed Young Nick and the others in through the fire escape on the third floor. The exact timing and nature of his entry into the building remained unproven, though, and I had no intention of meeting him ahead of the others. I'd wiped my memory of my previous visit to the building but, despite half my brain screaming at me that it was a terrible idea, in 2011, in the week following Mia's accident, I had picked John and Simon's brains regarding the events of that evening. It was precisely the thing I'd wiped my memory to avoid, of course. I hadn't wanted to go to my death knowing the details. That just seemed like a form of morbid self-destruction. But in the end I had been unable to leave it alone. Like picking at a scab.

John, of course, had been useless, but Simon's perfect recall, along with the coroner's reports, police records and newspaper write-ups, had furnished me with a reasonably clear picture of events. I even had some insight into the action in the restaurant, where Mia and I were the only surviving witnesses, but both with our memories wiped. Before erasing our memories in the park a few days later we had both let some details slip to the others. Simon resisted telling me. He said that I had told him never to speak of any of it, especially to me. I explained that a child had given him that instruction. A child twenty-five years from having to re-enter that building. And now a man was asking for answers. His oldest friend.

Simon spilled the beans, and being Simon he remembered every bean, including any that Mia and I had dropped in his path before we wiped the two weeks from our minds. One thing he recalled was that I'd told him how sick Demus had looked. Perhaps, like the hair, it was some nod to the idea that Demus had come back from the following summer where he had got radiation poisoning while arranging the time hammer at the nuclear power plant. But I felt fine; those events hadn't truly happened, or if they had it was in some strange loop of paradox. Even so, I had a role to play, so I had applied more make-up to create a sallow complexion and hollow, dark-ringed eyes. Maybe this was part of the message I was sending to myself: deliberately easing myself into the idea that I could play a role. Put on a performance.

I went to the restaurant first. The lights were off. No sound but the hum of refrigeration units. The thin beam of my torch swept the room, offering up tables and chairs. I let it linger on the table where the police report had surmised the fight between Ian Rust and 'John Doe' commenced, and tracked it across the short path of the struggle that had left both men dead, Rust from blunt trauma to the head and John Doe from blood loss associated with a machete being stuck through him.

I swung the torch beam to play across the spot where the report marked the body of Jean Arnot (fifty-two) as having been found sprawled in another pool of blood. The furniture hid it from where Rust and Mia would have been sitting. At least she wouldn't have had to see him lying there while Rust held his blade to her throat.

I moved slowly around the room, making a few adjustments here and there, then left with a last backward glance. The next time I entered the room would be my last.

Curiosity led me up past the mainframe room on the second floor, and I let myself in. The computers hummed away just as I remembered them. Or rather they hummed away less impressively now, since I'd seen more processing power in a 2011 wristwatch than was present in all the cabinet-sized mainframes looming around me. I turned to check the back of the door. Someone had hung a whiteboard on it, and written on the board in red marker pen was the legend 'Tower of Tricks'.

Simon had mentioned the curious coincidence, and part of me had wondered whether I, Demus, had written it before Young Nick arrived. But no, here it was, waiting for me. I shone my pencil torch across the board again and leaned in close. Simon said that I'd thought there was something familiar about the handwriting, and I still thought it; though, just as a quarter of a century earlier, I was unable to pin down exactly what it was. Déjà vu, maybe.

I left with a frown, closing and relocking the door behind me.

I went on up to the top floor, still creeping almost on tiptoe. Both the Rust brothers terrified me and no part of me truly wanted to be in that building save for the part of me that loved Mia, and that was all of me. It seemed that I was made entirely of paradox, though fortunately not the world-ending kind. I carried on, heart thumping, sweating despite the cold, doing that thing that we do our entire lives: not thinking about the inevitable death that we know is always waiting for us and might be around any given corner.

I found the skylight window that Elton would manage to get in through. I unlocked it for him. Then I went and hid myself in one of the offices close to the fire escape that they would enter by. I checked through my equipment, then sat down to wait.

That was the longest hour I'd spent in the whole forty years of my life: sitting in the dark, staring at the handful of lights visible from the window. Going over and over my plan, constantly interrupted by thoughts of the approaching psychopath, the severed head in his bag, the machete he had with him. Other thoughts intruded, too. Your life is supposed to pass before your eyes in the final moment before the truck hits you or gravity hauls you along the short journey from rooftop to concrete. Mine crawled by in a succession of bittersweet fragments over the course of that hour.

I was wearing the watch that Simon 'gave' me in 2011. I illuminated the dial to check the time every few minutes, or every thirty seconds as it more accurately informed me. My light in dark places, Simon had called it in his nerdy reference. Checking it in the dark had very rapidly become a nervous habit.

When Elton opened the fire door I nearly jolted out of my chair. I'd been so deep in contemplation that I hadn't even heard him pass by outside the office I was in.

The others came clattering up the fire escape to join him.

'You got in, then.' Young Nick, talking to Elton, I guessed.

'Catch on a skylight was gone. No alarms up there. Dropped down on to a posh desk. Probably John's dad's.' A pause. 'You sure they're keeping this super seekret chip here? It all seems a bit easy.'

'Let's find out.' Mia's voice, followed by the sound of feet as they all trooped off into the building to search for the computer room.

I sat back and carried on waiting, checking the time even more often now. It only took another three minutes and eleven seconds. Ian Rust came up the metal steps on feet so soft I almost missed his arrival entirely.

I heard the faint sound of heavy bags being set down and then nothing. I waited. Had he gone or was he still out there, also waiting, pricked by some animal instinct that told him someone else was nearby?

I found myself holding my breath and released it slowly. A minute crawled by, then another. I couldn't sit paralysed by fear all night. He must have moved off so quietly that I missed him going.

The handle creaked no matter how slowly I turned it. Expecting a machete in the face, I eased the door open and peered through the crack. Darkness. Either he had gone or was standing there as blind as I was.

I turned on my torch. An empty corridor! Just two Tesco bags abandoned by the wall, one bulging with something wet-looking, the other almost empty. I didn't have to examine them. The police report came with vivid photographs that I wished I had never seen. One contained the severed head of the drug dealer whose street name was Sacks. The other contained the hammer that would deal the killing blow to Rust and a hacksaw that had been used to decapitate the victim.

I retreated to the office once more. Young Nick would be in the computer room by now. Simon would be trying to find the combination for the safe holding the prototype microchip. Soon they would set to searching for the safe. My task was to wait for Young Nick's search to bring him to my door. I sat and went back to my watch-watching.

Fifteen minutes later I heard him coming, clomping along where Rust had slunk fox-like, a killer seeking prey. I heard the pause as my younger self registered the two bags, then went past my door to investigate.

'I wouldn't.' I stepped out of the office behind him, causing him to freeze and squeak in fright.

'Steady,' I said. 'It's only me.'

'Jesus, fuck!' He clutched his chest. 'What the hell are you doing here?'

'Helping. I arrived before you and disabled the alarms from the outside.'

Anger battled relief across Young Nick's slightly spotty face. 'If you were going to come here anyway, what do you need us for?'

I offered a version of the old explanation: this was the way it had happened, so this was what had to happen. We moved on to discuss the matter of the severed head, and that naturally led on to the alarming fact that Ian Rust had graduated to murder and was already in the building.

'That psycho's in the building?' With commendable bravery, Young Nick started to head back in.

'Whoa.' I grabbed his arm. 'Where do you think you're going?'

'To stop him!' He tried to shake off my grip. 'Mia's on her own in there. And the others.'

'This is what happens. Mia survives.'

'What?' Nick shook his head. 'You said you don't remember this. I'm supposed to wipe my memory.'

'I don't remember it happening, but I remember the aftermath. I've lived with it for more than half my life. I never asked about it, but some facts can't be avoided.' Actually, I knew a lot more than that, but I needed him to save Mia, whatever the cost, even if that meant lying to myself.

'The aftermath?' He was still trying to break free.

'This is the Tower of Tricks. There's no escape without sacrifice. There's a price to pay.' I let him go. Jean Arnot was the price, and no matter what the logic was it hurt as much to trade him for Mia as it had when I first realised that he was dead.

'Tell me what you know!' Young Nick raged. He was scared for all of them. I could see it in his face.

'I know that this way you can bring Mia back. Return her past to her and give her a future. I know that one day, that will mean more to you than everything. Anything.' That, at least, was a truth I could share with him.

'At what cost?' He had hold of my coat in both hands. 'At what cost?' His bike lamp fell to the floor, shadows spinning crazily.

'You lose friends here, Nick. I lose friends. And I've had twenty-five years to mourn that fact. There's blood on my hands. Whatever I do, there's blood on my hands.' Even now I wanted another way.

'Who? Who do I lose?' He slammed me back against the wall.

'Does—' I'd bitten my tongue and tasted blood on my lips. 'Does it matter? Would . . . Would it change what you do?'

'I . . . No! I'm not losing any of them. Tell me how to stop it!'

'You can't stop it.' He couldn't. I couldn't. 'It's the sacrifice. It's what she costs us. Her life saved. Others lost. One or many? Elton set you the puzzle already. And you ran from it. Ask me again how to stop it and I might tell you. But then you'd have to decide. I could tell you where to find Rust. One word. One word.'

'I . . .' Indecision twisted his face.

'Or let it play out. As it already *has* played out. Let my past be your future. And save Mia.'

'Mia.' He released his hold on me. I could see he loved her. I loved her more now, though. I was ready to go down there and let Rust attack me with that machete. And if that required manipulating this boy into playing his part, then so be it.

'I don't know what you do, Nick,' I lied. 'I don't remember this conversation. I remember the next week. I remember the shit I had to deal with. The bodies that needed to go into the ground. None of this is good. None of it can be. But it happened.'

'I can't play this game. I'm sorry.' Young Nick stepped away, bent and picked up the light. 'I need to unstick the future, jump us on to another timeline. We all need a chance. I can't walk your path. I'm sorry.' He glanced down the dark corridor. 'Your Mia is old. Forty. She's lived a life . . .'

I bowed my head. 'How easily the young sacrifice the old. When you get to forty, it won't seem quite so clear-cut. Believe me. But . . . Well, just remember that you told me the old were a price worth paying.'

'I didn't say that.' He frowned, though, as if realising that he had.

I pulled back my right sleeve. 'I don't have a scar here.' I drew a finger across the back of my wrist.

'What?' Young Nick looked bemused.

'I don't have a scar here. If you did . . . then you couldn't be me. Could you?' I covered my wrist with my sleeve again, not wanting him to notice the make-up covering my tattoo. 'I remember that three people die here tonight. Do it your way and maybe it will be more. Maybe fewer.' I met his gaze, narrowing my eyes against the light. Simon had told me Nick had found a knife during his search and that's how he cut the back of his wrist. 'It's in your pocket,' I guessed.

Young Nick reached into his coat pocket and took out a Stanley knife, setting the small blade to the back of his left wrist. The trick had worked. I still had that scar on my left wrist. It was the natural one to cut if you were right-handed. He would slice the skin and think himself free of me, no longer bound to become me.

'Think about it,' I cautioned.

'No time.' He made the cut, blood welling up immediately.

'Restaurant,' I told him. My one-word kill, like the D&D spell.

'Huh?'

'That's the killing word. That's where you'll find Rust and remake the future.' I didn't feel bad about the lie. I had done it to myself. Besides, things still might go wrong. I was manoeuvring the pieces but there were no guarantees.

Young Nick hurried away, eager to do the right thing on a night where there *were* no right things. 'You coming?'

'Why should I?' I called after him. 'It's not my future any more.' Let him think he was on his own.

He looked back from the corner. 'It still matters!'

'To you, maybe.' The truth was that every decision split the world's timeline and I only truly had enough compassion to care about mine, the versions of me and Mia and all the rest that I knew and remembered. 'That was the solution to your other problem, too, you know,' I shouted after him.

'What? What was?'

'In the Tower of Tricks. Someone had to die. You should have used Power Word Kill on the old man. Everything would have gone away. One old man dead.'

'Come on!' he hollered, and the sounds of his running feet faded into the distance.

With Young Nick dispatched to do his duty, unburdened of the idea that nothing he did would matter, I set off down the fire escape as fast as I could, pausing only to take the grisly hammer from Rust's bag.

I re-entered the building by the side door on the ground floor and hurried to the kitchens at the rear of the restaurant, unlocking any doors that were locked. I thought that Rust would already be there, having killed Mr Arnot, and perhaps Mia would unwittingly come in later and be captured; but as I snuck into the unlit back of the seating area I could see nothing. There was nobody sitting at the table where Rust should be.

I didn't dare go further into the room. Instead I locked the door behind me and crouched behind the rearmost table. I set my holdall beside me and waited. It seemed to be a night of waiting. I checked my watch. Checked it again. My legs were starting to ache by the time I heard Rust and Mia approaching, him snarling directions, her swearing and gasping in pain as her arm was twisted up behind her.

The doors banged open and he thrust her ahead of him, slapping the blade of his machete at the lights. The row closest to the entrance flickered into life. Mia cried out again as Rust tightened his hold, jerking her arm higher behind her back, and despite the insanity lancing from the black beads of Rust's eyes and the twenty-four inches of bloody steel in his hand, it still took considerable effort for me not to just rush him. Instead I kept my place and waited for him to settle. I continued checking my watch, for no good reason. Nerves, I guess.

Simon had reported that Young Nick said Demus rose from the shadows behind Rust and hit him with something heavy. A fire extinguisher, he thought. I had my fire extinguisher ready. I'd even taken a few practice swings. The hammer hung from my belt, ready for the coup de grâce.

I watched as Rust sat himself at the expected table with Mia in front of him, his blade against her throat.

'Now, let's just wait and see who turns up.' He sounded mildly amused. 'What were you searching for, Mia? Breaking and entering isn't Hayes's style. And why this place? It's just offices.'

'Electronics.' Mia swallowed past the pressure of the blade. 'They make electronics here.'

Rust was quiet for a moment, chewing on that one. 'And?'

'They want something special for a project. Him and the other brainiac. The fat one.'

'I don't—'

A distant bang cut him off. A door being opened at speed. Now the sound of someone approaching at a run.

Young Nick clattered through the restaurant doors, bicycle lamp in hand, and came to a stop under the entrance lights, taking in the scene with horror. He spotted Mr Arnot lying among the chairs, then looked across to where Rust sat with Mia.

'Little. Nicky. Hayes.' Rust put a cigarette in the corner of his mouth. 'Come to play?'

'You're mad,' Young Nick gasped.

Rust shrugged. 'If I kill all the witnesses, what has anyone got on me but rumours? People say I don't know where to stop. I say, if you never stop, they'll never catch you.' He moved the machete higher until the cutting edge pressed up under Mia's chin. 'We've been waiting for you to show up, Nick. I wanted you to see her die.'

'Don't. You don't have to do this!' Nick stepped closer.

'You mistake me. I *want* to do it,' Rust said.

I'd seen the same sickness in his brother, though buried a little deeper.

'Just don't.' Nick took another step. Five yards and half a dozen chairs separated them.

I edged forward on knees and one hand, holding the fire extinguisher close with the other, trying not to make a sound. I realised that the face of my watch was still lit up but lacked a free hand to turn it off. I just had to hope Rust didn't somehow spot it and screw everything up. Even if I got to him, I wasn't sure how this would work. If I hit Rust with the extinguisher Mia's neck could easily be sliced open.

'You've got a choice, Nick,' Rust said, his amusement growing. 'You can go back and turn on the main lights so you get a better view. That way, she gets to live sixty seconds longer. Or you can say no, and I'll do it now.'

'I . . .' Nick stood, agonised with indecision. 'Wait! I'll do it.' He started to edge back towards the doors.

'Quicker!' Rust pressed the flat of the machete blade to Mia's neck, making her cry out. 'Mia's dying for you to see her better.'

Nick was making quite a racket pushing chairs aside as he retreated towards the light switches. The noise covered my approach. I was close now, almost within striking range, but terrified to do it in case Rust cut Mia's throat as he collapsed.

Nick reached the switches and set his hand against them. 'Lower the blade.'

I stood right behind Rust now, extinguisher at the ready.

'Really? You're trying to give me order—'

I swung and hit him with all my might. Either he somehow managed to duck and take only a glancing blow or 'all my might' wasn't very mighty, because instead of collapsing into a boneless heap he hit the floor and rolled away, still clutching his blade.

At that point all the lights went on, leaving me blinking for a moment while chairs went clattering over on all sides. My vision returned just in time to see Rust staggering towards me, machete in hand, blood streaming down his forehead and murder in his eyes.

That's when I shot him with the taser I'd made a week earlier in my workshop. Blinded by the lights, Nick wouldn't see what I'd done. I pulled the hammer from my belt and threw myself on Rust as the surge of current died. The bastard still managed to hold on to his weapon even as his muscles spasmed and jerked, but a swift hammer blow to his hand saw him let go. I kicked the machete off among the fallen chairs as we went down together.

Even with Rust disarmed and still twitching from the taser, it took only a moment on the floor wrestling him to know that he was going to kill me within a matter of seconds. I'd had a small number of kinda-fights in my school days and on those occasions I had been a mix of scared and angry as I struggled with my opponent, but never in doubt that I stood at least a chance. Fighting with Rust was like being attacked by a savage dog, or a bear. There was an unmanning animal ferocity to him, and a blind strength of the sort that comes from rage rather than muscle mass. The sort that lets mothers lift cars off their children. Rust had that same strength of desire a mother has to save her baby, but in him it was a desire to hurt, maim and kill.

For a few horrifying moments I struggled to keep his thumbs from my eye sockets, then suddenly he was being pulled away from me, Nick hauling on his arm.

I took my chance and swung the hammer, landing the blow on the side of his head with a wet crunch.

This time he went limp, falling away with Nick, leaving me on the floor clutching a bloody hammer.

◆　◆　◆

A month after my final battle with Ian Rust, an illusionist named David Copperfield would walk through the Great Wall of China before a live audience standing on both sides and on top of it. I don't know how he did it, but it was pretty clever. I'm sure, though, that like many great illusions, it relies on the fact that we are all somewhat less clever than we think we are, and far, far less observant than we think we are.

A famous experiment has a man in a gorilla suit walk across the stage before an audience without any attempt to conceal himself. And because the performer on stage is focusing the audience's attention, almost nobody sat there watching actually notices that a man in a gorilla suit has ambled through the action.

I mention all this to explain why I had thought my plan could work.

Nick let Rust drop and ran to help Mia, who was on her knees amid fallen chairs, clutching her neck with crimson hands. My Mia in 2011 still had the scar from that shallow cut: a thin white seam, only visible when she tanned. A reminder of the day she had her throat sliced by a murderer.

'Mia?' Nick reached for her.

'I'm OK. I think . . .'

Meanwhile I was unfolding the hilt and four inches of blade that were hinged to a stiff rectangle of plastic under my shirt, moulded to my abdomen just beneath my ribs. That plate was secured by a band that ran around my torso and also anchored a similar plate on my back from which I hurriedly unfolded four bloody inches of 'emerging' machete blade.

The blood bags under my shirt had burst during the fight so all I had to do was pull open my jacket to expose the gore.

◆　◆　◆

Things had to happen as they had happened. But how had they happened? All that was certain was that I remembered things, and others had told me things. As long as that still happened then I had kept to the rules. The timeline didn't have to fork. The memories Young Nick stored from Young Mia would still be on the memory stick I'd left with my Mia in 2011.

I didn't need Rust to stick a machete through me. I needed Nick to *see* that he had and to tell the others. And as the Tower of Tricks had taught me long ago, the eyes can be deceived. People can be deceived. A lie can be used for good ends as well as bad. An illusion that is never dispelled is a reality all of its own.

I put a blood capsule in my mouth and bit down on it, letting the gore run down my chin. 'You'll have a . . . lovely scar.' I coughed to get their attention.

Nick turned to me, horrified. 'Are you . . . OK?'

'Three people die here tonight. Like I said.' I looked pointedly at the hilt of the machete jutting from my side.

'Shit.' Nick saw it for the first time. 'Look, don't move. I'm calling an ambulance!'

I caught his wrist. 'Don't. It's not you that calls them.'

He tried to pull free. 'Enough with that! I changed things. Remember? This isn't your time any more. I'm not even you.' And he showed me his left wrist, sticky with blood from the cut he made earlier.

I showed him the same scar on my own wrist, feigning growing weakness. 'You can always fool yourself, Nick.' I really hoped so, anyway. 'I showed you my right wrist before. You cut your left one. It's the natural way to do it. Three people will die here. Just like I remember.'

'But . . . you said I'd lose a friend.'

I nodded towards the body lying by the serving area. It still hurt me after all these years. 'Jean Arnot. You said you were prepared to sacrifice someone "old" for someone young. Elton never forgives you for it. I'm sorry. You lose a friend. It's silly. We were just kids, and I haven't seen him for longer than you've been alive . . . but I still miss him.'

'I don't understand,' Mia said.

I was about to give her a speech about having come back here to die for her out of love, but I noticed the taser wires dangling from her hand.

I gave an exaggerated cry of pain to distract her, but the damn girl followed the wires, thin wires that she shouldn't have been able to see lying there on the ground in the first place. She followed them under the chair and when she emerged it wasn't the taser that she had in her hand. It was Rust's machete.

'Two of them?' she asked.

'Dying . . .' I whispered, and then convulsed in what I hoped looked like agony. Unfortunately, the handle and blade section jutting from my abdomen hadn't locked in place as it should have when I unfolded it, and it chose that moment to fall over, folding back against my body. 'Shit,' I said, and sat up. 'Fuck it!'

CHAPTER 22

· 1986 ·

'Mia!' I couldn't keep the bitterness from my voice. 'For God's sake! You've *ruined* everything.'

Young Nick and Mia stood with their mouths open, staring at me in confusion.

'I don't understand . . .' Nick reached towards the machete handle swinging about on my side as I got to my feet. 'This is all pretend?' He glanced at Rust on the floor, then at Mr Arnot.

'No, they're dead.' I gave Rust a hefty kick. 'And this bastard truly deserved it.' I raised both hands in fists and let out a roar of anger. 'We were so close! So fucking close! And now it's all in ruins.' I'd been within touching distance of saving Mia. And who'd stopped me doing it? Mia herself.

'We've forked the timeline?' Nick asked.

'Forked it and fucked it.' I nodded. 'None of this matters to me now. None of it carries forward to the Mia I had to save in 2011.'

The here and now Mia, the fifteen-year-old one with the bloody neck and unreasonable powers of observation under stress, shook her head; still confused, apparently. 'Are you sure?'

'Yes, I'm sure!' I couldn't help shouting at her. 'This wasn't what happened at all.'

She shook her head again. 'I mean, are you sure they're both dead? Because I thought I saw Mr Arnot move his hand just now.'

I sighed deeply, glanced at the fallen man, then inhaled a breath to explain it to her again. But the words that actually came out were, 'Holy shit!'

All of us backed away rapidly as Mr Arnot pushed himself up from the pool of his own blood, the stuff dripping from his security jacket, then turned his face towards us.

I don't know who screamed. Might have been me, or both of me.

'Hey!' Mr Arnot raised a bloody hand in a placatory gesture. 'Mia. She'll explain it.'

'I will?' Mia asked, her voice faint.

'No. I will.' And Mia. My Mia. My wife, who in my mind should still be in her hospital bed having old memories repatterned into newly regenerated brain tissue, stood up from behind the food counter.

I took another step back, fell into a waiting chair, and laughed that kind of on-the-edge-of-insanity laugh. 'Would anyone else like to join the party?'

On cue, the main doors banged open to reveal John and Elton with Simon puffing up behind them. I guess the looks on their faces were as astonished as mine.

◆　◆　◆

'You look . . . well,' I said.

Mia came to join me in the centre of the restaurant. She did look well. No sign of the accident except for a pink scar on her forehead like a jagged Y.

'Thanks,' she said. 'You look like crap.'

'Make-up,' I said. 'Mostly.'

She came close and hugged me like she hadn't seen me in a hundred years. We kissed, and it was good.

213

'What?' Young Mia's slightly horrified voice broke into our reunion. 'Demus is Nick?'

The Mia in my arms broke free and addressed her younger self. 'He is. Now be quiet and think it through. You're a clever girl. You'll figure it out.'

Young Mia nodded, dumbstruck, and stepped back.

The others were all standing in a loose circle, watching us: Elton beside his father, having established that the blood on him was no more real than the blood on me.

'Are you still . . . you?' I asked, reaching tentatively to close my hand around 'old' Mia's arm.

'I think so.' She smiled, half-sad. 'How does anyone ever tell?'

'I don't know.' I felt lost. I wasn't entirely sure if I was me any more. 'What are you even doing here? How are you even here?' I was asking all the questions. Young Nick and Young Mia both seemed overwhelmed by the presence of centre-stage Mia.

'Well, it took me a while to recover. The best part of two years. And then a while to think it all through. I wasn't pleased with you, Dr Hayes. Not at all. But then I was looking through your notes and I had a great idea. So I fired up the time-rig—'

'But the barrier!' I could believe, after helping to send over a hundred travellers back, she could work the equipment on her own. The barrier, though – that should have stopped her.

'I figured out what you'd been up to before you left, then I went to see that nice young professor in Birmingham and persuaded him to see things my way. I am very rich, you know!'

'Professor?' I guessed that Elias Root had been promoted in a hurry. I pressed on with more important questions. 'Why? When? How?'

She grinned at my lack of eloquence. 'I came back to save you, of course.'

'Me?'

'I saw your designs for the taser and I understood what you were trying to do. It's very clever.' She took my hand.

'Thanks.' At that stage it hadn't been more than doodles and wishful thinking. I looked around at the disaster it had turned into and saw that it had never stood much chance, but I couldn't manage to be sorry about it. After all, somehow Mia was miraculously restored, and Mr Arnot was alive. I didn't know how that had happened, but the weight that had lifted off my soul because of it was immense, greater even than I had known, and I knew it was heavy. Even if it didn't last and paradox tore it apart, I was glad for the chance to have seen it. 'I gave it my best shot. It was quite clever, wasn't it?'

'Clever, but not as clever as it could be, because you, my love, might be good at sums but you've never been very good at lying, or acting, or—'

'Get to the point, maybe? We're standing in somewhere we're not allowed to be next to the body of a man I killed.'

'I saw what you were trying to do and I thought I'd go one better,' she said. 'You've got a suitable corpse, I assume?'

'In a van round the corner,' I said.

'Suitable corpse?' Nick asked: his first words since I'd confirmed we'd forked the timeline.

'I remember that I died here tonight,' I told him. 'All of us know it. But I didn't want to die here, so I faked it.' I knocked at the machete handle still swinging around on my side. 'And it would have worked, too . . .' I shot Young Mia a hard look, then softened the blow by adopting an American drawl. 'It would have worked if it hadn't been for you damn kids!' We shared a smile. 'Anyway. When you had all left the building my plan was to bring in the body I purchased illegally for "medical research", shove Rust's machete through his chest and then leave him. I've already bribed the pathologist who is going to carry out the post-mortems to write it up as if the wound was the cause of death and substitute some suitable photos of me into the records along with some of my DNA.' I had thought the bribery part was going to be difficult, but the guy had jumped at the money.

'And it was a great plan!' my Mia said. 'But what about poor Mr Arnot?'

'What could I do?' I twisted my face. 'I mean, if I survived, I was planning to build a time-rig and come back to you. I only landed back in '86 a few weeks back; there are no other memories of me that need making. With Mr Arnot . . . I mean . . . it's different. He's Elton's dad, for God's sake! He died! I remember it.'

Mia cocked her head and pursed her lips. 'You remember what?'

'I remember he's dead. I've seen the grave.'

'You remember being told that he died. Reading it in the newspapers. Seeing it in the police reports. Never seeing or hearing from him again.'

'But . . .' I floundered. 'How . . .'

'I arrived back months earlier than you, Nick,' Mia told me. 'I made a lot of money the same way you did. Bets and investments. Then I went and introduced myself to Elton's family. I showed them five million pounds in several suitcases to start with, and then bank accounts with similar sums in. I told them who I was. Explained everything. Proved it with tricks like predicting the Challenger crash and the football results. I said that I knew it was a big decision but if they would move cities and take steps never to let you know he was alive, then I would set them up with new lives and as much money as they would ever want.' She turned towards Elton. 'They were going to tell you all this tonight, before anyone told you your dad had been killed.'

'But . . .' I flailed, trying to seize some kind of sense from all this, '. . . that would mean Elton withdrew from our friendship . . .'

'To keep you from learning the truth,' Mia said. 'You had to believe Mr Arnot was dead.'

'But. No, this is nonsense. Rust killed Mr Arnot!'

'He probably would have if he'd bumped into him,' Mia said.

'But he was lying RIGHT THERE!' I pointed to the bloody puddle.

'He was, but not when Rust brought me in.' Mia smiled at Young Mia. 'Her, I mean.'

'He was there! I saw him!'

'Did you?' Mia shook her head. 'He crawled out while Rust was questioning me . . . her . . . from where he was hiding behind the counter with me and lay there where none of you could see him until you stood and looked round after all the fighting. That was all that was needed – for young you to see him and think Rust had killed him. If I hadn't come back and interfered, then yes, Rust would have found him and killed him. But this way everything is consistent with your memories and Mr Arnot gets to live.'

'So . . .' I boggled. 'You've got a suitable corpse, too?'

Mia nodded. 'In a refrigerated van around the corner. Plus, I managed to get the old pathologist reassigned and a new, rather corrupt and easily bribed one put in post. And my corpse actually did die of stab wounds and has been on ice ever since, so he's a damn sight more convincing than yours. Jean has already posed for the morgue shots. We had a special effects guy from Hollywood get him looking right.'

'Well . . . as nice as it is to argue in front of our young selves about who's brought the more convincing substitute corpse . . . we've fucked it up.'

'Is that a problem?' John found his voice. 'I mean, you're here. She's here, and recovered. Can't we just leave Rust and never speak of this again?' He looked most hopeful about the 'never speak of this again' bit.

'It wouldn't be a problem,' I sighed, 'except for paradox. This is all wrong. It doesn't fit. And because of the way our timeline is plumbed together, that small problem is apt to grow and grow and grow until a few years down the line it eats the world.'

'Oh,' said John.

For a few moments we all stood in silence, variously covered in fake or real blood, or just a thick layer of bewilderment.

'So,' said Young Mia. 'All this went wrong because I spotted those wires?'

'Taser wires,' I said. 'Yes. And sorry for being a dick. It was my fault, not yours. I should have made sure they weren't left in full view.'

'So,' said 'old' Mia. 'It was mostly bad luck and easily avoided.'

'Yes,' I said bitterly.

Old Mia turned to Young Nick. 'You've got those memory bands on you?'

'In a bag hidden in the car park,' he said, seeming almost hypnotised by her.

'Go and get them,' she ordered, and when he hesitated, 'Run!'

He ran.

'But they don't work,' John said.

'I got this.' Elton held up a black case. 'That's what we needed, ain't it?'

I nodded. 'Yes. It literally just needs to be clicked into place on the motherboard.'

Then Old and Young Mia, both of whom had always thought bigger and more devious thoughts than I had, spoke together. 'Stage the play then!'

'What?' I asked.

'Stage the play,' my Mia repeated. 'Set everyone where you need them. Wipe everyone's memories back to the point where things went wrong. Start again.'

I shook my head. 'That's crazy.'

'Not if it leaves us with the same memories we know we had. We should all go off and do what we remember being done. And this timeline will still be the one you and I came back from.'

The idea was fantastic, if it could be done: if we could replay the whole encounter so that Young Nick and Young Mia left the building remembering exactly what Mia and I remembered, then they would act as we had. They would live their lives as we had. And the fatal paradox would be avoided. It wouldn't matter *why* they remembered what they remembered. It wouldn't matter if the whole thing was a fake. As long as it was consistent, then we should be safe. This whole thing could still be salvaged, and left with a far more palatable secret underbelly where Mr Arnot survived to enjoy a wealthy retirement and Elton only pretended to blame me.

I still wasn't buying it. 'What moment could we go back to that would possibly work?'

Mia didn't even pause to think. 'When young you turns the lights on. You and Rust were on the floor. You can pretend to wrestle him. Nick hauls him off. You hammer him again. It all goes from there. Only this time we remove the real machete and the taser from the scene entirely.'

'What about John and Simon and Elton?' I looked at the trio, standing together by Mr Arnot.

'Well.' Mia frowned. 'We could wipe them back to the point Simon and Elton found John, and everything would be waiting for them just as it should be when they get here . . . But it would be tricky to get the headbands out there, and we only have two . . . Or we could just tell them now what we remember they did next and they could do that . . .'

'What, and just not tell me about it for the next few decades!' I boggled at the idea.

'Sure,' Mia said. 'You can keep a secret. Can't you, boys?'

They all nodded.

'But . . . but . . . this is monstrous!' I blustered. 'You mean that the John and Simon I left behind in 2011 remembered all this and have been lying to me practically my whole life?'

Mia pursed her lips and nodded. 'Pretty much.' She frowned. 'It was John who brought me the plans you had for the pretend machete when I was recovering in hospital.'

'But I didn't even think of that until after I came back!' I stared accusingly at John.

He shrugged. 'I guess that's something you need me to do in 2011, then. Memo to self: fake machete plans and give them to Mia in hospital twenty-five years from now. I need to know, though, do we have jet cars—'

'They knew it all worked out?' I couldn't keep from shouting. I strode towards Mia. 'And that you were here that night, all healed up? For twenty-five fucking years? And never told me?'

Mia shrugged. 'You're about to ask them not to, aren't you?'

I harrumphed disgustedly. 'I guess.'

'There's a problem with all this,' Young Nick announced. I hadn't seen him return, but he was breathing heavily and had the bag with the headbands in his hand. 'You stage the scene, use the two headbands to wipe Mia and my memories, and turn the lights on. Fine. But then there are the two of us – her lying on the floor there . . .' he pointed, '. . . and me standing over here.' He indicated the spot. 'Both wearing funky headbands. How's that going to work?'

The Mias thought for a second.

Young Mia spoke first. 'Elton stands behind you, and as the lights go up, he lifts the headband off you and backs through the doors. We'll keep it dark for a good while before so everyone is dazzled when the lights go on.'

'And I'll stand behind you,' Old Mia said to Young Mia, 'and take off your headband, then retreat to hide at the back of the restaurant. You and Nick will both be too dazzled and otherwise preoccupied to notice. Nick will remember being in the middle of a fight and you will still be wondering if your throat has been properly cut.'

'What about the timing?' Young Nick asked. 'How accurate are these things, and how do we even know what time to set them to?'

'Excellent points. Fortunately, we're in an electronics laboratory and I can tweak them for accuracy. Also . . . again fortunately . . . I was looking at my watch quite a bit, so I think I can judge the time pretty well.' I looked suspiciously at Simon. He'd given me the watch in the week after Mia's accident. He must have done it knowing full well I would need to be wearing one today.

'OK!' Old Mia took charge. 'Let's do it. Let's get this show on the road, people!'

◆   ◆   ◆

Before I got to work on the headbands, I went across to Elton. I felt awkward. Him a kid I hadn't really spoken to for longer than he'd been alive. Me a grown man, responsible if not for his father's death, then at least for the upheaval of his family's life. Albeit with the compensation of millions of pounds.

'I . . . I'm glad we found a way to work this, Elton,' I said, tentative, unsure of myself. 'I know this sounds lame . . . but I missed you.' To my horror I found myself far more emotional than I wanted to be, blinking rapidly to keep any suggestion of tears from my eyes.

'No, man.' Elton shrugged. 'It don't sound lame at all.' And to my surprise, he moved into the Nick Hayes no-hugging zone and broke the only rule. 'I'm gonna miss you, too. Mia explained how it has to be, but it ain't right. Ain't right at all. Not any righter than cancer. But the world's got plenty of that sort of shit in it.' He stepped back and grinned. 'Dunno what you're planning now, Doctor Who, but if you ever go back to the future like Michael J. Fox, then Mia says you can look me up. We can sit out on the balcony and have a few beers together like a couple of old men, eh?'

I grinned back, turned away and got to work. Those would be a few beers long overdue, and ones I was determined to have.

Mia said to get the show back on course, and so we did. We cleaned blood, we stood chairs back up, we readied the stage. With the headbands sorted, I lay down and arranged my fake machete so I looked transfixed by it. Mr Arnot returned to his blood pool. Mia stood behind Mia, hands ready to remove the headband. Elton stood behind Nick at the door.

We variously stood or lay in darkness waiting for our eyes to adjust, something that took much longer than I had expected. And then, at last, I had the deeply unpleasant task of hauling Rust's gory, cooling corpse on top of me.

'Everyone ready?' Old Mia asked.

A series of grunts and affirmatives.

'Three, two, one, action!' Old Mia shouted.

Old Mia and Elton hit the buttons that would wipe Young Mia and Young Nick's memories back to the moment of Nick's turning on the lights. A second later Elton hit all the light switches and slipped the memory band from Nick's head just as Mia slipped the other band from her younger self's head. Mia and Elton then withdrew rapidly.

Both Mia and Nick were on their own travels through time in that moment. Their memory of the last forty minutes had been erased. We had sent them back to the crucial moment simply by playing with their memories. It might seem a cheap trick compared to actually moving backward through time. But time is just a different kind of illusion. Though one seems fundamental and the other a human conceit, they are in fact deeply connected. Memory and time, time and memory. The universe doesn't care about time. We care about time. Because we remember.

In the next instant, a disoriented young Nick came stumbling through the chairs towards me and with a roar of effort managed to haul the already dead Ian Rust off me. At which point I hit the corpse with my hammer again.

Having done my job, I lay back against the chair pretending to be dying while Nick checked on Mia, who before the memory wipe had washed her drying blood off her own neck and replaced it with fresh fake blood from the supply Old Mia had brought along for Mr Arnot.

Soon enough, with no taser wires to distract Mia, both she and Nick were fussing over me and asking questions. My answers led them back to Mr Arnot who Mia hadn't yet seen, and they both stood contemplating his apparently dead body in silent horror.

'Mia . . .' I lifted a hand to the hilt jutting from my side. My voice fell lower still. 'I can't speak to her. But you will, Nick. You'll understand.'

'You never did have a plan to go back,' he said.

'No,' I whispered heroically.

'You need to be in hospital . . .'

I shook my head. A trip to hospital was the last thing I wanted. 'The two of you have to erase today from your minds, Nick. It's important. You can't know these things. They'll poison you both.'

'But . . . I *die* here?' He looked horrified, and I knew exactly how he felt.

'I knew this was the end for me, but I didn't know how. I'm not brave enough to have done it knowing all the details, and to let it happen just as you saw it. Rub those memories out.'

'Christ.' Mia knelt beside me. 'Nick? You came back to do *this* . . . for me?' The way she looked at me then was the first time I could really see my Mia in those eyes. 'You came here to die for *me*?'

I coughed and looked away. I tried to offer alternatives that might take the sharp edges off for her. 'Maybe my cancer returned. Maybe I found out after I came back that time travel may only work on living things, but they don't live long afterwards. It's not a gentle process. The truth is that neither of you should know what I gave up or why. Neither of you want to know.' I lay back and tried not to over-act the death scene. I knew my Mia was crouched not far away, judging me from the perspective of a successful film actress. I sucked in a breath I intended to hold until they were gone and used part of it to whisper, 'I've given you what you need. Take away the memories. Give yourself back your future. Live your lives.' A little grandiose, maybe, but not bad for off the cuff. Young Mia had tears in her eyes. The other Mia was probably crouched behind a table trying not to laugh.

CHAPTER 23

1986

Young Mia and Nick hurried off and out of the restaurant doors, away to their rendezvous with John, Simon and Elton. I now viewed all three of those young men in a very different light, part of a decades-old conspiracy that Mia and I had instigated and yet been wholly ignorant of until this night.

Mr Arnot helped Mia bring in her substitute corpse while I ran off to put the bag with the memory bands back into the bushes where Young Nick would be expecting to find them. After that we waited until all five of the teenagers had headed off in search of a taxi, and then brought in the corpse that was to stand in for me.

Between the three of us we staged a convincing crime scene and removed as much as we could of any evidence that pointed towards a different story.

And, finally, we went home: Mr Arnot to his millions and me and Mia to her luxury Richmond flat overlooking the Thames.

◆　◆　◆

'Are we safe now?' Mia had asked. 'From the paradox, I mean.'

'Everything I remembered happening has happened. Young Nick has seen exactly what I saw. His life should unfold the same way mine has. Sure, from our side of the curtain, those events look totally different and have a whole new interpretation, but from his side, and in my memory, nothing has changed.'

◆ ◆ ◆

We lay in bed that night watching the stars in the black sky over the river. Even in London a few stars shine bright enough to be seen.

I watched them for hours with Mia sleeping beside me. Mia who had saved me from myself and then come back to save herself, weaving a deeper and wider illusion of her own around the one that I had tried to fool myself with.

I thought about where and when we might go next. Where and when our story had started and the time and place it might end. It seemed to me that those weren't questions that could be answered, however much you knew. The stories of our lives don't behave themselves; they don't have clear beginnings, and even death isn't a clear end. We just do what we can, we take what kindness and joy we find along the way, we ride the rapids as best we're able.

Time and memory. Memory and time. The forking of timelines might seem to take away meaning from our own path, but surely it's the ultimate comfort. We can look at ourselves and say that this isn't everything we are. We know now that all of us are explored across an infinity of universes, and that's the big kind of infinity, not one of those pokey countable infinities. We are all of us endless. Every possibility gets its chance. The best and the worst of us walk the stage. All of our choices sampled. Every mistake made and avoided.

I lay there and I wasn't sure of my past or my future. But I was sure of my present, and it was good.

'Hey.' Mia rolled sleepily against me. 'Still awake?'

'I am. Can't sleep.' I put an arm around her. 'We did good today. I'm so glad Mr Arnot didn't die.'

'And you,' she mumbled, stroking a hand across my arm.

'Me, too,' I agreed. 'But I owe Mr Arnot. After all, it was him who told me to kiss the girl.'

'Silly.' Mia snorted and kissed me. 'I told him to say that. Some things you just can't leave to chance.'

ABOUT THE AUTHOR

Photo © 2010 Nick Williams

Before becoming an author, Mark Lawrence was a research scientist for twenty years, working on artificial intelligence. He is a dual national, with both British and American citizenship, and has held secret-level clearance with both governments. At one point, he was qualified to say, 'This isn't rocket science – oh wait, it actually is.'

He is the author of the Broken Empire trilogy (*Prince of Thorns, King of Thorns* and *Emperor of Thorns*), the Red Queen's War trilogy (*Prince of Fools, The Liar's Key* and *The Wheel of Osheim*) and the Book of the Ancestor series (*Red Sister, Grey Sister* and *Holy Sister*).